AUGUST
GAMBLE

Linda Hall

NOV 0 6 1997

Published by
Bethel Publishing Company
1819 South Main Street
Elkhart, Indiana 46516

Cover Illustration by
Ed French

Editing and Typesetting by
Grace Pettifor

Printed in the United States of America

ISBN 0-934998-62-0

Dedicated
to
Rik, Wendy and Ian
the three most important people
in the world
to me

ACKNOWLEDGMENTS

Chester, Alberta, Canada and all its inhabitants are ficti-
tious. If you drive twenty miles east from Calgary on Highway 1, you will encounter rich fields of canola and grain, but
no Chester. The city of Azuyo, Nevada doesn't exist either,
except in the pages of this book.

Thank you to Sergeant Dennis Grotkowski of the Barrhead
detachment of the Royal Canadian Mounted Police for his
advice and information.

As well, thank you to Sergeant Clint Dykeman for giving
me the "royal tour" of the Fredericton detachment of the
RCMP, and for answering my many questions.

A very special thank you to Rhett and Carla Tindall and
sons, Grayson and Trent, for three indescribable days spent
on a houseboat on lake Mohave, Nevada.

CHAPTER 1

It was hot—that torrid kind of August heat that threatens to suck the planet of its very life. Not even the merest whisper of a cloud hung anywhere in the pallid sky. Trees stood like paper props left too long on an elementary school stage. No breeze rustled their limp leaves. It was the kind of day when everyone you meet says, "Hot 'nuff for ya?"

When Pris McNinn left the cool confines of Pfeiffer's Independent Grocers where she'd been scanning groceries all day at checkstand number two, she was unprepared for the sauna blast that hit her square in the face. Just after 4:30 and the heat showed no sign of abating.

"What a scorcher," she said out loud, shading her eyes. Despite the cardboard windscreen with the giant sunglasses, her eleven-year-old Ford would be as hot as an oven. Hot enough to fry an egg on the dashboard, she thought. The drive home would be a killer. She couldn't afford air conditioning—not on her salary. Not with three half-grown kids who required every penny and an ex who refused to pay child support living somewhere up in Edmonton.

The rank smell of refuse in the nearby dumpster assailed her nostrils. Why don't they pick up this garbage once in a while, she thought as she waved away the flies. She opened her car door, leaned across the hot vinyl and opened the passenger door to let some air through—as if that would help with the temperature in the high nineties and humidity to match. Smelling sour cigarette butts, she decided it was time she emptied the ash tray. Mr. Peiffer would kill her if she dumped ashes in the parking lot. Better take them over to the dumpster, she grumbled to herself.

Pris was short and lifting the heavy green dumpster lid was some feat. And—oh, the smell. With one hand holding up the lid, she sprinkled her cigarette remains on top of the knotted plastic bags full of coffee grounds, lunch leftovers, rotting cabbages and mucky hamburger buns. Something in the far back caught her eye—a thing familiar, yet out of place. The tops of three spongy-looking grayish fingers pointed up between molding zucchinis and oranges. Probably one of those fake body parts you can buy at Halloween. Intrigued, she grabbed a stick from the ground and gently probed, nudging a slimy grapefruit and a paper-filled cardboard box away from the fingers. And that is when she began to scream and scream and scream.

* * *

Corporal Roger Sheppard of the Chester, Alberta, detachment of the Royal Canadian Mounted Police sat in shorts and a tank-top downstairs in the coolest room of his house, an iced Diet Coke beside him. It was his day off. Next to him a plastic wastebasket was three-quarters filled with crumpled papers. As he stared at another blank sheet, he wondered how he ever got himself into this.

In a reluctant moment—a very reluctant moment—he had said yes, sure, he'd be delighted. Well, he hadn't said it in exactly those words; it was more like, "I guess I could." Then Hank Pfeiffer had taken one of Roger's hands in both of his large ones and shook and shook it. "Thank you, brother. We'll be looking forward to what you have to say, really looking forward."

What he had done in that moment of supreme weakness was volunteer to give a speech at the Christian Men's Breakfast Club. He would be the featured career moment. He was supposed to talk for ten minutes on what it means to be a Christian in his particular line of work. In mid-September, more than a month away, he was scheduled to speak. Already the thought of getting up in front of all those people was making him sweat. Well, the heat wasn't helping either.

Kate, his wife, had said, "But Rog, you go in and talk to schools all the time about drugs and bicycle safety and stuff. How is this so different?"

He couldn't explain it. It just was. It was more like preaching, somehow. And he wasn't a preacher.

Then she said, "You've been teaching Sunday School for years. Why don't you just pretend they're all grade four boys?"

Why not, indeed, except they weren't.

Undaunted, she continued, "People respect you, Rog. Everyone around here respects the RCMP. It's not like L.A. or anything." She smiled, "Just show them your gun, that'll impress them."

The paper in front of him remained devoid of coherent thoughts, empty of words. What was he supposed to tell that group of businessmen? That small-town Chester whose biggest problem used to be parking violations and the occasional speeder seemed to be overrun now with drugs and related crime—B and E's, armed robberies, even prostitution? That he was called almost daily by the high school principal to "get these drug-dealing hoods off the school grounds"? And that arresting a few of them just caused more to come out of the woodwork?

He could blame it on the fact that Chester was just twenty miles from the city limits of Calgary. But he had met with officers in Okotoks, Airdrie, and Cochrane, who were similarly distanced from Calgary, and they did not seem to have the magnitude of the problem that his detachment dealt with on a daily basis.

Even the Christian community was feeling the effects. Early this spring, they had raided a teen "bush" party down in the ravine where they found drugs, plenty of alcohol and two sixteen-year-olds from Roger's church—Chester Community Church. He thought of his daughter, Rebecca. At age fourteen, she was struggling with issues of right and wrong. She could have been there.

Recently, Roger had been appointed to head up an investigation into the drug problem—Chester's own version of drug wars.

Upstairs the screen door slammed. It would be Rebecca. Kate wasn't due home for half an hour. Kate worked two days a week and every other Saturday morning at a local real estate office. Their other daughter, Sara, who was eighteen and newly graduated from high school, was spending the summer in Spain on a youth mission project. She was helping to build a small, rural church. The thought of Sara without her curling iron and wearing work boots made him chuckle.

He downed the rest of his Coke. "Hey, Beck," he called up the stairs.

He could hear her rattling around the kitchen. She was obviously ignoring him, probably still pouting. The previous evening she had begged for permission to go to a rock concert in Calgary on Saturday. Roger and Kate were firm.

She had screamed at them, "All of my friends get to go out all the time. I'm fourteen! What do you want to do? Keep me a baby forever?"

At precisely 5:02, the phone rang.

"Dad, it's for you," yelled Becky.

"I'll get it down here."

CHAPTER 2

By the time Roger arrived on the scene, three squad cars and an ambulance van were already at the site. Yellow plastic tape warning *Police Line Do Not Cross* had been tacked up on telephone poles and light standards. A crowd was gathering—groups of threes and fours shading their eyes and straining for a look. Senior Constable Clayton Lavoir stood just inside the tape and talked with them. He was a large, gentle man. If anyone could calm their trepidation, Clayton could. Roger knew it wouldn't be long before Clayton was promoted to Corporal and transferred out of Chester. Roger would miss him.

The local coroner, round little Dr. Ansen Ridley, stood on tip-toe and leaned into the dumpster, his back end jutting out like the hind end of a piglet nuzzling in at feeding time. The back of his bald head was pimpled with sweat.

Constable Dennis Mayweather, the police camera's viewfinder firmly pressed against his eye, shot the scene from a variety of angles. Another constable, Duane Castelli, talked to two EMTs who lounged against the back of their ambulance, arms crossed across their chests, smiling over some private joke.

In the shade against the building on a faded green slatted bench, Constable Roberta St. Marie was sitting close to a frightened-looking blowzy blonde in a pale blue smock who kept pulling at her earrings and smoothing her hair. He guessed this was the woman who had found the body.

Mayweather was the first to notice Roger.

"Corporal," he said, "We already called Calgary. They're on their way."

"What's the story?" asked Roger, flipping his notebook to a clean page and walking toward the dumpster.

"That woman," Dennis indicated the blonde on the bench, "is an employee of Pfeiffer's. She saw a hand sticking up out of that dumpster. The hand was attached to a body. This body," he said pointing down, "very much dead."

Roger peered into the dumpster. The open eyes of the dead man stared up at him, one bullet hole neatly in the center of his forehead.

"Recognize him?" asked Duane.

He nodded, "Tom Anderchuk. It's nice when they kill their own. Makes our job a heck of a lot easier." He sighed.

"No great loss, eh?" asked Dennis.

Roger frowned. Tom Anderchuk was well-known to both the Chester detachment and to many Chester residents. He was the town's bad kid, the drop out, the drug taker, then drug dealer. This was the "hood" that the principal called him about.

Under the hot sun, sweat pooled on Roger's forehead and he wiped it away with his fingers. In his small notebook he began meticulously describing the scene; the position of the body, the time of day. Under the word *temperature*, he wrote one word, *hot*. With Staff Sergeant Roy Laird on vacation, the duty would fall to Roger to oversee this investigation. He was determined to do it well. Knowing who the victim was, he was almost certain this crime was drug-related, so it would be his responsibility anyway.

"He's all yours," said the doctor, stepping away from the dumpster. "Doesn't take a genius to figure out he was killed by a flying bullet."

"Time of death? Any guesstimations?" asked Roger.

"Little lividity, skin cool to the touch—as cool as can be in this weather—rigor mortis already resolving, although this heat may have sped up the process. An autopsy will tell, however," said the doctor pulling off his surgical gloves.

"Can you give me that in English?"

"My guess would be sometime last night. To be more precise, I would say that sometime between the hours of 10 P.M. and—oh, say—1 or 2 A.M., he got his head in the way of a bullet."

Duane, Dennis and the two EMT's rolled the stretcher over to the dumpster. Before they loaded the body, Roger pulled on a pair of surgical gloves and made his own examination. The victim was wearing jeans, no socks, Nike running shoes and an oversized gray and red plaid sports jacket over a Calgary Flames tee shirt. He fingered the jacket. Wool. Why anybody, dead or alive, would be wearing wool on a day hot enough to melt asphalt was beyond human comprehension. From the victim's back pocket, he pulled out a grimy, mustard-colored nylon wallet. In an empty array of plastic sleeves meant to hold credit cards and wallet photos, Roger found his driver's license. Unlike most other provinces and states, the Alberta driver's license was in two sections, neatly folded into its own plastic case. Roger pulled out the paper part of the license. In the center he felt a slight bulge. He unfolded it. Neatly wrapped around a coin was a U.S. $5.00 bill.

"What is it?" asked Clayton walking over.

"A U.S. bill. Five dollars."

"A *loony* in there?"

It certainly felt like it to Roger. "I think so," he said.

They were referring to Canada's dollar coin, affectionately referred to as the *loony* because it featured a picture of a loon.

However, when Roger unwrapped the bill, he found—not a loony—but a silver token of some kind. He examined it in the sunlight. Around the outside edge of one side he read, *One dollar gaming token. For use by player only.* He turned it over. *One dollar gaming token, Acceptable only at the Riverboat.* Across the center of the coin was a picture of an old fashioned paddle boat and the words, *Azuyo, Nevada.*

"Who's F. Schmidt?" asked Clayton.

"Who?"

Clayton spread the U.S. bill open on the hood of the car. In the lower right corner the name *F. Schmidt* was scrawled clumsily in blue ink.

Roger bent his head over the bill.

"It could mean nothing," said Clayton. "Could've been there a long time."

"Nevertheless it'll be worth checking out. Ever heard of a place called Azuyo, Nevada?"

"Azu, who?"

"Azuyo," said Roger holding up the coin.

"A gambling token," Clayton said looking at the coin, "I've heard of Vegas, Reno, but never Azuyo." He added, "There are dozens, no hundreds, of small gambling towns up and down Nevada. I imagine Azuyo's just one of them."

"It looks like whoever killed him, cleaned out his wallet," said Roger.

"Just enough left to ID him," said Clayton.

"But they forgot to check the inside of the license," added Duane from behind.

"Maybe they weren't from Alberta."

Roger waved the flies away and made notes of the name *F. Schmidt, the Riverboat, Azuyo,* and then placed the wallet, the bill and the token in a clear plastic evidence bag. It would go to the crime lab in Calgary along with the victim and all of his clothing.

Roger ducked back under the tape and walked over to Roberta who now had her arm around the blonde who was blubbering into a tissue. A group of employees were huddled together by the back door, arms crossed and talking seriously and quietly. Standing in the doorway and looking very confused was Hank Pfeiffer in a white smock. When he saw Roger, he stumbled across the asphalt toward him.

"Roger," he said, putting a hand on his shoulder, "Terrible thing, terrible thing. They say a body was found. Is that true?"

"Can we talk?"

Hank looked as if he might faint. His large-featured face became suddenly pale, and he leaned against a nearby telephone pole for support. "Terrible thing," he said shaking his head, "Terrible, terrible thing."

Hank kept stealing glances toward the crowd around the dumpster, back at his group of employees, and at the laden stretcher being lifted into the ambulance. His face blanched when he saw the body and Roger wondered if Hank might be sick. But then Hank straightened slightly and seemed to recover some of his color.

"Hank," said Roger putting his hand gently on Hank's arm. "I'm going to need to talk to you and to every one of your employees privately one at a time. Do you have an office or some place I can use?"

"Certainly, Roger, certainly." His voice was barely above a whisper. Roger kept his hand on the large man's arm as they made their way across the parking lot to the back door of the grocery store. Hank's walk was unsteady, his nose twitched and he kept shaking his head.

The blonde who had found the body was now standing in the center of the group of sober-looking employees. One woman lit a cigarette. Clayton and Roberta met with Roger briefly before they set off for the address on the license to find the next of kin, if there was any. A large RCMP van pulled in behind them, stopping next to the yellow tape. Two homicide detectives from Calgary jumped out and headed toward the constables at the dumpster, their black tool kits in their hands. He knew they would spend the next few hours sifting through the mounds of garbage, and examining every inch of ground around the dumpster.

The coolness of the store was a welcome relief from the outside heat. Roger and Hank walked into a coffee room which contained the usual array of unwashed coffee mugs with names on them, a half-filled coffee pot, a long table cluttered with old *Peoples* and *Calgary Heralds*, a variety of mismatched chairs and one broken-down couch. Beyond the coffee room was Hank's office, or what he referred to as his office. It was little more than a windowed cubbyhole and it didn't seem to have one square inch of empty, usable space. Floor to ceiling boxes lined the walls; stacks of paper haphazardly covered the desk. Files were strewn on the floor. Roger half-expected Hank to jump back in horror exclaiming, "Someone's ransacked my office!" But he didn't. This was how it was supposed to look, apparently.

"Here, you can use my desk and chair," he said lifting a case of chicken noodle soup off the chair and setting it on top of some boxes. Hank, himself, sat on a rickety chair in the corner. His color was back, but he kept clasping and unclasping his large hands in his lap.

After Roger sat down, he realized a computer was perched on the right corner of the desk. The monitor face was covered with little yellow sticky pad notes.

"Hank," said Roger, clearing a place in front of him and flipping open his notebook, "I'm going to be asking you a lot of questions and I want you to think very carefully before you answer." He paused and Hank nodded.

"What time did you arrive at the store this morning?"

"Around eight, maybe eight-fifteen. No, I think it was more like eight."

"So you arrived at eight this morning. You drove?"

"I always drive."

"Where did you park?"

"In my spot. Next to the back door."

"Your car's there now?"

"Yeah," Hank grunted.

"Did you see anything unusual, anything that struck you as being out of the ordinary?"

"No, not really."

"Strange car? Dumpster with its lid up instead of down, or down instead of up?"

"I don't think I even looked at the dumpster."

"So, nothing unusual this morning. How about last night? What time did you leave?"

"Last night? Around seven. Store closes at six, but I usually stay a bit longer to finish up orders and loose ends."

"Did you see anything then? Anyone? Anything unusual?"

"Nothing, nothing," he said shaking his head and running a hand through his hair. "I just got into my car and drove home."

"And the next time you came to the store was this morning about eight?"

Hank looked down at his hands, paused, seemed to consider something and then said quietly, "That's right."

"And when you left at seven you noticed nothing out of the ordinary?"

"I wish I could help you, but no, I don't remember anything at all. Nothing." He bowed his head, his shoulders shaking. "I'm sorry. It's all so frightening, lunatics running loose in my parking lot."

When Hank left a few minutes later, Roger looked out of the office door to see the rest of the employees sitting close

18

together on the rose-colored couch, whispering seriously. Someone was up making a fresh pot of coffee.

Next was Priscilla McNinn. Roger invited her in, closed the door and began. "Mrs. McNinn, can you go over once again what happened this afternoon?"

"It was like I told that lady policeman," she said sitting down heavily. "I went over to the dumpster to dump out my ashes and I saw this hand sticking up, the fingers sort of curled over like this," and she held her hand up to demonstrate. "At first I thought it was one of those rubber hands."

"Rubber hands?" wondered Roger aloud, raising his eyebrows.

"Those fake rubber hands, you seen 'em, you stick 'em out of your trunk and people think you got a dead body hanging out of your car."

How amusing, thought Roger dryly.

"So that's why I moved the cardboard away, so's I could see what it was."

"You picked up a stick from the ground?" said Roger reading from the notes Roberta had given him.

"Yeah, I'm not digging in all that slime with my bare hands, am I? And that's when I seen this weird-colored face with these bug eyes staring up at me. I'm gonna have nightmares for a long time after this."

"What did you do with the stick then?"

"I guess I dropped it. I don't know."

She sniffed into her tissue and dabbed her eyes. Rivers of blue eye makeup ran down her cheeks. Her hands shook. Roger wondered if she needed a cigarette. She looked like the type who needed cigarettes.

"Do you smoke?" he asked.

"Pardon me?"

"Do you smoke? Do you ever go out back and have a cigarette?"

"Only on my breaks."

"Did you go outside today?"

"Yes."

"What time was that?"

"Around two. That was my break on account of I had my lunch between eleven and eleven-thirty."

"When you were out there at two, did you notice anything unusual—strange car, person, anything?"

"No, but I was sitting on the bench. I couldn't see the dumpster with the cars in the way and all. I didn't stay out there very long on account of it was so hot. Didn't even finish my smoke. I hate this no-smoking thing, you know. Used to be we could smoke in the coffee room. Now? Nowhere. So in the winter we freeze—stand out there in thirty below—and in the summer we die of heat."

"So, sitting on the bench you didn't have a clear view of the dumpster?"

"No," she said, "On account of the cars being in the way."

"This morning when you came to work, you didn't walk over to the dumpster?"

"No."

"During the times you were in the parking lot, nothing struck you as being unusual? I want you to think very hard."

"Nothing. I didn't see nothing."

"Last night you got off work at what time?"

"Yesterday was my day off."

Roger wrote briefly in his notebook, then rose and handed her his card. "Thanks, Mrs. McNinn. Call me if you think of anything else."

"I can go now?" she asked. "I got my kids at home. Probably wrecking the place by now."

He watched her lumber out of the office and into the blistering heat to head for home.

About three quarters of an hour later he had interviewed

all of the employees. There were several time periods unaccounted for, and Roger made a note of these. Although he was fairly sure the body had been in the dumpster since last night, he couldn't rule out the possibility that it had been dumped there today. Not one of the employees had seen or heard anything unusual in the back lot. A few of the stock boys had reported throwing more garbage into the dumpster, burying the corpse even further.

Roger had no further reason to stay. He walked to the front. Hank was spraying a bin of oranges with a fine mist.

"Thank you," he said to Hank. "I may need to call you again."

"No problem, brother."

The two IDENT detectives from Calgary were kneeling and examining the ground a couple feet away from the dumpster when Roger approached.

The shorter of the two was scooping up small samplings of some brownish dirt and gravel into a plastic evidence bag. He stood up when Roger approached.

"Corporal Sheppard, I'm Alec McGann."

"Roger Sheppard."

"Looks like blood," said the other one. "I'm John Woods, by the way. I think we've met before."

Roger nodded. "Blood on the ground?" he asked.

"He could have been shot here and then his body put into the dumpster."

"Shot here," said Alec pointing with a gloved hand, "and then dragged. Do you see those marks in the gravel? Almost obliterated now by traffic, but still there."

John added, "We're thinking this was one person. Two people wouldn't drag a body, they would lift it."

"Murder weapon?" asked Roger.

"Nothing yet. Your constables are looking in the dumpster now," said Alec nodding toward the dumpster where Duane and Dennis were knee-deep in muck.

"How come there's so much garbage in here?" asked Duane, holding up a McDonald's take-out bag. "That's what I'd like to know. We've got half the garbage of Chester and Calgary combined. You got your McDonald's, your Wendy's, your Pizza Hut," he said, holding up the appropriate containers.

At that moment from behind him, Roger heard a voice he recognized.

"Hey, Corporal!"

Roger sighed. The voice belonged to reporter Chad Williamson from CKJY-TV, Calgary. Ambling behind him was a long-haired camera-man wearing a sweat-blotched black tee shirt which read *No Animal Testing*.

"Wanna tell me what's going on here?" asked Chad.

"Not really," answered Dennis.

"We heard a possible homicide."

Roger took over. "A body was found in this dumpster around 4:30 this afternoon, and please, stay behind the tape. You'll contaminate the crime scene."

"Anyone we know?"

"Next of kin haven't been notified."

"Gun shot? Strangling? Stabbing? Natural causes?"

"The autopsy hasn't been completed."

"Natural causes—like the guy's going to have a heart attack in a dumpster. Where's Laird?"

"Vacation."

"So you're in charge now, huh?"

"Lord, help me not to strangle this, this . . ." Roger prayed silently.

Dennis looked up from the dumpster. "Chad, if you and your hippie friend don't turn around and crawl back under whatever rock you came from, you'll be wearing this watermelon."

"Can I quote you?"

Duane made ready to throw the watermelon like a football, thought better of it, and put it down.

"Let's set this up," Chad said to the camera-man. A few minutes later the camera's red light was blinking and Chad began, "Chester RCMP are tightlipped about a body found in this dumpster behind a grocery store in Chester at about 4:30 P.M. today. Police spent most of this evening going through garbage to try to find . . ."

As the taping continued, Roger stood and waited. He should be the one to answer Chad's questions, not Duane or Dennis who might have difficulty remaining cool.

A few moments later the microphone was shoved in Roger's face. "A body was found," he heard himself saying, "in this dumpster abut 4:30 this afternoon. We are waiting for next of kin to be notified and the autopsy to be completed before we can comment further. We are not ruling out foul play."

The two turned and walked back to the large mauve van with TV-CKJY scrawled artfully across the side. Since leaving the grocery store, Roger was perspiring heavily, and there was Chad, his cotton shirt neatly pressed, his blond hair freshly styled. No wonder the *Calgary Herald* in one of their lighter moments had dubbed him Calgary's Most Eligible Bachelor.

CHAPTER 3

He had told her it was stupid to want to change her name.
Her real name, Madeline, was perfectly okay. But he had
never understood how important it was that she change her
name. He would just shake his head and aim the remote at
the TV. She was thinking of Mary or Madonna—Madonna
was nice, it was a real name, someone told her. Mothers
actually named their daughters Madonna. She liked playing
around with names, letting them roll around her tongue, writing them down on scraps of paper with little hearts as *i* dots.
Erica Jeanette. Madonna Juliet. Cherise Erica. She had finally settled on Madonna Juliet—not the rock star Madonna,
but the mother and baby. She had a picture in her mind,
remembered from some magazine's long-ago December cover,
of a sad-eyed young woman shawled in blue and holding a
sad-eyed baby. Tom told her it cost money to change your
name. But she couldn't, she *wouldn't*, go through the rest of
her life with the name of Madeline.

She scolded herself, as she did every night, that tomorrow
she would go to the Chester town hall and ask how to change
one's name. She was making all these plans while standing at
the sink in the tiny kitchen and pouring water into the kettle
for tea. She dropped a scrunched-up tea bag into her mother's
faded china cup with the dark roses around the rim. She
smiled a little. Mrs. Smith would have a fit. To be *proper*,
loose tea—never bags—was to be placed in a china pot which

had been rinsed first in boiling water.

Back in the front room, she settled herself on the couch, wrapped herself in a ratty beige quilt and aimed the remote at the TV. Oprah would be on soon.

She sipped the hot drink; her supper until Tom came home. There was hardly anything in the refrigerator anyway—half a jar of sweet pickles and some mayonnaise was about it. She'd ignore her grumbling stomach and wait for him.

Tom hadn't been home in a week; well, if you didn't count last night—that half hour when he had waltzed in, eyes bright, acting like a crazy person. He made a phone call and then had run out again.

Maybe she should call her friend, Janice, from next door. If she went over there, Janice would give her something to eat. Janice always had lots of food at her house, and expensive stuff, too, like frozen waffles and Sara Lee cakes.

The tea was hot going down and seemed only to accentuate her hunger. But she'd wait for Tom. He always brought food when he came, take-out bags from McDonald's or Arby's, or those wrapped-up burritos from the Seven-Eleven. She shivered. It was hot; her arms and legs felt sweaty, but she shivered, and wrapped herself more tightly with her quilt.

"I'll be back, Madeline," Tom had told her last night. "I'll be back in half an hour. Wait up for me." Then he had moved restlessly from room to room and back again.

"Why are you wearing that stupid-looking jacket?" she had asked, hardly looking up.

"Why not?" His eyes had blazed. Then he leaned his head back and laughed. "Why not! It's a perfect fit!"

Madeline had just shrugged and sighed and gone back to her program. All night she waited for him, watching the movie of the week, the nightly news, the late-night talk shows and the late movie. She waited and waited.

On the opposite wall above the TV hung his autographed

Calgary Flames poster. Rows of smiling faces. Scrawled names. Tom never missed hockey. "Please come home, Tom," she whispered. "Don't leave me. Please, please, please come home." Why did she suddenly feel so cold?

In the middle of a Pampers commercial she heard someone knocking on her front door. Maybe it was Janice. She rose and undid the locks.

* * *

Roger was alone in the detachment office. It was late. After he called Kate to tell her he'd be a while yet, he dug out his notes, sat down at Adele's desk and switched on the computer. Adele, the detachment's receptionist/secretary, had the office word processing computer on her desk. Their detachment had three computers; one of them hooked into police and RCMP detachments Canada-wide, another had the capability to call up information worldwide, and the third, the one on Adele's desk, was mainly used for word processing. He opened the Diet Coke he'd bought at the Seven-Eleven and placed it on the desk beside him. He began typing:

The body of Tom Anderchuk, white, male, age 23, was found at approximately 4:35 P.M. by Priscilla McNinn, an employee of Pfeiffer's Independent Grocers on her way home from work. The victim was lying on his back in a dumpster used by Pfeiffer's Grocery Store. He appeared to be shot once through the head. Medical examiner Dr. Ansen Ridley estimates the time of death between 8 P.M. and 2:00 A.M. Little blood or tissue was found underneath the body. Examination of the scene suggests that the victim was shot about three feet to the right of said dumpster and then dragged to the dumpster. He was shot from the front and preliminary examination of the body shows no signs of a struggle.

Roger paused, his fingers on the keys. *Store employees were questioned and none report seeing anything out of the ordinary. The victim was wearing Nike running shoes, no socks, jeans, a red Calgary Flames tee shirt and a extra-large wool plaid sports jacket.*

Roger was a careful and slow typist. He leaned back in his chair and took another long drink out of the can, warm already, but at least it was wet. He took his notebook out of his jacket pocket and copied word for word his interviews with the store employees.

Keying in the other computer, he called up the police records on Thomas Brian Anderchuk. On the screen he read: *possession of narcotics, impaired driving, resisting arrest, break and enter.* Tom Anderchuk was born in Chester and had grown up here. He seemed to have had nothing but problems since day one—school truancy, possession of alcohol, numerous school suspensions, possession of narcotics at age fourteen, (the same age as Becky). The report stated that he had spent time in the Young Offender's Centre in Calgary and two stints at a youth detox center in Edmonton. A psychiatric evaluation at Alberta Hospital when he was sixteen showed no signs of mental illness. As well, the reports listed various social workers, counselors and psychiatrists who could furnish further information. He printed it off, then moved the arrest record into his word processing file and edited it for his report. What emerged was the life history of a very troubled young man.

Roberta and Clayton had left word that Tom had lived with a young woman named Madeline Westmier who had given them the name of Leslie Ferguson, sister of the deceased in Red Deer, Alberta. His parents, apparently, lived in Ontario. He incorporated these statements into his report as well.

By the time Roger pulled into his own driveway it was 11:15. The house was quiet and dark.

"Everything okay?" Kate stood in the kitchen doorway in a long cotton nightgown.

"As well as can be."

"The news said the police haven't ruled out foul play."

"Ah, you heard your friend and mine, Chad Williamson." She smiled. "Well, that's how us ordinary folk find out what is going on. This was supposed to be your day off."

"Yeah, well, the murderer didn't ask me if it was my day off."

He sat down at the kitchen table, suddenly realizing how tired he was.

Kate pulled up a chair next to him. "Is there a crazy person roaming the streets or what?"

"There are cities full of crazy people roaming the streets at any given time."

"Who was it?"

"You ever heard of Tom Anderchuk?"

"Tom? Yes. He was the one killed?"

Roger nodded.

"Who killed him?"

"We don't know."

Kate rose and stood, her back to him at the kitchen sink. "That's so sad," she said quietly. "I remember him as a teenager. Just a few years ahead of Sara in school. Always getting into trouble. She told me he got kicked out of his house when he was thirteen, and used to sleep in grain bins."

"Sara knew him?"

"This is a small town. The kids hear things. But everyone knew he was into drugs and alcohol. Does he have parents, a family?"

"Just a sister in Red Deer. Parents live in Ontario somewhere. They're being notified. He was living with a Madeline something."

"Does this have something to do with drugs?"

"I don't know, but I think so. It was sort of like he was executed—one bullet hole through his forehead. Far too neat for your average drunken brawl death. Not even any signs of a struggle—just shot once cleanly through the forehead. He would have dropped instantly."

"So he was facing his killer, maybe talking with him, then all of a sudden the killer pulls out a gun and shoots him?"

"That's what it looks like."

Kate got up and walked to the open screen door. She looked out into the silent night and ran a hand through her thick, dark hair. Tonight her long unruly hair was held off her shoulders by a large white barrette.

"It's so sad," she said again.

After a long pause, Roger asked, "How's Becky?"

She turned to him, almost relieved, it seemed, to have the subject changed.

"In a royal snit as usual," she said quietly.

"Is that news?"

"She still wants to go to that rock concert in the city—the Dark Hearts one. I said no."

"Good. You heard about the riot, two injured in Hamilton when they performed there a couple of weeks ago."

"That's what I told her. She said that had nothing to do with the group. Apparently she has a free ticket. Some friend of hers, Carrie, had an extra ticket. It seems her mother was going to go with her and now has to work. Can you imagine? A *mother* going to a Dark Hearts concert? So Carrie gave the ticket to Becky. For free. She doesn't even have to pay for it."

"We can't let her go."

"I agree with you."

He rose and stood beside her.

"You look tired," she said. He put his arm around her and she leaned against him.

Together they looked out into the dark night. Somewhere in the distance, a dog barked.

* * *

Roger poured hot coffee from the office coffee-pot into a large black mug with **DAD** inscribed around it in large red letters. He couldn't remember which of his daughters had given it to him. Beside him, Clayton was depositing a large Tupperware container of blueberry muffins on the coffee stand. Clayton's wife regularly baked muffins, donuts or other delicacies for the detachment.

Only 9:30 in the morning, but already the underarms of Clayton's short-sleeved tan shirt, the summer uniform of the RCMP, were darkened with sweat. The building was air-conditioned but it didn't feel like it.

"Tell me about this girlfriend of his," said Roger to Clayton, "Did you get a sense of her at all?"

"She was scared out of her socks," said Clayton breaking open a muffin and smearing it with butter. "And she calls herself Madonna Juliet. Seemed real insistent about it."

"Were you able to get a look around the apartment?" asked Roger.

"We did," said Roberta, walking over with a coffee mug in her hand. "Madeline, or Madonna, well, she totally broke down when she heard the news. Totally."

"We got very little out of her," added Clayton. "She was practically incoherent. She did give us the name of that sister in Red Deer. A Leslie Ferguson who's coming down later to ID the body."

"But she did say one thing," said Roberta. She kept saying, 'I warned him, I warned him.' That was it. When we asked what she meant, she just broke down. We couldn't get anything else out of her."

Roger nodded and Clayton added, "We only found a few things in the apartment—a drawer full of his clothes, a razor in the bathroom, a thing of Mennen Speed Stick. But nothing else. No papers and no drugs, nothing. For a drug dealer, he certainly wasn't living the high life."

A lazy fly flew in front of Roger's face and he brushed it away. Out front the telephone rang and he could hear Adele's muffled voice.

"We think someone should go back today," said Roberta. "I'm worried about her. I don't think she has anyone."

"Corporal," Adele leaned around the partition of her office. "One of Pfeiffer's employees from yesterday remembers something."

"Thanks Adele," he said picking up his desk phone.

"Is this the policeman I talked to yesterday?" asked the timid voice on the other end.

When Roger assured him it was, the voice continued.

"Hi, I mean, hello, sir. This is Brent Simonsen, I work at Pfeiffer's. A stock boy. I talked with you yesterday."

"Yes," prompted Roger.

"Remember how you told me to call you if I remembered anything?"

"Yes?"

"Well, I don't know—maybe this isn't important or anything, but I do remember something . . ."

"Go on."

"Well, remember when I told you that I drove around the parking lot that night on my way to Wendy's?"

"Yes?"

"Well, I was lying in bed last night going over what happened and all, and I remembered that when I was driving around the corner of the building, I was sure I saw Mr.

Pfeiffer's car parked there, well, his van actually. I mean, I don't know but I thought it was his. It looked like his."

"What time was this?"

"I was awake about two o'clock last night, it was."

Roger smiled. "No, I mean, what time did you see this van?"

"Oh, yeah, sorry. I think it must have been a quarter after ten or so."

"Where was his van parked?"

"Parked? In his usual spot, I think."

"And you're certain it was his?"

"Well, I'm not real sure, but I think so—his blue one, 'cause I remember thinking to myself, Mr. Pfeiffer must be working late or something."

"Mr. Simonsen . . ."

"Yeah?"

"I wonder if you would mind coming down to the detachment to talk to one of the constables here."

"No problem. Mr. Pfeiffer says we're supposed to help you all we can."

CHAPTER 4

When Madeline was a child, she lived in lots of houses. Most were little more than two-room or three-room apartments, but she called them all houses. Because they moved so often and so quickly, Madeline learned to pack her things hastily, stuffing all of her clothes and a Teddy Bear named Harold into a scuffed white suitcase with a hinge missing that her mother had brought home from the Salvation Army store. Her dad would throw their bags, beds, a couple of dilapidated dressers, a few chairs and a kitchen table into the back of their old truck, and they'd be off to some new house.

The first place that she had any memory of was a few rooms in a basement, underneath a large house with lots of children and pets. Madeline remembered standing on tiptoe on her bed and looking out of her ground-level window at a black and white cat hunkered down in the dirt in the basement window-well. He was always there; in the morning when she woke up he'd be there, and in the afternoon when she went to take her nap he'd be there, and at night when she went to bed he'd be there, sitting, licking himself all over or staring in at her with his big expressionless face, his tail wagging gently.

Then there was the house with the stairs. They lived in the top couple of rooms of an old three-story house. The only way up was a set of rickety wooden steps which wound around the building. Around eight years of age at the time,

Madeline wondered why people would build a house with no inside stairs. She conjured up images of evil people banished to this place forever. She would imagine a time when the house, instead of being chopped up into lots of little houses, was all one house—a castle—for she couldn't imagine one family living in a house so grand. There would be lots of laughing children all dressed like the girls in Little House on the Prairie. They would chase each other through the rooms. There was also an evil man-witch who would sneak in the basement window and try and snatch the children. But the mother of the house was too smart and strong for him, and she would grab the man-witch, throw him outside and make him climb the 54 stairs up to the attic (Madeline counted them once) and be alone forever. Then the mother and the children would burn the stairs so the evil man-witch could never escape. However, sometimes the children would hear him. Cuddling together in bed on dark nights, they would hear him scratching at the ceiling and crying.

In those days her mother cried a lot. Late at night Madeline would wake up and hear muffled sobs coming from the front room. That would mean that her father, the man-witch, was out again. So Madeline would tiptoe out of her room and stand in the doorway. There would be her mother, small and scrunched-up in her quilt, wiping her eyes with its edges. Madeline would move toward her then and her mother would lift up a part of the blanket and Madeline would crawl under, putting her arms around her mother's neck until gradually her sobs subsided. They would stay that way for a long time, the two captured children. Sometimes Madeline would fall asleep and wake up in the morning tucked in securely in her own bed. But, more often than not, the two of them would stay together on the couch waking up to the pale sunlight filtering in through the curtains. Sometimes in the early morning Madeline would hear her father stumbling up the 54 stairs.

She'd leave the couch and move soundlessly toward the kitchen. Through the smudgy window in the door, she would see her father stumbling up the stairs, cursing loudly and swaying from side to side against the railing. She'd watch him with no emotion, like the cat in the window-well. When he got within ten stairs of the door, she'd run silently to her bedroom and slip under the bedcovers and close her eyes.

Madeline seldom cried in those days. It wasn't until her parents were both gone that Madeline learned how to cry. One of the things she'd taken when she left was her mother's quilt, and now, as the pallid morning light came in around the cracks in the venetian blinds, Madeline wrapped herself tightly in that quilt and cried for her mother.

She hadn't slept last night. Even though the police told her Tom was dead, she wouldn't believe them. All night she sat with her face pressed against the window between two venetian blinds waiting, waiting for him to come home. For surely he would. He promised.

Earlier that night a lady officer had put an arm around her and asked if there was anyone she could call for her.

"No, thank you."

"Brothers? Sisters?"

"I'm an only child."

"Parents?"

"Both dead."

The police officer had looked at her sadly then. "I'm so sorry," she said. "Can I call a friend or a neighbor?"

"Maybe Janice from next door."

When Janice came over, they hugged and hugged and cried and sat close together on the couch all evening while baby Samantha toddled throughout the three rooms dragging around a noisy pull-toy. Eventually, Janice rose and made coffee and then toast. Then she talked a lot about the police not doing their job and about people not being safe on the streets anymore. Finally, at eleven, Janice had left.

"I've got to get Sam into bed," she told Madeline, a hand on her arm. "But I'm right next door. You need anything you just holler, or punch the door and I'm right over, you hear?"

Madeline nodded numbly and Janice continued. "I'll be over first thing in the morning. I'm gonna bring you something to eat when I come, so you go to bed and try to sleep, you hear? You want some sleeping pills or anything?"

Madeline shook her head. She had some she said, and thanks, she'd be all right.

As the sun grew brighter she heard a knock on her door. Janice entered with two Egg McMuffins and two large coffees.

* * *

"The van? The old blue one?" said Hank to Roger on the phone later that morning. "That vehicle's always there. It's one of my old ones and most of the time I leave it at the store."

"In your statement you said you got in your car around seven and drove home. That's true then?"

"Certainly. I leave that van parked at the store for any off-hours delivery. I'm surprised it being there even raised an eyebrow."

"And the next time you drove to the store was the following morning."

"Right."

The detachment was quiet when Roger hung up. Clayton and Roberta were out on the house-to-house investigation and Duane and Dennis were checking out all of the *F. Schmidts* in the area. Some of the other constables were scheduled to come in on later shifts or were off for the day. Sergeant Laird was still away.

Adele was on the phone when he fetched the Diet Coke

that he'd brought in earlier. She waved at him as he walked by. He smiled back. He liked Adele. She was a single mom. Her husband, an RCMP constable, had been killed while on duty near Whitehorse in the Yukon. Alone on night patrol, he had pulled over a speeding pick-up truck. The truck contained two escaped convicts who shot him point blank. He died instantly. The two in the truck were picked up just outside of Yellowknife in the Northwest Territories. They were given life imprisonment with no chance of parole, which meant they'd probably be out in a couple of years, he thought sourly.

Adele and her two-year-old son, Sean, moved from Whitehorse to Calgary to be near her parents. When the job of detachment receptionist/secretary came open in Chester, Adele applied. That she would choose to work in an RCMP detachment always amazed Roger. Sean was now eight.

Back at his desk he got out his notebook to review his interviews and notes.

"Clayton and Roberta just called in," Adele called to him. "A few more people in the neighborhood reported hearing a sound like a shot the night before last. Most thought it was a car backfiring or fireworks—people don't think of gunshots— around ten forty-five, some say it was closer to eleven."

She continued, "Your wife called, too, while you were on the phone. She said to remind you that you're supposed to have supper at Pfeiffers at seven tonight, but if you're too busy with the new investigation, just let her know early enough so she can call them. You got that?"

"Oh, yes. Supper. Almost forgot."

"Is it about the investigation?"

"No. A couple of weeks ago they invited us out for a barbecue."

"They've got a pool don't they? And a hot tub?"

"I think so. I've never been out there."

"I'm told it's quite the place. Have fun."

"I'll try."

He and Kate had attended the same church as the Pfeiffers ever since Roger was transferred here five years ago. Hank was on the church board. They had never socialized much with Hank and his wife, Rose. Roger felt this dinner was a sort of "thank you" for agreeing to speak at the CMBC next month. He'd do his best to be out of here by seven.

Opening his folder he went over his notes again, puzzling over the name F. Schmidt. The skinny Chester phone book had yielded no "F. Schmidts." There were three in the Calgary book. He'd also begun making inquiries about Azuyo and the Riverboat. Maybe he'd get a handle on a bit more of this tomorrow when the full forensics report was due to arrive from Calgary.

By mid-morning, with a few more notes added to Tom Anderchuk's already-thick file, he decided to head out to Madeline Westmier's. Looking down at the address which he had scrawled on a three-by-five card, he nearly collided with a small, serious-looking, fortyish woman wearing a pair of oversized horn-rimmed glasses.

"Sorry," he said reaching for her arm to steady her.

"Not at all," she said, extending her hand formally. "I think you probably want to see me. I'm Tom Anderchuk's sister."

"Mrs. Ferguson?"

"Leslie, yes," she said.

A few minutes later they sat across from each other in Roger's office.

"This is all so unpleasant," she said clasping and unclasping her hands, pushing her glasses up on her nose and running a hand through her long graying hair.

"I'm so sorry," said Roger gently. "I know how hard this must be for you."

"It's such bad timing, all of this . . ."

She looked down at her hands folded on her lap and said, "We've got that houseboat booked in British Columbia on Shuswap Lake. We've been saving for such a long time. I would hate to lose it. You don't suppose they'll give us our money back under the circumstances?"

Roger stared at her.

"I take it you and your brother were not very close," is what he finally said.

"Oh." She looked up sharply, "I guess you could say that."

"When was the last time you saw him?"

"Maybe three, four years ago."

"No Christmas get-togethers, birthdays?" He was aware that his line of questioning was going slightly beyond the call of duty, but this family-life or lack of it intrigued him.

"No. As I said before, we weren't very close."

"I see. Your parents?"

"They live in Ontario, but they're flying out. Should be here today sometime."

"Tom wasn't close to them either?"

"Our parents moved to Windsor when Tommy was thirteen. He decided he didn't want to go with them, so he came to live with Jeff and me. I was already married at the time. You see I'm sixteen years older than he is. Was."

"Do you have any idea of who may have wanted to do this to him?"

Leslie shrugged, sighed and a little chuckle escaped her throat. "Let's face it. Practically everybody."

"Can you name anyone specifically?"

"No, I can't name anyone specifically now. I mean, he left home, left Jeff and me when he was around fifteen. I mean, we couldn't keep him the way he was, could we? Playing hooky all the time, getting into trouble, cops coming over all the time . . ." She paused and looked down at her fidgeting fingers. Then she said, "I mean he wasn't one of us anyway."

"Excuse me?"

"He was adopted if you must know. And unfortunately for us, we got one with bad genes. Happens sometimes with these adopted kids." She paused slightly before continuing. "My mother almost died having me, so the doctor said no more kids. Unfortunately, Dad wanted a son, someone to carry on the name—too bad about that now, eh?" she shrugged. "So I'm sixteen years old when they go down to the adoption agency and pick up three-month-old Tommy Trouble."

She was describing it the way you might talk about going down to the SPCA to pick out a puppy, only with less compassion, thought Roger. He had to change the subject or he would start throwing things.

"How well do you know Madeline Westmier?"

"Her? Try my best not to. I was there this morning. Left as soon as I could. She's crying like a banshee. She was mainly the one that got Tommy in trouble when he was a teenager."

Roger scrawled notes as she talked. The room was getting stuffy. He breathed out a puff of air on his page, shaking his head slightly. Leslie rose tentatively from her chair. "If that's all you need . . ."

"For now. I may call you again." She extended her hand to him but he ignored it.

On the way out, she asked, "Oh, and when is the body going to be released? I've got to get it driven up to Red Deer somehow for the funeral."

"Two or three days. In cases of violent death, such as this, the entire body must be examined, inside and out, for evidence. Physicians look for debris left under fingernails, hair and blood samplings, marks on the skin, anything. Since it was a gunshot wound to the head, the skull must be thoroughly examined. The bullet exited the skull at the back, but a good forensics expert can even discover the caliber of the gun, just by examining the wound itself. It really is amazing." He was hoping that his rather long and graphic and totally unnecessary explanation would bring on even the tiniest flicker of passion from this woman, but she just stood there like a piece of gray granite, expressionless, emotionless.

"I understand," she said. "Someone will let me know when we can get it up to Red Deer?" She shrugged and muttered, "I suppose we will have to pay some sort of transport cost. The RCMP wouldn't, I suppose . . ."

Roger glanced at his notebook pretending he didn't hear. With a sigh she turned to leave.

To her retreating figure Roger said, "With any luck, all of this unpleasantness will be over and you won't have to miss that houseboat vacation."

CHAPTER 5

The apartment wasn't an apartment at all but a converted row of motel units, sagging and faded. Along a facing wall of what was probably once the office, the words, *Starlite Motel* were still readable, although just barely.

The grass around the units was yellowed and stiff and patched with brown dirt. A varied array of rattle-trap bicycles, tricycles, and baby strollers with cracked seats and rusting wheels leaned against the small cement porches which led into each unit.

Most of the doors were open in the heat. As Roger walked past, he saw undershirted men sitting at kitchen tables and tee-shirted women on couches watching the late morning offering of soap operas and talk shows.

The door to Apartment 23 was shut tight, the curtains drawn. He stood looking at it for a few seconds.

"You looking for Madonna?"

A woman sat smoking on the cement steps of a neighboring apartment, eyeing him warily. Her dark-rooted, fuzzy yellow hair was fastened back in a rubber band. She wore a bright pink halter-top and black shorts that looked as though they had been through a couple hundred washings. Her feet were bare. Her arms were bony.

"Are you Madeline Westmier?"

She leaned back and laughed until she coughed.

"Heck, no, wait'll I tell her someone thought I was her.

No, Madonna lives in twenty-three. I'm Janice. In twenty-four."

A chubby, fair-haired baby smudged in dirt and wearing only a sagging diaper toddled toward him, smiling and extending a large kitchen spoon.

"Samantha!" yelled the woman, "Get back here!"

The baby turned and ran whining back toward Janice who placed her down in the dirt beside the steps. She began to dig.

"Madonna ain't in the mood for no company, I can tell you that much."

"Is she in, do you know?"

Janice drew deeply on her cigarette which was now just about a quarter of an inch long.

"She's in all right. Afraid to leave. I been keeping an eye on her. Poor little thing. The sister's been in and out, but the sister's a jerk; Samantha, don't eat the dirt!"

The baby suddenly let out a wail. Janice leaned over and hoisted the child up onto the stoop. "I just hope you catch that guy that killed Tom," she said, carrying the child into her apartment through the open door. "Tom was a nice guy."

Roger rapped on the door to Number 23. About two minutes later, it was opened a crack. Through the safety latch, Roger caught a glimpse of a pale face, devoid of makeup with very red-rimmed eyes.

"Madeline Westmier?"

"Yes, but my name's not Madeline. I don't answer to that name. Not now, not ever. My name's Madonna Juliet."

Even though her speech was blunt, almost brutal, there was a softness about her words, a hesitancy, a fear, maybe.

"I'm Corporal Roger Sheppard from the RCMP. I'd like to ask you a few questions."

"I already talked to the cops—a lady, and another person."

"May I come in?"

She stared at him for a few minutes. Her face seemed more than empty of makeup; it seemed to be barren of any color at all, almost translucent. Her hair was straight and blonde and fell to her cheekbones. It was very light, a white blonde and to Roger's inexperienced eye, it looked natural. He could see that she was a pretty girl, and her face seemed to lack an edge of hardness that he saw in so many other young people.

"Oh, what the heck," she said undoing the latch. He entered a dim, stale-smelling living room. A faded quilt lay haphazardly across the couch. On the floor were a couple of empty cartons from McDonald's. He guessed she had just gotten up.

Roger followed her into a small kitchen.

"You want some coffee?" she said filling a battered flowered kettle with water. "I know I could use some."

The sink was jammed with dirty dishes. She had to stack them precariously on the counter in order to fit the kettle under the tap. She wore cutoffs and an oversized white Calgary Flames tee shirt. He guessed it was one of Tom's.

"Yes, thank you, Miss Westmier. That would be very nice."

"Instant okay?"

"Instant's fine."

He settled himself into an aluminum chair at the small table which was shoved against the wall. The room was unbearably stuffy and hot, yet all of the windows were closed and the curtains drawn.

She set the kettle on the burner and turned it on. Then she sat down at the table across from him.

He flipped open his notebook and began, "I know this is difficult for you, but last night when the officers were here, you said that you warned Tom. Can you tell me what you meant by that?"

"Nothing."

"Nothing?"

She shook her head and looked past him into the living room.

"Nothing," she said again.

He said gently, "I'd like to help you. What were you warning him about?"

Roger waited. Long silences had never bothered him.

The kettle began to screech. Madeline rose and filled a mug with boiling water and set it down on the table in front of Roger along with a spoon and a big yellow jar of generic instant coffee.

"You like anything in yours?" she asked.

"Just a bit of cream or milk."

"I don't have any milk. Sorry."

"Black's fine then."

She fixed her own coffee in a delicate china tea cup imprinted with dark red roses. It seemed somehow out of character for her, for the place.

"That's a pretty cup," he said.

"It was my mother's."

"Were you close to your mother?"

"You could say that."

"I'm sorry, Madonna."

A few moments later Roger tried again, "What did you warn him about, Madonna?"

She looked away and bit her lower lip, her eyes glistening.

"Nothing. I didn't mean nothing by it."

Then she got up and pulled a paper towel sheet off from a plastic reel near the sink and dabbed her eyes. Her hands shook.

"Madonna," he said gently, "We want to find whoever it was that killed Tom." He paused, debating whether or not to take notes. He decided against it. "I know you can help us.

You told the officers that the night Tom died he came home briefly."

"Yes."

"Exactly what happened that night? I'd like you to go over that again for me."

"Well, he was acting real jumpy-like."

"Jumpy-like?"

"Yeah, like he couldn't sit still."

"Did he say anything?"

"Not much."

"Do you remember anything he said?"

"Not really."

She looked away then, and chewed on her lower lip. Then she said, "He went into the kitchen and made a phone call. I don't know to who. I didn't ask. I was watching TV. The only thing I remember him saying on the phone is something like, 'I'll give you one last chance,' something like that."

"I'll give you one last chance."

"Maybe. Something like that. I'm not sure."

"And he didn't tell you who he was talking to?"

"No."

"Tom was wearing a large plaid jacket. Was it his?"

"No, I never saw it before." She looked down into the blackness of her coffee and stirred it with a spoon.

Another long silence. Roger pointed to an autographed Flames poster on the wall. "Tom a Flames fan, was he?"

She brightened slightly, "You're telling me! I couldn't disturb him at all if hockey was on. We went to a lot of the games, too. He met Lani MacDonald when he was a kid. Got his autograph, even. He was a Flames fan, all right. How did you know?"

"Is that his shirt?"

She looked down, "Yeah, I guess it is." And then she said quietly, so quietly that Roger had to strain to hear, "I keep thinking, I keep thinking he's going to come walking through that door like always. I can just see him there, you know, with that big, stupid smile on his face." She paused and looked down at the table. "He wasn't a bad person, Mister," she said quietly. "You may think he was, but I know he wasn't."

"Madonna, we want to find out what happened to Tom. You can help us by telling us everything you know. You were warning him about something. What was it?"

"I don't know. I told you that already. I can't talk anymore," she said backing away from him and blowing her nose into the paper towel. "I was in a state last night. I could have said anything."

Roger took a sip of the coffee and looked at her. She was shivering. He looked around the apartment and became aware of the emptiness of it. Oh, the rooms were cluttered with things—dirty dishes, grimy towels, and clothes draped on chair backs, but it was fundamentally empty. In his experience with death and funerals, people always sent a lot of flowers and brought over casseroles. There were no flowers or casseroles here.

"Have you seen Leslie?" he said.

"She came last night. She's gone now and good riddance. She's organizing his funeral in Red Deer. His parents are flying out from Ontario. Except his parents hated him and he hated them. They didn't even take him with them when they moved to Ontario. He was only thirteen and they didn't want him. I think they were glad to be rid of him. And now they're flying back here like the good, devoted mommy and daddy."

He took another sip. "Did Tom ever talk about a place in Nevada called Azuyo?"

"Nevada?" She looked startled.

He nodded.

"No, he never told me where he was going. He went to

Nevada?"

"He may have."

Both of her hands were around the tea cup as if to transfer the warmth from it. Roger noticed she was shivering uncontrollably. "I never heard of Azuyo," she said, still shaking.

"If Tom were to go down to a place like Nevada, how would he get there? Would he drive?"

"No, he took the bus mostly. Greyhound."

"Ever hear of someone called F. Schmidt?"

She paused, "No."

He stayed with her a few more minutes and finished his coffee, but she said little more. When he left, he gave her his card and told her to call him any time, day or night, if she needed to talk.

Driving through traffic on his way back to the detachment, Roger thought, is this what I talk about at the Christian Men's Breakfast Club, about people whose friends die and no one sends them flowers or brings over casseroles? Lives of the Poor and Unknown. Do I tell all of those successful Christian businessmen that?

* * *

Madeline could only remember one happy time in her entire childhood. Only one. She was around nine or ten, and her father was working. During her childhood he worked at a variety of odd jobs, never keeping one for very long. She remembered long stretches of time when he sat all day in front of the TV in a white tee shirt and gray sweat pants watching cable sports on TV and lifting hand weights. But this particular time, this one happy time of her life, he was like other dads and was gone during the day and then home at supper time.

School had just begun again for the year and it was still

quite warm with a whisper of coolness around the edges. She was walking home from school when her mother met her at the door taking her hands and dancing her around the front stoop.

Her mother was a small woman like Madeline herself, fine-boned and thin. On this particular day her mother wore a pair of faded cut-off jeans and a mustard-colored sweatshirt turned inside out.

Madeline always thought that she had the prettiest mother in the world, with her long, shiny yellow hair, not fat like the other mothers on her street.

"We're going to the movies tonight!" said her mother breathlessly. "Daddy just called. Do you want to know what he said? He said, 'Do my two favorite ladies want to go out to McDonald's and then to the movies?'"

Madeline stopped dead still and unwound herself from her mother's arms. It wouldn't happen. Her father had made promises like this before.

She turned her back to her mother and walked into the house and up the stairs to her room quietly, slowly, without a backward glance. She knew her father would not come home. He would stop off somewhere with his friends and get drunk and not come home. She knew that in about two hours she would descend the stairs to find her mother leaning into the couch and sobbing. Then Madeline would go into the kitchen and make peanut butter sandwiches for her mother and herself.

Nevertheless, an hour later they were squished into a McDonald's booth with a full tray of fries and burgers and drinks between them. At first she watched her father warily. He was a big man, with strong shoulders and arms. He always wore white tee shirts with the sleeves rolled up enough to reveal a small heart tattoo on his left arm. She had never seen him in anything else, even in the winter. That night he smiled. He was handsome when he smiled, thought Madeline. He had a dimple in his right cheek and one curl of his dark hair fell forward onto his forehead.

They arrived early at the movies and, after buying more drinks and a big red cardboard box of popcorn with extra butter, they took seats in the middle of the center section.

"The best seats," said her father sitting down. "The ones in the middle are always the best."

Madeline couldn't remember the name of the movie. What she did remember was a lot of shooting and people screaming and blood. She shut her eyes tight for a lot of it. Glancing around she didn't see any other children her age there. She had a vague feeling that this really wasn't a movie for kids.

After the movie they walked for a while along the darkened city street, her mother holding her right hand and her father holding her left. Madeline felt happy and proud. She hoped she would run into Miss Parsons, her teacher, or Mr. Adley, the school principal. She wanted them to see her with her parents and have them comment to each other, "Look at Madeline's nice family. Doesn't Madeline have a nice family?"

Later they stopped for ice-cream. Her father bought her a double scoop of bubblegum, her favorite. Her mother giggled and said, "Madeline, you can't eat all of that."

"Oh sure she can," said her father, handing her the big cone. "She's not a little wimp like you."

Her mother chose one scoop of chocolate ripple and her father had a triple of French vanilla. Madeline didn't finish her ice-cream after all, and her father finished it for her.

At home Madeline went to bed by herself and left her parents sitting in front of the TV. Later she heard the door slam and knew that her father had gone out. Sometime during the night she woke up to the loud sounds of arguing and cursing. She pushed her fists into her ears. She wished that ears had ear lids, like eye lids, and that just by closing them you could shut out the bad man-witch sounds.

Then she heard her mother crying.

Like Madeline was crying now. Janice was next door, probably Samantha was taking her afternoon nap. The policeman was gone, his card propped up against her phone. Leslie was gone now, too. Leslie had said that she would call their parents in Ontario, and she'd arrange with the police about Tom's body, and that she'd plan for the funeral in Red Deer. From the tone of her voice it was clear to Madeline that she was not invited. That was fine. She had never liked Leslie anyway. Neither had Tom.

CHAPTER 6

The day after Tom Anderchuk was murdered, Marjorie
Romaine sat at her kitchen table working through her second
pot of coffee of the day. At 1:30 in the afternoon, she was
still in her dressing gown, a faded blue peignoir with many
layers of nylon that swept the floor and fanned around her
scuffy pink mules. The kitchen TV was on, news on cable
she neither watched nor heard. Spread out in front of her on
the table was the *Calgary Herald,* her coffee cup sitting
squarely on a full-color feature in the life section on jam—
"Make the Most of Summer Strawberries."

Marjorie tried to remember if there was a time when she
cared about strawberries. If there was, it was probably when
the kids were small and still at home. The back of her mind
held a dim memory of strawberries—the four of them, she
and Wes and the children, Lisa and Derrick, filling plastic
buckets with the berries that grew down by the ravine. She
couldn't remember if these were strawberries or raspberries
they had picked that day. She hadn't been back there in
years.

On that day she had filled a plastic bucket with berries. It
took a long time, and Marjorie remembered wishing she had
brought a sun hat. Wes had half-filled his bucket before he
left. Even then, he left early from things. Hours later the
children brought their offerings to her—a few berries lolling
around the bottom of their plastic buckets—the red juice

dripping from their mouths betraying their guilt. She wasn't sure what she did with those berries. Perhaps she had made jam and lined her pantry with glass canning jars in neat rows. Perhaps she had made pies, as the article suggested. Perhaps she had washed them, drying them on paper towels to be scooped by handfuls for breakfast cereal. Perhaps she left the buckets on the back porch, finally throwing them out when they rotted.

Absently, she stroked her ankle where she'd fallen last night and closed the paper, carefully straightening it, as if there would be people who would come to her house and care whether newspapers were neatly stacked. She glanced at the front page again, the story about the murder here in Chester, the body found behind Pfeiffer's. Earlier that morning, hours ago, she had read the entire story and something about it bothered her, striking some familiar chord. The article said Tom Anderchuk had a police record, but anyone could tell that just by the mug shot they printed of him—black and white, dull eyes, scornful expression like he was daring the camera to come any closer.

Below the eyes Marjorie could see a spattering of freckles across his cheeks. She imagined that if he smiled he would look mischievous, impish, innocent. Like Wes. But he wasn't smiling, probably had never smiled in his life, and now would never smile again.

The phone rang. She ignored it. On the fourth ring she heard Wes on the answering machine, "Marj, I know you're there. Pick up Marjorie." How could he be so certain she would be there? She sat very still, as if movement in her kitchen would betray her presence.

"Okay Marj, if you're going to be that way, I called to say I'll be home briefly before I leave for Ottawa. Pick up my good shirts from the cleaners, would you? I'm in meetings."

In meetings. He was always in meetings, either that or off

on business trips or conferences. She'd taken to checking up on him so she knew the Ottawa conference was legitimate—unless the receptionists down at the town office were all in on his deceptions. Just two days ago she had called down to the Chester Town Office where Wes served as an elected town councilor.

"Hello, Paula," she tried to sound official. "This is Marjorie Romaine. I just want to check on this Ottawa trip. Wes mentioned that he was going to Ottawa, and I'm trying to sort out things—don't know if that's to do with his town council work or his business . . ."

"Oh, yes, Mrs. Romaine, it's the annual city and town government conference in Ottawa. Let me see here." Marjorie could hear the shuffling of papers. "Yes, he and the mayor are scheduled to go."

She gave Marjorie the dates, in a business-like voice but Marjorie knew that Paula wasn't fooled by her ruse. She imagined the office gossip when she hung up—*Marjorie Romaine isn't even going to Ottawa with her husband. Well, are you surprised?—I heard that he beats her up—I heard that she beats him up—I heard—I heard . . .*

The problem was, Wes hadn't always been like this. There was a time when he was kind, a time when he smiled. But now he had become like the picture of that boy who was killed, an unsmiling face forever washed in a bath of sadness.

And now he was changing again. A couple months ago he had gone from the passive husband who was never home to the angry, argumentative husband who shoved her around occasionally—well, not really. Last night he had pushed her. Could he know that she would stumble against the stone fireplace and injure her ankle?

She put her forehead in her hand and leaned over the table staring down at the picture of the freckle-faced boy who was murdered, wondering why he looked so familiar.

* * *

Madeline closed and locked all the windows and put the safety latch across the door. Surely it would be hot in here but that was a small price to pay. Then she dragged a kitchen chair over and hooked the back of it underneath the door-knob. It didn't look like it would keep anyone out, but she'd seen people do it on TV, so maybe it worked.

Just twenty-four hours earlier the police had come and told her that Tom was dead, and today Janice had told her some-thing else that made her afraid. Juggling Samantha on her knee, she had sat on Madeline's couch with a cigarette in her hand and said, "Too bad the police won't do anything about poor Tom . . ."

"What do you mean?" asked Madeline, startled.

"Look at it this way, Madonna. Tom—although you and I know that he was a nice guy—he isn't on the cops' 'favorite people of all time' list."

Madeline looked at her questioningly.

"Let me put it another way. Suppose the mayor had a kid who was murdered. They would be putting major energy into solving that one, let me tell you."

"So you're saying that since Tom had a record they're not going to try to find out who killed him?"

"That's exactly what I'm saying. I'm only saying this 'cause I'm worried about you."

"Don't worry about me."

"I'm worried this guy's gonna come and get you next."

Madeline was so tired now. Her entire body ached, yet she was afraid to close her eyes, afraid of what might be waiting for her in her dreams. Aside from the short nap this morning, she had not slept since Tom had run out yelling, "Just one more thing, Madonna, and we're home free."

Through the thin walls she could hear Janice's TV. She could also hear her loud laughing. She was probably on the phone. Madeline aimed her remote at the TV and clicked it on. She was supposed to go to work today. She worked at Chester's Best Fried Chicken four days a week, but today she hadn't shown up. A little while ago she called her boss and told him that she wouldn't be able to make it in for a couple of days. Her boss, Mr. Hendricks, muttered something about being sorry about Tom, and when could he expect her back. Madeline hung up without saying anything.

A swim meet on the sports channel caught her attention. She watched the team of women, a red maple leaf on each white bathing cap, glide through the pool. There was a time when all Madeline wanted to do was to swim in the Olympics. She was good at most sports. She and Tom played on a mixed fastball team in Chester, but it was in swimming that she excelled.

Growing up near Lake Winnipeg probably helped, plus all the swimming lessons she'd taken as a child in school physical education classes.

As a youngster, she always out-shone everyone in swimming. In both formal and informal races, she usually won. Watching the swimmers move through the pool, arm over arm, it was suddenly ten years ago and Madeline was standing beside the pool at the local recreation center. She was eleven years old and competing for the Grade Six Swimming Award.

She flexed her fingers. When the starting gun cracked she surface dove into the water and glided quickly to the other side. She felt good. And when the times were posted she was miles ahead of her nearest competitor, Jennifer Hadecker.

Following the swim meet, the award qualifiers were given half an hour to complete a twenty-question multiple choice test on water safety.

Madeline always struggled with her written work, but she was determined to do well on this test. She bent her head over the questions. Concentrate, concentrate, she told herself. But the words were hard. She was certain they'd never had some of them before. Around fifteen minutes later, Jennifer walked up and placed her paper on Miss Parsons' desk. Madeline looked around her. She couldn't have finished yet! Madeline was only on question 9. Fifteen minutes later, Miss Parsons asked for her paper. Madeline looked around and was chagrined to find that she was the only one left in the room. She was only on question 16.

Outside, the test was quickly forgotten when everyone congratulated her on her time. Her best friend, Jillian, said that the whole class *knew* that Madeline would win the Swimming Award.

"Oh, Maddy, that's wonderful! Of course we'll come to the assembly. Daddy and I will both come," said her mother that evening. "I am so proud of my little girl being the fastest swimmer in the whole school!"

With the assembly less than two weeks away, all Madeline thought about was the award. She even cleared a space on her dresser for the trophy. Every morning the first thing she would see when she opened her eyes was the little gold trophy that was going to be there with her very own name on it—Madeline Westmier.

Madeline had never received an award before. Every year she sat through the Awards Assembly and watched everyone else walk up to receive Math awards, Science Fair awards, English Composition awards. This year would be different. This year she'd get to go up in front of everybody and shake Mr. Adley's hand while everybody clapped. This time it would be for her.

On the day of the Awards Assembly, Madeline wore her best jeans and cleanest shirt. Her mother and father said they would be there by two.

All morning long she endured spelling, arithmetic, science and then lunch. One more class and then it would be time for the entire school to file into the auditorium. She held her hands in fists at her sides to keep them from shaking. Full of nervous excitement, she talked loudly to Jillian as they walked down the hall toward the assembly until Miss Parsons had to shush her with her finger against her mouth.

"You're going to get the Swimming Award, I just know it," whispered Jillian in her ear as they took their seats in the gym.

They stood and sang *O Canada* accompanied by Mrs. Martin on the tuneless upright. She turned around. She couldn't see her parents. There were too many heads in the way. They were probably sitting at the very back.

Finally, Mr. Adley, the principal, was welcoming the students, the parents and the guests. The Math Awards were first. The Science Fair Awards were next. Madeline watched impatiently while all the moms and dads ran up and snapped pictures of the Science Fair winners on the stage. This was taking forever! The Scholastic Achievement Awards were followed by the Music Awards, the Most Improved Students Awards and the Citizenship Awards. Finally it was time for the Sports Awards. Jillian grabbed Madeline's arm.

"This is a new award," explained Mr. Adley, "for the student who shows the most leadership in swimming. It is based, not only on speed, although there is a race involved, but on leadership and on the basis of a written test on water safety."

Get on with it. Get on with it, thought Madeline who was sitting on her hands to keep them from shaking.

"This year's recipient of the Grade Six Swimming Award goes to—Jennifer Hadecker! Jennifer, I might add, scored 100 percent on the Water Safety Test!"

Something wrong had just happened, Something terrible that wasn't supposed to happen had just happened. Jillian let go of her arm. Madeline didn't look at her. Instead, she held on to the sides of her chair and looked down at the space on the floor underneath the chair in front of her. Her stomach churned and she felt sick. Clapping all around her was thundering in her ears. To keep herself from getting sick, she memorized the pattern of dust and scuff marks on the floor. The rest of the ceremony was empty of meaning.

As she lay huddled underneath the blanket watching the meet, she wondered if Jennifer Hadecker was one of the television swimmers. After the assembly, she remembered walking past Miss Parsons who was taking a picture of Jennifer standing besides her parents and holding all of her awards.

Her own parents never came. Not even her mother. After school she had shuffled home alone. The house was locked and she unlocked it with the key she always kept on a chain around her neck. It was quiet. She made herself a jam sandwich and sat down in front of the TV. Hours passed. Still she was alone.

Finally, late at night her mother and father came jostling home, hanging onto each other, laughing and talking loudly. Madeline knew by the sounds that both of them were drunk. They tripped over the doorsill and when they saw her sitting on the couch, her mother said, "Oh, we have a daughter." Then she giggled, leaned against her husband and laughed again. "I almost forgot we had a daughter. Did you remember we had a daughter?" More peals of laughter.

When her father got drunk, he became abusive and angry. When her mother got drunk, she acted so stupid and loud that Madeline was embarrassed for her.

Madeline never mentioned the Awards Assembly again, and neither did her parents. A year and a half later her mother was dead and she had moved to Chester to live with the Smiths. By age fifteen when she had dropped out of school, no one in the whole world knew that Madeline had almost won the Grade Six Swimming Award.

The swimmers were finished and Madeline punched the mute button. She turned then and pressed her face into the heavy brown fabric of the couch, smelling the dense, oily smell of it. Quietly she sobbed until the swimmers were replaced by a home repair show which was replaced by the news.

* * *

The evening was still; there was no breeze at all. Hank and Roger were sitting on the Pfeiffer's cedar patio surrounded by multicolored lights which reminded Roger of Christmas. The remains of a steak barbecue—crumpled up pieces of baked potato foil, steak bones and crusts of garlic bread—were being dutifully cleared away by Kate and Rose. The four of them hadn't talked much about the murder investigation. On their way in, Hank had taken Roger aside and said, "This whole thing, this murder thing is upsetting to Rosie, especially since it happened near the store, so I'd appreciate it if we kept conversation about it to a minimum." That was fine by Roger.

Roger was only half listening as Hank talked on and on about investments, portfolios, earnings and how you never get ahead working for someone else and merely earning a salary.

Hank was a big man and if Roger hadn't known for certain he was a teetotaler, he would have described Hank as possessing a beer belly. Besides owning and managing Pfeiffer's Independent Grocers, he had also made money on various real estate transactions throughout Chester and Calgary. Hank seemed more relaxed than yesterday, not quite so shaken.

"You sure have a nice place here," said Roger, reaching for his iced tea on the table and hoping to change the subject.

"Worked hard for it," said Hank leaning back in his chair. "None of this stuff just arrives magically from the sky. I've put in my days of scrounging, of wondering where my next dollar is coming from, but now it has paid off. The Lord's been mighty good to us, too. That's for sure. But like I said before, Roger, you never get rich earning someone else's money for them. Take yourself for example."

Roger would have preferred that they didn't, but Hank continued, undaunted. "What do you have, ten more years with the force before you retire? What is it, twenty years and then full pension?"

"Twenty-five."

Hank leaned forward conspiratorially. "You've got to be thinking about a business then, something you can get into. You'll get full pension, but it'll hardly be enough to buy the groceries then. You take my advice and begin planning now. Have you any idea what you want to do when you retire?"

"Move to the west coast, buy a boat and sail around the world."

Actually, the idea had never occurred to him before, but suddenly it sounded very appealing.

"Yeah, and who's going to finance this grand adventure?"

"Haven't got that far yet," said Roger smiling. "Say," he said looking up, "Do I see coffee coming through the door?"

Rose and Kate emerged with a tray of coffee mugs and a plate of fruit, crackers and various kinds of cheeses. The difference between the two women couldn't have been more striking. Kate was tall and slender, and Rose was softly rounded and much shorter.

"The coffee has arrived," said Rose.

When they were comfortably seated, Kate said to Hank, "Rose tells me that Susan's two daughters won some award in gymnastics or something."

Hank chuckled, "They're just about the brightest little grand-daughter twins that a grandpa could ever want. Mother, go inside and get the album, will you?"

Roger could see Kate wincing behind her coffee mug. He knew that was one of her pet peeves—husbands who call their wives *mother*.

"The day you start calling me *mother*," she had laughingly told him once, "is the day I pack my bags."

Running a close second with Kate were husbands who call their wives *the wife*. Such as, *"The wife* and I would be glad to come over," or "I'll have to see what *the wife* is doing tonight."

"Kate, my name is Kate, not *the wife* and certainly never, never *mother*."

"That's fine with me, wifey," he had said, dodging her playful punch.

A few minutes later Rose returned with a thick photo album. Kate moved to the wicker couch to sit beside her.

"Now, there's Ashley and Amanda," said Rose pointing, "they're identical, you know. They live down in the States."

Roger leaned over pretending to be interested in the picture of the two towheaded little girls in pink tutus.

"How often do you get to see them?" asked Kate.

"About twice a year—not often enough for this grandma," answered Rose.

Kate exclaimed over every picture and Roger wondered if this was a female thing—this being interested in other people's photo albums, people you hardly knew. Kate could spend hours looking at the wedding pictures of complete strangers. "So how's the best man related to the groom?" she would ask. "He must be related to the ring bearer. I can see a resemblance there. No? And peach, she chose peach and lime for her colors. How unique!"

Kate was doing the same thing now with the Pfeiffer family album.

"And is this your son?"

"That's Robert, yes. He's in Chicago. A pastor there. They have two children, eighteen months and two months. We just got these pictures in the mail—was it last week, Hank?"

"I think it was last week."

"Oh, it must break your heart to be so far away from your grandchildren," said Kate. "And look at his eyes. That's an adorable outfit. How much did he weigh?"

"Nine one."

"Ohhh, a big guy. Look, Roger. What's his name?"

"Matthew. The older one is Jeffrey."

"Matthew and Jeffrey. So close together in age. Will you get to see them soon?"

"We're flying down the end of September."

"Do you have any other children?" asked Kate.

"One other daughter, Carol. She's in Calgary. Works in a dentist's office."

The chatter went on and on. Roger only half listened as he sat on the spacious all-weather cedar patio surrounded by dozens of hanging baskets and planters and lights. To the right of them, an eight-person hot tub and a kidney-shaped swimming pool reflected the colored lights. Behind him was a spacious six-bedroom home with three decks and two fireplaces. Roger began to think of another home—a squalid, hot, little apartment that used to be a motel—and of a girl who called herself Madonna Juliet for whatever reason, a fair-haired wisp of a girl who had no flowers. And of a young man who *was not one of us,* who was scorned by an elder, jealous sister, and abandoned by his parents.

CHAPTER 7

"Florence Schmidt is a little old lady who has about a million cats. Frieda Schmidt is an aerobics instructor. We interrupted her morning exercises. She kept at it with the video the whole time we were questioning her, and Fellowes Schmidt is . . ."

"*Fellowes* Schmidt?" asked Roger looking up from the desk.

"Fellowes, that's his name, the name on the name plate on his door—*Dr. Fellowes Schmidt, Head of Something*," answered Duane. "He's a university professor studying the habitat of the earthworm."

"He gave us a tour," said Dennis.

"You took a tour?"

"We couldn't get out of it," said Duane. "He says the earthworm is the key to saving the environment, global warming, the holes in the ozone layer, the whole nine yards."

"You took a *tour?*"

"We couldn't get out of it."

"He was a nice guy."

"He just kept talking."

"We couldn't get out of it."

Roger shook his head. "So now the two of you are so knowledgeable about earthworms that if we ever get a crime that we suspect is committed by earthworms, we'll call you up, okay?"

"Hey, don't get so touchy," said Duane.

"None of them had anything to do with Tom Anderchuk, Corporal. We weren't even close."

"There is a connection," said Roger tapping his notebook with his pen.

Duane said, "Look, I probably shouldn't be saying this but . . ."

"Then don't."

"Well, what I mean is," he continued, "you have us running off on wild goose chases and we haven't even heard from Calgary yet. It might not even be his handwriting."

"I'm willing to put money on it," said Roger. "Go out and check all the F. Schmidts you can find in all the surrounding towns—Red Deer, Edmonton if you have to. Go and find that blasted F. Schmidt!"

Duane and Dennis gave each other looks as they walked back to their desks.

As Roger rose, his chair scraped loudly on the floor. On his way out the door, he yelled to Adele, "Get Calgary on the phone and tell them that I need that forensics stuff out here yesterday."

Roberta called, "Corporal, another thing came up, a reported domestic dispute out at Romaines; caller said she heard loud yelling and thumping."

Roger stopped momentarily, "That would be Wes Romaine, our alderman?"

"The very same."

"Well, get someone on it, you don't need me for that." And he was gone.

It was this heat. That's what was the matter with him. No, it was more than that, he thought, walking toward his '87 Chevy. It was the fact that he'd been at this drug thing for half a year and hadn't made any progress. And now a murder, right in his own backyard. A young drug dealer named

Tom Anderchuk had been shot execution-style, his body dumped. And everything was clean; his apartment was clean, and his girlfriend, if she knew anything, wasn't talking, or was too afraid to. And that sister of his.

Roger's car wouldn't start. He turned the key again. His car often had trouble starting in the summer. The opposite of most cars, his operated better in the winter than in the summer. Great. Just great! He pounded his fist against the steering wheel. He needed a new car, he couldn't afford a new car. His house needed a new roof, and Sara was going to university in the fall. And where was the money going to come from for that? Maybe Hank was right. I should be thinking about investments, about doing something for me for a change.

A few minutes later he got the car going and pulled out of the lot. What I really need, he told himself, is a vacation. That imaginary sailboat moored on the coast was looking better all the time. Maybe I should just pack it all in and go into business, open up a car dealership or a donut shop, he thought. A former cop with his own donut shop, now wouldn't that be the end-all?

Roger didn't often blow up like this. He was always the cool one, the non-emotional policeman, the Christian cop. Keeping the world safe for its citizenry. Yeah, right. Keeping the world safe for the criminals was more like it.

Morning traffic was heavy and his air conditioner wasn't working. It needed to be refilled with freon—or was it freon that was bad for the environment? Wasn't freon replaced with something else? Probably something that caused cancer, Roger thought glumly. Earthworms! His officers were wandering around ooohing and ahhhing about earthworms while a murderer was running lose in Chester, probably handing out drugs to kids. He stopped at a traffic light, bent his head on the steering wheel and began to send a soundless prayer to heaven, a prayer of David, remembered from his morning devotions. *Why do the unrighteous prosper and mock God's people?*

Roger wondered why this particular murder upset him so. Tom could well have been a murderer himself, with all the drugs he'd dispensed in Chester during the past decade. But he couldn't get Madeline Westmier's eyes out of his mind— haunted, frightened, empty. What dreams lay behind those eyes? What sorrows? What fears?

As he moved ahead through the green light, he was conscious that his angry prayer was being replaced with a calmness, a peace in God's presence. Whatever happened, God was ultimately in control. God was sovereign.

"Help me Lord," he prayed, "I blow it so often."

* * *

Roger fixed himself a tall iced tea with extra ice and took it out to the small deck off their kitchen. Kate was out in the yard hosing down her vegetables. The tomato plants loved this heat and as long as they were kept watered, they grew in abundance. Lawn sprinkling in the drought was prohibited, but residents were allowed to water their gardens by hand between the evening hours of seven and ten.

Roger watched her. There were few mosquitoes this summer, unlike other summers when sitting outside in the evening was practically impossible. At least the drought had one good side-effect.

Roger had been right. The *F. Schmidt* on the dollar bill did, in fact, match the handwriting on Tom's driver's license. By the time Roger had returned to the office that day, much cooled down and ready to begin again, the nine-page forensics report was on his desk. After apologizing to Duane and Dennis and Roberta and Adele, he carefully studied it page by page. Tom's fingerprints were on the token, the license and the bill, suggesting that Tom, himself, had carefully wrapped up the token and placed it in the inner pocket of his driver's license. Did he suspect he was going to be killed and was he leaving clues, or was this something else?

He also puzzled over Tom's clothing. His tee shirt, jeans, underwear and running shoes were purchased locally in Alberta. The jacket, however, was U.S.-made. They were still trying to trace it. Roger grabbed a scratch pad from the kitchen table, took it out on the deck and proceeded to make some doodling, notes, diagrams. If he could see a connection on paper, maybe he could grasp the connection in his mind. Bent over his paper, he was unaware that Kate had walked up behind him. She put her arms around his shoulders. Her fingers smelled strongly of green tomato vines.

"Working on your speech, Corporal?"

"Speech?"

"For the CMBC. You were in such deep thought over that paper, I thought you were working on your speech."

"No, it's this drug thing—this Tom Anderchuk thing. As for the speech, I'm actually thinking of phoning Hank and canceling out. Things are getting heavy here in Chester. Something's happening. I just can't put my finger on it. I want to be here when the whole thing blows."

Kate sat down in the chair next to him. "You have no idea who killed that boy?"

"None. But I'm more concerned with the why. He was executed. But what for? We've never had an execution-style murder like this in Chester before."

"You think maybe Tom had information on someone and was blackmailing them?"

"It's possible. But I'm not sure about that either. Tom has been involved with these people long enough to realize that you can't blackmail them without getting fitted for cement shoes and being dumped in the river."

"Maybe he thought he could outwit them this time. He was always a cocky kid."

Roger looked down at his doodling. Ever since he joined the force some fifteen years ago, Kate was his prime confidant. They had a special relationship when it came to Roger's confidential police work. Kate had a shrewd mind and he respected her.

She pulled her chair closer to his. "Tell me what you have so far, and let's see if we can figure this out."

Before Roger had a chance to tell her about F. Schmidt and Azuyo and the large jacket and Madeline, Becky appeared at the door.

"Mom, Dad," she said hesitantly. Her voice was low and non-confrontational. She was obviously trying a new tack. "I know you think I'm too young to go to that concert, but I want you to think about it. All of my friends are going, even my church friends. I really think I'm mature enough to go to the concert with my friends. All of my friends' parents are letting them go . . ."

Roger and Kate exchanged glances. Kate began, "Becky, you're only fourteen. From what you've said, there will be no adult supervision."

Becky's tone was changing. From soft-conversational to whining-confrontational.

"You just don't trust me. You never have! This just proves it!"

"Becky," Roger said, "Have you ever listened, really listened, to the lyrics of Dark Hearts?"

"Nobody listens to the words, Dad. It's just the music. You just don't understand."

"Plus," added Kate, "two people were seriously injured, Becky, at their concert in Hamilton."

"I know. You've told me that a million times. You'll never

let me forget it, but it had nothing to do with the group. Two people just got trampled. Dad, you should know, the group was not responsible at all."

"Becky, you know the answer has to be no," said Roger.

"You just don't understand! I'm not a baby! Just because you're a cop, you always look on the bad side of everything!" And she stormed off.

Kate and Roger looked helplessly at each other.

Kate spoke, "I was pretty rebellious as a kid, Rog. And I turned out okay. We just need to give her some time—and pray for her."

Roger nodded. Kate took his hand and together they stared out onto the gardens, the flowers, the grass, the daylight fading into darkness, each thinking their own private thoughts, praying their own private prayers.

Their other daughter, Sara, had never given them a moment's worry. An honor student, she breezed thorough high school, was president of the Youth Group, maintained an active witness for Christ and now was on a youth mission project to Spain. Then along came Rebecca four years later who was everything Sara was not. A poor student—*She's not slow, she just needs to apply herself*—was the message they had heard from grade five on.

And she was playing on both sides of the spiritual fence.

"Come on," said Kate rubbing his shoulders. "Let's go in. It's getting buggy out here"

* * *

It was her daughter's morning phone call that started Marjorie thinking, that actually made her decide to do something about Wes. The previous evening after Wes left, she had lain down on her bed and stared at the ceiling. After several hours she drew herself a hot bath and lay there, quiet tears mingling with the bath water. This time he had actually hit her, striking her cheek with the back of his hand. She had accused him of seeing someone else.

"You know nothing about it!" he had yelled, a note of near-desperation in his voice. "Nothing at all!" Ironically it was his wedding ring which bit into her cheek and left its mark.

This morning Lisa had called from Calgary.

"How are you, Mom?"

"Oh, just fine," she said wearily.

"You don't sound fine."

"I am fine, dear. And how are you?"

"Did Dad leave already?"

"Yes, he left last night."

"Mom, I worry about you rattling around in that big house when Dad is away. You sure you're okay?"

"I'm fine . . . well, not totally fine, perhaps."

"What's wrong, Mom? Is it stomach pains again? I told you to see Dr. Billingsly the minute you have a problem. He said that, too."

"Well, maybe . . ."

"Mom, I know you're afraid. It's natural. But knowing is *always* better than not knowing."

"I don't know about that. Sometimes knowing may not be better, not in all situations."

"Mom, no. You have to know, okay? And I'm sure it's nothing."

"Perhaps I should, Lisa, find out I mean."

"Of course you should, Mom."

The fictions were firmly established. As Marjorie vacuumed and dusted the already-clean house, she caught a glimpse of herself in the hall mirror and placed her hand against her cheek. Maybe Lisa was right. Maybe she should find out. If there *was* another woman, maybe knowing who it was would help her deal with it.

Marjorie had always been a strong woman. A respected woman in Chester. While her husband served the community as an elected official, Marjorie served in other ways. For two terms, the maximum, she had worked hard on the library board. She volunteered at the Food Bank. Could that be where she'd seen that poor boy who was killed? She still served on the hospital auxiliary and, for two hours a week, she volunteered her time teaching an elderly lady to read and write.

Marjorie carefully put her vacuum cleaner away in the closet and decided to find out for herself who it was that Wes was seeing. Climbing the stairs to the master bedroom, she pulled out his dresser drawers, one by one. His socks and underwear drawer held nothing but socks and underwear. His tee shirt drawer just held tee shirts. The pockets of his pants and jackets yielded nothing. The top of his dresser was empty.

She descended the stairs and entered the guest room. Wes had a lot of his personal belongings there. He'd taken to practically living there. The hide-a-bed was folded into the couch position. Another fiction, thought Marjorie. The few visitors they still entertained would pass this room on their way to one of the downstairs bathrooms and the folded-up hide-a-bed would conceal the fact he hadn't slept with Marjorie in the master bedroom upstairs for many months.

On top of the small desk in the guest room was his lap-top computer. Odd that he didn't take that to Ottawa, she thought. She had no idea how to operate one of those things, but was certain it held the secrets of her husband's life. She was afraid that if she turned it on and fiddled with it, Wes would know that she'd been in there checking up on him. She didn't know much about computers, but one thing she did know was that they didn't lie. Not like her husband.

On the floor leaning against the dresser was the black

leather briefcase that held the computer for travel. She sat down on the hide-a-bed couch and opened the case. Within the case itself were various pouches containing wires and a battery pack. One outside pocket was empty. Another contained a rubber-banded stack of his business cards—*Wes Romaine Holdings*. She flipped through them but the backs were empty. Other zippered pockets were empty. She was about to put the case away when she reached into a small Velcro'd pocket along one end. Marjorie pulled out six flimsy Visa receipts paper-clipped together. Carefully she undid the clip and spread them out on the couch. All of them, all six of them, were for food, drinks and lodging at a place called the Riverboat Casino in Azuyo, Nevada. She stared at them, puzzled and confused.

CHAPTER 8

Madeline had first met Tom when they were both thirteen and in junior high school in Chester. In fact, it was Tom who had ultimately helped her run away from the Smiths. The year before, when she was twelve, was the year her mother died. It was Madeline who found the body on a Thursday afternoon after school. The police dragged her away, screaming and incoherent, to Social Services where she stayed overnight in a youth shelter. The next morning a social worker had taken her back to the house to help her pack. In a daze, she had crammed all of her belongings into two gray duffel bags. As an afterthought, she grabbed her mother's favorite china tea cup and her mother's quilt. The social worker grew impatient when Madeline went crying from room to room searching for Harold. The policeman finally told the social worker they had to leave. They were contaminating the crime scene. Harold was never found.

The next day they sent her far away to Alberta, to Chester. It was for her safety, they told her. Two days after her mother died, Madeline went to live with the Smiths. She went to the Smiths accompanied by a different social worker. Madeline stood small and alone, feeling as if everything under her feet was falling away. Mrs. Smith didn't even look at her or talk to her at all, but just to the social worker. She referred to Madeline only as *the girl*. "We have a room for *the girl* in the back," she said, and "I'm sure *the girl* will be quite comfortable here."

Mrs. Smith was a large matronly woman who wore a lot of gray. When the social worker left, Mrs. Smith sat Madeline down on a kitchen chair and she sat opposite her, not touching. Never touching. The whole three years she was there, Madeline never remembered Mrs. Smith touching her.

Madeline sat with her coat still on, the threadbare woolen coat that her mother had picked up for her at the thrift store. Beside her on the floor were her two duffel bags.

"This is a Christian home," said Mrs. Smith, her voice edged with sternness. "And because it's a Christian home there are certain things that will not be tolerated—modern music, dishonorable TV shows, movies, the wrong associates, lewd dancing, and, it goes without saying that smoking and imbibing are forbidden."

Madeline fingered a loose button on the coat and stared at it. She had absolutely no idea what Mrs. Smith was talking about. What was imbibing?

"Do you own a Bible, Miss?"

Madeline didn't respond.

"I asked if you owned a Bible. Do you?"

Madeline stammered. Her face felt hot. Her voice came out in a croak, "A . . .a . . .a what?"

"A Bible. Never mind. I thought not. Mr. Smith and I have one that you may borrow while you stay here," she said rising heavily. Her gray skirt crinkled when she walked.

She rummaged around in a bookshelf and returned with a little leather volume with tiny writing on crinkly pages. She handed it to Madeline. *The Holy Bible* it said in gold letters on the front.

"We expect you to read a chapter of the Bible every single day."

Why? Madeline wanted to ask, but didn't. Instead, she trudged along a dark hallway following Mrs. Smith and struggling with her bags and the little leather book.

At the very back of the house was a small bedroom. It contained a single bed topped with a faded yellow chenille bedspread, a wooden desk, one dresser and a closet. The room was clean and smelled of new paint. The walls were bare and white except for a single painting over the head of the bed. Madeline would remember that picture. It was the only thing she would treasure from her time at the Smiths. It was the profile of a little girl on her knees, her hands together in prayer, her eyes upturned. But it was her hair which caught Madeline's attention. It was very fair and wispy, with sprigs of light blue flowers pinned throughout. Madeline touched her own hair. It was white-blonde and baby-fine. Even at age twelve it was still baby hair. It always slipped out of barrettes and braids no matter how tightly her mother braided it. Looking up at the little girl with the pug nose and curly hair, Madeline almost felt a kinship to her. Mrs. Smith, following her gaze, said, "Social Services examined this room and said that it was adequate. They had one suggestion, however, that Mr. Smith and I put up a few posters or prints. I found this particular one at a garage sale."

"It's very nice," said Madeline, her small voice barely above a whisper.

"I should also tell you that we attend church, and that also is a requirement."

A requirement for what? Madeline wondered. But she nodded and placed her bags on the bed.

"I will leave you, Madeline, to get settled in. Supper is at six sharp each evening. The bathroom is down the hall. You are free to use the towels on the rack farthest from the tub. That will be your rack. The one in the center is Mr. Smith's. Mine is the one closest to the tub."

With that Mrs. Smith walked out of the room and closed the door behind her. Madeline sat down on the bed in bewilderment and wondered what she was supposed to do now.

Eventually, she unpacked her bags and placed her socks and tee shirts and underwear into the empty wooden drawers. Then she lay down on the bed with her head at the foot end and stared up at the painting. She named the girl Bethany after a heroine in a TV movie that she and her mother had once watched.

"Bethany," she whispered, "Why did my mother leave me? What did I do wrong, Bethany?"

When Mrs. Smith finally came for her, her cheeks were blotchy and wet. Mrs. Smith frowned and led her wordlessly to the dining room for supper.

She held very few pictures in her mind of Mr. Smith. In the mornings he mostly grunted behind his newspapers. In the evening he watched the news and couldn't be disturbed, Mrs. Smith said. Madeline seldom spoke to him.

Only once did Madeline pick up the Bible on her desk. About a week after she moved into the back bedroom she was talking once more to Bethany—Bethany who always prayed. Maybe if Madeline knew how to pray like Bethany did, her mother would come back to her, and her nightmares would stop. Many nights she would wake up sweaty and desperately afraid. Many nights she saw her mother lying there on the kitchen floor—blood on her face, blood all over the floor. In little puddles, like after it rains. Maybe if she could pray like Bethany did, the awful pictures in her head would go away.

She picked up the Bible and opened to the first page. But Madeline, always a poor reader anyway, couldn't understand a word. Not one. She wondered if it was written in another language that Mrs. Smith thought that she knew.

When her social worker came for periodic visits, Madeline didn't have anything to say. Yes, she had enough to eat. Yes, she had lots of new clothes, more clothes than she'd ever had. No, there was nothing wrong that she could name, yet Madeline had never been so profoundly unhappy in all of her life.

It was Tom who gave her pills that finally stopped her terrifying dreams. Tom was exactly her age and in most of her classes. He was a poor student, like herself, who laughed and talked out loud in class and pretended it didn't matter. But Madeline knew it did. It always does. Everyone said he had *an attitude*. Tom lived with his sister, who didn't care where he went or what he did.

It was Tom who told her she could look so much better if she combed her hair a certain way, and wore different clothes and more makeup. Then, to Mrs. Smith's utter horror, she did just that.

But every night without fail, she talked to Bethany and told her all about the things she did that day and how she felt about everything. She told Bethany all about Tom, too, how smart and nice he was. He was also very rich. He always had tens and twenties in his wallet. Compared to the measly allowance she received from the Smiths, Tom seemed like a millionaire.

When she was almost fifteen, Tom persuaded Madeline to leave the Smiths forever. One evening when the Smiths were at a church meeting, she pulled her two bags down from the closet and stuffed her clothes into them. She left most of the new, plain clothes that Mrs. Smith had bought her. Tom was buying her clothes now and she much preferred his choices. She wrapped her tea cup in her mother's quilt and packed it carefully in one of the bags. She debated about taking Bethany, but decided against it. She would leave Bethany for the next girl who would come to live here.

"Good-bye, Bethany," she said. "You've been my best friend."

That night they moved into a downtown Calgary apartment with some of Tom's friends. She never saw the Smiths again, but she somehow doubted that they missed her.

* * *

In the very early morning, Madeline sat up on the couch and peeked out through the curtains. Dawn was just beginning; it was that quiet, half-light time of day when the late-night partygoers are finally in bed and the first morning-shift workers haven't risen yet. Her body ached and her stomach felt sour. She didn't feel like she had slept at all last night, even with three pills rather than the one or two she normally took. She was hungry. Her night had been filled with memories of Tom. She rose feeling like an old woman, joints creaking and head aching. It took a few minutes to straighten her body before she padded into the kitchen to boil some water for coffee.

The place was a mess. Flies were congregating in the sink. Garbage was on the floor, under the table and where she had kicked it into a corner. All of the ash trays were overflowing with stale butts. She turned on her radio but kept the volume low so it wouldn't disturb Janice and Samantha next door. Then she set to work.

Madeline got out a dozen little plastic grocery bags and filled them with the ashes and refuse. Then she found the broom and swept the debris from the kitchen floor into another bag. It was too early to borrow Janice's vacuum, so she vigorously swept the hard brown carpet in her front room. She tied the handles of the garbage bags together and carried them outside to the apartment garbage. It took her three trips to get the place cleaned up.

Then she made herself a cup of coffee and washed the dishes. Filled with a nervous energy, she bagged up all the dirty clothes into two pillow cases. Momentarily, she sat down and hugged a dirty sock of Tom's, pressing it close to her face. It seemed unfair, somehow, that a person who had died would still have dirty clothes that needed washing.

Then she added the sock to the top of one of the pillow cases. If she got to the Laundromat now, it wouldn't be busy. She grabbed a handful of quarters from a jar in the kitchen and the keys to Tom's car from the hook near the door. She thought it was strange that the police didn't ask about his car. It was really Tom's car, but because Tom had so many moving violations, the car was registered in her name. But she hadn't lied about the bus. For the past few months, Tom hadn't driven his car illegally.

Madeline opened the driver's door and flung the pillow cases into the back. The car was Tom's pride and joy, a 1994 black Camaro. As she got behind the wheel she noticed his portable CD player lying on the passenger seat. Next to it was Tom's small cassette player with a broken playback button. She remembered Tom had wanted her to take it somewhere to get it fixed.

She picked up the cassette player trying to remember where Tom had wanted her to take it. She turned it over and checked the battery compartment. Empty. She remembered that sometimes Tom kept batteries in the back.

Carrying the cassette player she got out and opened the hatch. There was the usual array of tools, spare tire, oil, old rags, but no batteries. Just before closing the hatch, she noticed a Nike shoe box wedged up at the back underneath a couple of rags. It didn't look familiar. She pulled it out and lifted the lid. There on top was a three-folded glossy brochure, an advertisement for the Riverboat, Azuyo, Nevada. She was perplexed. Hadn't that cop asked her about Azuyo, Nevada? A sticky note was placed on the top with one scrawled word, *Goldy*. Madeline recognized Tom's uneven handwriting. Under the brochure was a map of the Western States and Provinces, and at the bottom of the box was a thick stack of U.S. hundred dollar bills rubber-banded together. Rattling around the bottom of the box was an odd-shaped blue key. Absently, thinking about the money, she dropped the key into the cassette player's battery compartment. A perfect fit. She laid the broken cassette player next to the spare tire and flipped through the money, her hands shaking. There was a lot of it, which at once excited her but made her desperately afraid. She knew very little about Tom's dealings. She put the money back into the shoe box and carried it inside, locking the door behind her. Carefully, she drew the curtains, her hands shaking.

At her kitchen table she dumped out the box. She counted ten thousand dollars! What was Tom doing with ten thousand U.S. dollars? She sat quietly for a few moments and looked at the bills spread out on the table. Next door she could hear Samantha beginning to whimper. She didn't want to believe Janice. She wanted to believe that the police would find out who killed Tom. That cop, the older one, the one with the grayish-brown hair who had been over yesterday had nice eyes. And he had even sent over a flower, which arrived at her door yesterday afternoon. Would he really help her as he said he would?

She looked over at the slim vase in the middle of the table with one long-stemmed white rose. No one had ever given her a flower before, not in her whole life. Could she trust him? She got up, walked over to the phone where she had placed his business card and dialed his number. She would trust him. To a point.

* * *

Early Friday morning, Roger walked into the detachment office.

"Claire make more muffins?" he said to Clayton who was standing by the coffee pot munching on a confection that was full of chocolate chips.

"Yeah, you want one?" said Clayton shoving the box toward him.

"Maybe later. I've got my heart set on passing the physical."

Clayton grunted.

"Anything from overnight dispatch?" Roger asked picking up a sheet of paper.

Because Chester had less than 7,000 residents, overnight RCMP calls were answered in a central office in Calgary.

"You got two calls from someone who calls herself Madonna Juliet and—this is interesting—did you know that Tom Anderchuk worked for Hank Pfeiffer for a while?"

"Really?"

"That's right. Duane got that last night just before you left."

When Roger reached Madeline on the phone she said, "I don't know if what you said is true, about you helping me and all . . . but I found something you might want to see."

"What did you find, Madonna Juliet?"

"Can you come over, do you think?"

It was still early but already warm when he pulled up to the Starlite apartments. Another scorcher, he thought. As expected, the door to Apartment 23 was still closed, the drapes drawn. He knocked.

Roger heard scuffling as if furniture was being moved, then she drew back the chain and let him in. She looked even thinner than the last time he had seen her. Her short hair was clipped back off her forehead with a couple of silver barrettes and she still wore the same cutoffs and tee shirt. But that was all that was the same. The place was surprisingly clean and smelled fresh. The fast food containers were gone, the floor shone, the ash trays gleamed, and peering through to the small kitchenette, Roger could see that the sink had been emptied of dishes. On the table next to the wall stood a single white rose in a tall vase. She saw Roger eyeing it.

"Thank you for the flower." Her eyes darted from Roger to the floor and back again.

Walking over to the couch, she picked up a tattered Nike shoe box and handed it to him.

"I was cleaning up and found this box in the back of the closet."

Roger took the box and Madeline sat down in a ratty maroon arm chair. From the pocket of her cutoffs she produced a package of cigarettes and a lighter. American cigarettes, noted Roger.

"You want one?" she asked.

"No, thank you."

Roger sat down, the box on his lap. At the top of the box was a glossy three-folded brochure from the Riverboat Hotel and Casino, Azuyo, Nevada. It advertised cheap rates, casinos, good meals, and fine entertainment. Roger read through it carefully. The name of the proprietor, Goldy Bassino, was scrawled on a small square yellow sticky.

"That's Tom's writing," said Madeline, pointing.

Underneath the brochure was a small stack of U.S. hundred dollar bills, ten of them rubber-banded together. A thousand dollars. He was slightly disappointed. If Roger expected a signed statement from Tom with names, dates and Chester drug connections, he was sorely disappointed.

"You found this in your closet? This much money and you didn't know it was there?"

"That's right." Her hands shook.

"Why are you showing this to me? You could have kept the thousand dollars. It's a lot of money."

"I thought it might help you catch Tom's killer. Maybe it

was this guy, Goldy, that killed him."

"What do you know about Goldy?"

"Nothing. I never been down there. But there's something you should know. You won't believe it, but I got to say it anyway. This is what I was afraid to tell you before: Tom wanted to turn them all in. He was going straight. I warned him not to do it. That's what I was warning him about."

Surprise showed in Roger's eyes.

"I knew you wouldn't believe me. Tom said you wouldn't believe him either. That's why he said he had to get all the evidence before he handed it over to you."

"What evidence, Madonna?"

"Well, this is all I have. But Tom was going straight. That much I know. I don't know nothing else but I know it had something to do with this place," she said pointing to the brochure with her cigarette.

"Why would he decide to go straight all of a sudden?"

"He was changing. He was getting his life together. He was even going in for God." She rose. "I got a paper about it somewheres. I can show you."

From underneath a pile of paper bags, she pulled out a folded piece of paper. It was a church bulletin. Roger recognized the church immediately. Calgary City Church and its affiliate, the Shepherd Centre, were well known for their work in Calgary's inner core. A church on the cutting edge of ministry, they operated shelters for the homeless, battered families, drug addicts and runaway teens. He had read in the paper just the other day that their latest project was going to be a hospice for AIDS patients.

"Tom was involved with this church?" Roger was baffled.

"He wasn't the bad person you thought he was. He went to that church all the time. Just about everyday. They even gave him a Bible," said Madeline. "He couldn't read it very good though, that's when they got him hooked up with college. I decided to go, too. We were going to go together."

Madeline handed him two registration forms for Alberta Vocational College, Calgary. One was made out for Tom Anderchuk and the other for Madeline Westmier.

"Me and Tom were going to school in September. We were all signed up and everything. Both of us never finished high school. Tom could write his name and all, plus a few words. I can read—mostly—but I have trouble with some words."

Roger was so baffled that he was practically speechless.

"Tom was going to church and you two were registered for school?"

"That's the truth."

"Were you going to this church, too?"

She laughed, "Me? Heck, no. I had enough of religion when I was a kid."

CHAPTER 9

"You're here about Tom." Roger stood in the small office of Reg Sorensen, the senior pastor of Calgary City Church. Reg was dressed casually in corduroy slacks, brown loafers and a short-sleeved plaid shirt with a button-down collar. His hair was short and graying and he reminded Roger of a college professor on vacation.

"Yes, I understand that you knew him."

"We did. We heard about his murder just this morning. I was sitting here wondering if I should call you, and now you're here."

He continued, "Tom was in our drug rehab program. One of our lay counselors, James, knew him better than anyone. Hildy," he said turning to a young woman in jeans who sat at a desk working at a computer terminal. "Is James here to-day?"

"Yes he is," she said looking up from the computer. "He's in the first prayer room. Said he needed to pray. Tom's death has him pretty shaken."

Roger followed Reg down a brightly lit hallway flanked on either side with offices and small classrooms.

"To get to the prayer rooms we go past the men's shelter," said Reg, "This is part of the Shepherd Centre."

At the end of the hall they entered a large room where a few men lounged in front of the television. Roger thought he recognized the Christian movie which was plugged into the video. A ceiling fan lazily whirled the warm air around the room. The walls were papered with posters, most with an anti-drugs, anti-drinking or Christian message. One man was dusting the shelves. He flashed a toothless grin.

"Morning, Pastor Reg," he called out.

Reg waved. "Good morning, Isaac."

They walked past a gaunt man in a wheelchair who was probably younger than he looked. An open Bible lay on his lap. He didn't look up as Reg passed, but the pastor put both arms around his thin shoulders and whispered something to him. The man smiled.

Down the hall and out of earshot, Reg said, "That was Ralph. He has AIDS. He stays with us between hospital visits. Lately he's in the hospital more than he is here at the home. Ralph is the reason we are asking God for an AIDS hospice with full-time medical staff."

Roger raised his eyebrows and Reg continued, "Ralph's family has rejected him. A long time ago they rejected his lifestyle, and now that he is dying they want nothing to do with him. There are many like him, who die alone."

Roger was interested. "How did he come to be living here?"

"One of our lay counselors—all of our lay counselors are fully trained by the way—one of our counselors who ministers at the hospital met him there, led him to the Lord and brought him here. Now he's a permanent resident, well, as permanent as he can be. Like all of us, our permanent residency is with Christ."

Roger nodded.

"Ahh, here we are," said Reg, leading them into a small room. Like all of the other rooms in the complex, it was pleasant and well-cared for. A large open window overlooked an alley. A broad green viney plant on the windowsill had spread its tendrils up and to the outside. Kate would like this window, thought Roger. She was always bemoaning the fact that modern houses didn't have the wide old-fashioned windowsills where plants could grow and enjoy the sun and the outside air. A bookshelf against the far wall held a variety of Bibles and Christian books and little pamphlets called tracts.

The man behind the desk appeared to be in his late twenties. His hair reached his shirt collar and he wore round, wire-rimmed glasses, jeans and sandals.

"Hi," he said, rising and extending his hand. He looked as if he had been crying. "I'm James, James Bonfiest. You're here about Tom."

Roger nodded. After they were seated and Reg had left, Roger took out his notebook, "How well did you know him?"

"Fairly well. About seven, eight months ago I was out one night with another counselor doing street ministry. I met him in a pub along Electric Avenue."

His voice was very soft and gentle. He paused and then went on.

"We were sitting there, my friend and I, waiting for the Lord's leading, and that's when I noticed Tom, felt drawn to him, actually. He was alone and he looked so troubled. It was as if the Lord was telling me *Here is a troubled person.* When I went over, we ended up talking until four that morning. I finally brought him back here. He was really searching, really troubled. A couple months later he accepted Christ. He came to Christ with a lot of excess baggage, not to mention a long and dangerous addiction to drugs." James said.

"Do you have any idea why someone would want to murder him?" asked Roger.

"Tom was uncovering evidence, evidence that he said could 'put a whole bunch of people away for a long time.' I begged him, pleaded and prayed with him not to do this. 'Give what you have to the police right now,' I told him, but Tom has . . . had a bit of a stubborn streak."

"He wanted to be a hero."

"No, I wouldn't say that," countered James. "He genuinely wanted to come clean before the Lord, and this is how he planned to do it."

"Do you know what kind of evidence he had? Did he leave anything with you?"

James smiled, "If you mean did he keep a log and journal with names and dates and phone numbers and information, forget it. Tom couldn't read and write very well, but like everyone who has literacy difficulties, he had a phenomenal memory. It was all in his head."

"And died with him," said Roger frowning.

James nodded.

"Does the name F. Schmidt mean anything to you?" asked Roger.

James thought for a moment. "No, I'm sorry. I can't help you. As I said before, he kept it all to himself. He wouldn't tell me anything, even though I told him how dangerous it was to carry around this kind of information."

"You ever hear of Azuyo, Nevada, or the Riverboat?"

"I'm not sure," said James opening his palms in an attitude of helplessness. "All I know is that he made several trips to the States in recent months. He took the bus because his license had been revoked. But I really don't know where he went. He told no one."

"How well do you know Madeline Westmier?"

"Ahh, Madonna Juliet. I take it you've met her. I met her only once. She refuses to have anything to do with us here at the Centre. She and Tom have known each other practically since grade school I understand. She's quite dependent on him and he's quite protective of her. We were helping Tom and Madeline to enroll in school. Reg has asked Jenny, another one of the counselors, to visit her. I should mention that she is at the top of our prayer list here at the Centre."

On the way back to the detachment in Chester, Roger's mind was a snarl of confused thoughts. Tom, a Christian! Tom, down in Azuyo, Nevada. Tom, with information about some drug operation, information which probably had something to do with a proprietor of a gambling casino named Goldy Bassino. Someone named F. Schmidt was also involved. Tom, planning to take this information to the police. Tom, murdered before he could.

Back at his desk, Roger called Hank.

"Didn't you think it was important to tell me that Tom Anderchuk worked for you for a time?"

"I guess it slipped my mind. He did, but I had to fire him. He was helping himself out of the cash register."

"When was this, Hank?"

"Oh, let's see, five, maybe six months ago, I think. Maybe longer."

"And why didn't you report it?"

"I thought it was best dealt with internally." Roger could hear Hank sigh across the wire. "You try to do something nice for these people and they just end up taking advantage of you."

He was hanging up the receiver when Constable Tim Erickson approached his desk..

"They've traced the plaid jacket, the one found on the body, to a men's clothing store in the United States. They've even got a specific town," he said.

"Let me guess—Azuyo, Nevada."

"Huh?"

"Never mind. Where is it from?"

"Spokane, Washington."

* * *

Madeline placed the phone back in its cradle and surveyed

the room. She did not want to, *would not,* talk to that Jenny lady from that church place that Tom was hooked up with. She had taken the rest of the money, the nine thousand dollars, and had hidden it in one of Tom's socks. She had also kept the map. The beginning of a plan was forming around the edges of her thinking. Suppose, by herself, she could find out who killed Tom. She wished now that she had *made* Tom tell her what he was doing and what he had found. As she walked around the two rooms, the map of the Western States and Provinces in one hand, Tom's sock in the other, she reasoned that none of this would have happened if he had not become involved with that church.

Five and a half months ago Tom had begun to change. He started talking about God and Jesus in a way that confused her. When he showed her his New Testament, she really became concerned.

"I got to learn how to read this," he had told her. In her mind she saw Mrs. Smith's little black book, a nonsensical book with thin, delicate pages—a book that she was supposed to read because it was *required.* A person named James was reading the Bible to Tom and Tom was memorizing it. He began spending more and more time at the Shepherd Centre.

About a month ago Tom had come home one night and said, "Madonna, I don't think we should be living together anymore."

Madeline had flown into a rage. "What! You got somebody else? Somebody at that church. I knew it! You been spending so much time there, I should have wised up! Boy, am I the schmuck of the world, or what!"

"No, no, nothing like that. It's just that, well, living together like we are, well, it ain't right in God's eyes."

"*Whose* eyes?" she demanded.

"Well, God's, Madeline."

"And don't call me Madeline. Don't ever call me Madeline!" She had stormed out of the apartment. An hour later Tom found her sitting in front of a beer at the Chester Inn. Over the noise of the country band, he said very gently, "I don't have anybody else. What I was thinking was maybe we should get married or something."

Open-mouthed, Madeline stared at him. "What do you mean?"

"Married, like *I do,* like ordinary people. I checked it out with James. He said we could probably get married down at the Centre."

There it was again, those people controlling his life, changing him. Wanting to control her now. Her expression darkened. She withdrew her hand from his and stared into her drink. "I don't want to get married at that place. Not now. Not ever. Don't you remember the Smiths? They were religious, too."

"The Smiths were *out to lunch.* I know that now."

"They made my life miserable for three years with that Bible crap! And that's all you can say, 'they were out to lunch'?"

"Madonna . . ."

But she had walked away. In the end Tom had stayed in the apartment, but began sleeping on the couch, the place where she had slept since he died. He was changing, though. He never came home drunk or stoned anymore. He never yelled at her anymore. And even though she had no interest in the Shepherd Centre, she did promise to go to school with him in the fall.

That seemed so long ago. Now Tom was gone forever. Like her mother. She threw a few clothes in her gray duffel bag along with her mother's tea cup, the quilt, the vase with its flower, the money and the map of the Western States and Provinces. She locked the door behind her.

She had a long drive ahead of her.

* * *

He would have preferred to eat inside, in the coolness of an air-conditioned lunch cafe, but Kate liked it outside. So they sat sweltering underneath a big umbrella with *Pepsi* printed across the top of it.

"I'm inside all day, Rog. It's nice to be out."

The outside eating area was little more than a fenced-in area of the sidewalk along the front of the restaurant. It was decorated with little round tables each with its own umbrella advertising *Coors, Pepsi* or *Budweiser.*

Roger always thought the place was pretentious, this eating outside where passersby could look over the fence and watch them munching on fries and burgers.

". . . and besides all that, she says it's hot but she's enjoying herself and meeting a lot of new people."

"What?"

"Roger," she put down her salad fork, "You haven't heard a word I've been saying have you?"

"I'm sorry. Go on."

"It's that case isn't it? That poor kid who was killed."

"There are so many loose ends that don't make sense. But go on, you were talking about Becky?"

"Sara. I was talking about *Sara.* We got a letter this morning. Becky brought it in to work. Sara and some of the others have formed a singing group of some sort. They sing in the evenings at different places. One of them plays the guitar. Sounds like she's having the time of her life."

"Great. Good for her."

"Here," she fished in her purse, "I'll let you read it for yourself. It sounds like our little girl is really growing up." He put the envelope with the row of exotic stamps into his pocket and adjusted the umbrella so that it shaded more of them. Half an hour ago they had started in the shade, now he was mostly in the sun. So was Kate, but she didn't seem to mind. As well, his ice water glass was empty and he longed for more. He looked yearningly through the door into the darkened, cool restaurant interior.

The two of them tried to get together for lunch at least once a month. And it was usually at this cafe, which Roger called *Chester's Outdoor Yuppie Paradise.* As if to confirm his thoughts, he spotted a couple of young business-types seated in a far corner, gym bags and squash rackets on the ground beside them, and on the table between them were two bottles of Perrier.

"What's Becky doing today?" he asked between bites of his burger.

"She's at Jody's. They're watching videos. I think she's resigned herself to the fact that she can't go to the concert. Jody's not allowed to go either. I spoke to Gladys earlier. Becky was actually pleasant this morning before I went to work."

"Nice change. Boy, I could sure use some more water . . ."

"Oh, Rog, just sit and enjoy the rest of your meal."

"I'll be back in a minute," he said easing out of his chair.

The interior of the restaurant was just as cool and dark as he had imagined. Their waitress must have gone on her break or gone home because she was nowhere in sight. He stood by the bar for a minute wondering if all the waiters had gone home for the day when a calendar hanging on the side wall caught his eye. He reached across the bar and tore it from its hook.

The calendar was like a hundred other Alberta calendars, with photographs of grain elevators, wheat fields and mountains. That wasn't what interested him. Underneath the photos was printed, *Philip 'Flip' Schmidt's Deli & Fine Meats, #53 South East Bow Highway, River Valley Mall, Calgary.*"

"Can I help you sir?" A red-aproned waiter had returned.

"This deli, do you know it?"

"Not personally. People are always leaving their calendars and business cards with us." The waiter was looking at him curiously, a uniformed member of the RCMP asking about a deli.

"Is there someone here who knows this Flip?"

"You want me to get the manager?"

"If you would, please."

The waiter returned with a young man in a short-sleeved shirt and pleated pants. "You wanted some information about this deli?"

He probably thinks I'm in charge of the office barbecue this year, thought Roger. "Yes, please, do you know the proprietor, Flip Schmidt?"

"Not personally. We purchased some deli meats from him a while back and he must have sent us his calendar. Was there a specific question you had?"

"Was the meat good?"

"Certainly. We've had no complaints."

"Can I borrow this calendar?"

"Certainly, sir."

Back out in the hot sun, he leaned under the umbrella

"Did you find yourself a glass of water?" asked Kate.

"No, but I have to leave. You want a ride back to your office?"

"I can walk."

Halfway to Calgary, he realized that he had left Kate to pay for the lunch.

* * *

The River Valley Mall was a small strip mall containing a dry cleaners, a couple of stand-up sandwich and sub shops, a hardware store, a variety store, a video rental place and a large Safeway. Flip Schmidt's Deli & Fine Meats was on the corner, next to the submarine sandwich place which was advertising a lunch special of a hot Italian meatball sandwich and a drink. The mall was technically inside the city limits of Calgary, but Roger noted, it was as close to Chester as it could be.

A bell clanged when Roger pushed open the deli door and stepped into the cool interior. It had that peculiar, clean raw-meat smell. Along one wall were open freezers of plastic-wrapped ground beef, pork chops, chicken parts and fish sticks. On the other side were shelves of seasonings one can't buy in a regular grocery store—Swiss style steak seasonings, European soup mixes, sour Dutch candies, salsa concoctions from Mexico and South American coffees. Along the back, a glass case was filled with freshly ground hamburger, chunks of stewing meat, hunks of roasts and steaks and prepro-cessed, uncut rolls of sandwich meat and cheeses. A girl behind the counter was slicing ham. Roger wondered who it was for. He was the only one in the store.

She was the palest girl he had ever seen—colorless, wa-tery eyes, pallid skin, and long, lank, light hair which was fastened back in a pink rubber band. She looked as if some-one had tipped her upside down and dipped her headfirst into a vat of paint-remover. Her name tag announced her as *May*. He judged her to be mid-twenties. She had most likely worked here since high school. Roger guessed she would probably spend the rest of her life slicing boiled hams.

"What can I do you for?" she asked. Her voice was sur-prisingly deep and resonant.

"I'm looking for Mr. Schmidt."

"Sorry, he's away. On vacation. Won't be back till next Monday."

"Do you know where he went?"

"Sorry, don't know." She looked at his uniform quizzically and then continued, "You need to see him about something?"

Roger nodded.

She wiped her hands on her apron and marched into the back room through a swinging door.

The pale-haired girl returned a few minutes later with a short burly man.

"There a problem?" he asked.

"I'm Corporal Roger Sheppard of the Chester RCMP. I'd like to talk with Mr. Schmidt."

"What do you want to see Flip for?"

"He may have some information that we need."

"He's on vacation. Can't help you. Come back Monday."

"Do you know *where* he is vacationing?"

"Down south. States somewhere."

"Didn't he say he was going gambling somewhere?" asked May.

Abe gave her a look, paused and said, "Yeah, but who knows where."

"Vegas?mn Reno? Azuyo?" offered Roger.

"Azuyo, isn't that it?" offered May.

"Could be," said the man. "Like I said. He don't tell me where he goes. I don't tell him where I go."

"Can you give me his home address?"

"Yeah, Chester, somewhere. I can get it for you, but ain't nobody going to be there now."

"Do you by any chance have a picture of Mr. Schmidt?"

"Of Flip?"

"Yes, Flip."

Abe's eyes narrowed, "He in some kind of trouble?"

"Just routine. We're just looking for information, and he may be able to help us. Do you happen to have a picture of him?"

"I don't think so."

May said, "What about those old business cards of his, Abe, the ones with his picture on them? Any more of them kicking around?"

Abe looked steadily at her and said, "Why don't you check, May?"

She returned a few minutes later with a small card advertising the deli. Half of the card was a photo of a smiling Flip Schmidt, in a white apron standing behind a counter surrounded by sausages. He looked about five nine, five ten or so, a thick-bellied, curly-haired man, with a wide smile and lots of teeth. Roger took it, thanked them and left. On the way out, he noticed a blue station wagon quickly pulling away from the side of the deli. He could have sworn that it was Chester alderman, Wes Romaine, who hastily turned down the highway heading toward Calgary.

CHAPTER 10

Roger was finding it hard to concentrate. All around him in church, people were standing and singing. He stood next to Kate and held the hymn book while Hank, up in front, led them in the rousing song with generous sweeps of his arms.

I serve a risen Sa-a-vior, He's in the world toda-a-y. Roger could hear Hank's loud bass booming through the speakers.

He had spent all day yesterday, Saturday, searching out Philip Schmidt. His driver's license had come back clean, not even a speeding ticket. Nothing. He was past president of the Chamber of Commerce and a Rotarian. He was a widower with six children, all grown and gone. What had Roger been hoping for? Drug priors? He should be so lucky. And Phillip Schmidt was not registered in any of the hotels or motels in Azuyo or Las Vegas or Reno, or half a dozen other hotels and motels in Nevada. At least not under that name. He had driven by Flip's home in Chester. He had no search warrant so he couldn't go inside, but he drove by slowly. It was an ordinary white bungalow with hanging baskets of geraniums in the front, like a hundred other homes in Chester.

I know that He is li-i-ving whatever men may say . . .

Still, there was that Romaine thing. On Friday Roger was sure he'd seen him at Flip's Deli. And yet when he called the Romaine residence once he got back to the detachment, Marjorie had answered and said that Wes was down in Ottawa at a convention. Town Hall confirmed this, and so did the convention people in Ottawa. "Yes, Mr. Romaine picked up his delegate's packet the day before yesterday," said the convention secretary.

I see his hand of me-e-e-rcy—I hear his voice of ch-e-e-eer—and just the time I need Him . . .

The organ and piano swelled with the crescendo. The pianist, Roger noted, was adding many flourishes to the song, embellishing it for all it was worth.

Roberta, who had originally answered the domestic dispute call, told Roger that something about it bothered her. "Her face was bruised. When I asked her about it, she said she fell down the stairs. I told her there were people who could help her but she still insisted that she fell. Who knows? Maybe she really did fall."

And what did any of this have to do with Tom Anderchuk? Why would Tom scrawl Flip's name on a U.S. bill?

He walks with me—And talks with me—along life's narrow wa-a-ay . . .

But the shocker had been Kate's little revelation yesterday. After he called her in the afternoon and told her why he had run out with a calendar in his hand, she had done a little snooping in her own office and discovered that Wes Romaine had purchased Flip's deli a month ago. It seemed that Flip's little business was on the verge of bankruptcy and Wes Romaine stepped in to save the day. So what?

And then there was Madeline's disappearance. Clayton and Roberta had specifically told her to stick around Chester, and now she was gone. She had not shown up for work.

"She's about to lose her job," said Don Hendricks, manager of Chester's Best Fried Chicken. "I know that low-life boyfriend of hers was killed, but I've got a business to run."

Low-life boyfriend. Low-life *Christian* boyfriend. What did Tom know that got him killed? Roger wished he had more to go on than just a bunch of loose puzzle pieces spread all over the table.

The song over, Roger closed the hymn book and placed it in the rack in front of him and sat down. Across the crowded church he could see Becky's friends leaning together and whispering. Becky was not with them.

He whispered to Kate, "Where's Becky?"

She looked over and frowned, "I better go and look for her."

"No, you stay. I'll go this time. She's probably sitting out in the foyer. No doubt she'll have some excuse."

"Maybe we should make her sit with us today."

Becky wasn't in the foyer. She wasn't in the basement. Nor was she in the nursery, the junior church room or the youth lounge. He walked down the hall toward the washrooms in time to see Mrs. Fisher come out of the ladies' room.

"Mr. Sheppard, hallooo," she called.

She had a broad face and a smile which revealed several missing teeth. She was one elderly lady who still always wore hats to church. Today's creation was a purple thing with lots of lace and miniature yellow flowers.

"Mrs. Fisher, did you happen to see Becky in th . . .?"

"You know, I've been meaning to tell you how proud we all are of Sara. You must be so proud, too."

"Right. But I was wondering, was Becky . . .?"

"Just the other day I was telling Mrs. Swanson, that's my neighbor, she moved into the old Ballantine place across the way, well, I was telling her what a sweet girl that Sara was, how she always used to come over and have tea with me. And you'll never guess! She wrote me a letter. I got it just yesterday."

"That's nice. I'm looking for . . ."

"Such a sweet girl. You must be so proud. And you know

I even gave money for her. I'm glad to do something."

"And we all appreciate that . . ."

"Well, I better be getting back to my seat. The ladies' trio will be singing soon and I don't want to miss them."

"Mrs. Fisher," he called, "Did you happen to see . . .?"

But she didn't hear him. She was already through the door and back in the sanctuary.

A few seconds later Becky and Jody emerged from the Ladies' room laughing and giggling. When she saw him, her face immediately changed.

"What are you doing here?" she asked.

"Looking for you."

"I can't go to the bathroom without your permission?"

"Becky, please . . ."

"I can't believe you came out here!"

"We'll talk about this later," he said trying to quiet her. "Just go back and sit down now and we'll talk about it later."

Becky stormed back into the sanctuary with Jody following. As soon as Roger opened the door he heard Hank saying, ". . . When our own Corporal Roger Sheppard of the Royal Canadian Mounted Police will be speaking about what God means to him as a police officer. I'm sure you men will want to attend the September meeting."

The next Men's Breakfast meeting was less than a month away! His speech. He was no further ahead in preparing it. He still had no clue about what he would say. As he took his seat he decided that he would spend the afternoon getting that speech done.

Later that day, after a Sunday lunch of barbecued hamburgers, he settled down in the shade of his patio with an entire pad of empty paper. He would get that speech written today if it was the last thing he did.

* * *

Outside the car window the endless yellow fields of Alberta had been replaced by the wooded hills of Montana and Idaho. Still only morning and the pavement was already sizzling, but Madeline felt cool and comfortable in Tom's air-conditioned car. For once in her life she didn't have to worry about money. Before leaving Chester, she had divided the money into nine bundles and had hidden them all over the car—under the seats, behind the junk and screw drivers in the glove compartment and in back with the spare tire. She also put one in her purse, one in her duffel bag and one in the tea cup which she had wrapped up in newspapers and put under the seat. She felt very proud of herself. If someone robbed her, she'd hand them the nearest packet of bills and say, "Here, take all my money!" Losing a thousand would be no big deal. She'd still have thousands left.

Friday evening when she reached Lethbridge, Alberta, Madeline had stopped in at a mall and bought three new tee shirts, two pairs of brightly flowered bicycle shorts, a couple pairs of earrings, and some new Nikes. She had left most of her old stuff at home. She had enough money, she reasoned, to buy all new things. She experienced a little flurry of worry while handing the cashier a U.S. hundred, but the dozy cashier didn't blink an eye. She just took the bill, looked up the exchange rate on a card next to her cash register and handed the change back to her. She also bought the new Dark Hearts CD, a six-pack of Pepsi and half a dozen bags of assorted chips and candy bars. She didn't buy any cigarettes; Tom always told her they were cheaper in the States.

The large map of the Western States and Provinces lay opened on the passenger seat beside her. She, who had never been out of Canada before, was now heading down alone to Azuyo, Nevada. A sense of excitement filled her, and she sang along with a haunting Dark Hearts melody on the CD.

Yesterday morning when she had crossed the border into Sweet Grass, Montana, she experienced a moment of panic. She had forgotten about border crossings. Did she need a passport or something? Would they search the car? What would she say if they found the money? But the uniformed attendant had seemed tired as he leaned out of his cubicle and droned:

"Where are you going?"

"California," she lied.

"Where are you from?"

"Edmonton."

"Canadian citizen?"

"Yes."

"Are you bringing anything in to leave in the U.S.?"

"Uh, no."

"Any firearms, tobacco or alcohol?"

"No." Firearms! There was an idea.

"Have a nice day."

Lights and sirens on a highway patrol car passed her on Interstate 15 going in the opposite direction and Madeline immediately slammed on her brakes. The car ignored her and sped past her as she bent over the steering wheel. Settle down, settle down, she told herself. Nobody here knows anything about you. Janice doesn't even know where you are. No one's going to come looking. You're safe.

She glanced at the map beside her. According to her calculations she would take Route 15 right down to Las Vegas. Then she had to get on Highway 95 and eventually she would end up in Azuyo. Looking at the map she had no idea how long the trip would take. Two days? Three? A week? But she had lots of money and she could stay in hotels or motels along the way. She had stayed in two already and it was really no problem. If you paid ahead in cash, no one even asked any questions.

Madeline had no clear idea of what she planned to do once she got there, but she figured she had a lot of driving hours ahead of her in which to come up with something. Firearms? Hmmm.

* * *

"I'm sorry, Mrs. Romaine, but I can't divulge that information. Guest records are confidential. I'm sure you can appreciate that." Charles held the phone to his ear with his left hand and with his right doodled on a piece of Riverboat stationery with a green felt pen. Squiggles and lines, squares inside of squares inside of circles, odd-angled flower stems. He felt sorry for this woman, but rules were rules and Mr. Bassino was very strict about rules.

"No one is to receive any kind of guest information without my express approval," he had told Charles on more than one occasion.

"I know that he is your husband. I understand that and one thing I can say is that he's not here now." He paused. This was a part of his job that he found disturbing. Mr. Bassino called it *The Nosy Wife Syndrome,* and laughed about it, but Charles felt sorry for these wives who called, their voices a study in controlled panic, asking about their husbands. Nine times out of ten, the husband *was* there with a much younger female on his arm. They would book in one of the Premier Suites, and by the end of the week these confident businessmen would have gambled away their children's education savings, their entire businesses, or at the very least, the grocery money. As Mr. Bassino always said, it was a well-known, well-researched fact that the house always wins, so if people were going to be foolish enough to gamble away their kids' education, well, that wasn't his problem. "That's capitalism at work," he'd tell Charles. Still, it bothered him that Mr. Bassino and others like him were getting rich off another's misery. He tried not to think of the fact that his own summer job depended on the same thing.

Charles had worked for Mr. Bassino for three years and he'd received three raises and had gone from desk receptionist to Mr. Bassino's office assistant. Her wasn't quite sure why. He suspected it had a lot to do with his seriousness. Also, Charles wasn't particularly noteworthy in the looks department. His mother always said that Charles had a face that made people trust him.

"Please, I'm not checking up on my husband," he could hear Mrs. Romaine plead, "It's just that he asked me about his receipts, asked me to get the dates straight for his income tax."

Charles knew she was lying and he felt sad for her. He was sitting behind Mr. Bassino's desk and lining up his gold pens in a row. Out in the reception area someone was ringing the bell for service. Somehow he had to bring this conversation to a quick end. Lucia, the receptionist on duty, had run into the smoke shop to buy him a chocolate bar. Just my luck someone comes to the desk now, he thought.

"I'm sorry Mrs. Romaine, but the guest list must remain confidential." He paused, "But let me do this. If I can come up with anything, I'll call you. I'll check with my boss, okay?" He took her name and number. That placated her.

The truth was he remembered Wes Romaine as a serious sort from Canada who never *did* gamble away any of his money. He had arrived alone. Previously, Mr. Bassino told him to get a Premier Suite ready for him. He spent a lot of time with Mr. Bassino on the private terrace off his office. Charles had assumed that they were business partners or old friends and had basically ignored them both.

A middle-aged couple dragging behind them about four

suitcases each were impatiently waiting at the desk when Charles approached. After he got them settled with a key each and their complimentary drink chits, he went back into Mr. Bassino's office to finish up the paperwork he had to complete before Mr. Bassino returned from California.

He came across an envelope with a stamp from Canada and automatically put it aside. He'd take a look at the stamp later and see if it was one he needed for his collection. Charles collected stamps and his specialty was Canadian stamps. The stamp took him back three months ago to university and his new friend, Josh. He had met Josh this past year when Josh transferred in from another state. They were both entering their final year in Computer Science. They lived next door to each other in the dorm and quickly became friends, sharing an interest in software and stamps. Josh's specialty was early American stamps, Charles' was Canadian stamps.

Josh was different than the other friends Charles had. He seemed to have just as much fun as the other guys, yet there was something fundamentally different about him. Charles would call it *happier,* but no, it wasn't that. Josh got as hurt and upset as the next guy. Maybe Josh was somehow more at *peace*. Yes, that would describe it.

A couple of times Josh had invited Charles to something called Campus Fellowship, a group of Christians who met one lunch hour a week to study the Bible. The first time Charles went, he was dumbfounded. He had never met thinking people who believed the Bible was more than just a collection of Christian mythology—quaint little stories with moral endings. Many nights he and Josh discussed the Bible and God and Jesus into the early morning hours. By the end of the school year he had told Josh that he just couldn't accept the Bible the way Christians did, as the true words of a living God.

"I can't, Josh. I just don't see it. I can't accept that sacrifice part. I still can't see why God had to die."

He remembered Josh's last words to him, "I'm going to be praying for you every day this summer, Charles . . ."

Somehow, although he didn't believe, that gave him comfort.

"Hey, you, deep in thought. Are you creating a new computer program that's gonna get us all rich?" It was Lucia at the door with his candy bar.

CHAPTER 11

"How would you like to take a vacation, just you and me and the sun . . ."

Kate looked up at her husband quickly. "Let me guess—a nice little gambling town by the name of Azuyo, Nevada."

Roger grinned, "How'd you guess?"

"That's just part of my profound astuteness. You're not serious, are you?"

It was evening and they were taking one of their rare walks through the Chester residential area. It was warm, but not unbearable. It still had not rained. They passed neighbors taking advantage of the cooler evening to water lawns and weed gardens. Many of their neighbors were sitting out on their porches, testifying to the fact that it was cooler outside than inside.

"I am, Kate. The sergeant and I had a long talk today. I think it might be a good idea to head down to Azuyo. Maybe stay at the Riverboat, see what I can find out."

"You are serious," Kate stopped walking and looked into his face.

Sergeant Roy Laird had returned that morning and had agreed to Roger's idea. He would get in touch with the Azuyo County Sheriff's Department.

"It was my idea, actually. Laird's calling Ottawa for approval. He's pretty sure he can convince them. I think the Chester drug connection is somehow linked to something going on down there in Azuyo. It's been almost a week since Tom was murdered and we've come up with nothing. Duane and Dennis plus our Calgary people are working overtime, but we don't have anything. We don't even have a murder weapon. Tom was trying to tell us something. I think we should be listening."

"And you want me to go, too?"

He brightened, "I would love that."

"It may be more convincing if I'm there, you know, the good wife and all."

He grinned.

"I don't know if I can get the time off just like that," Kate considered.

"You've got some time coming though, don't you?"

"I guess I do. And we're not too busy now. When would you want to leave?"

"Wednesday."

"Wednesday! That's the day after tomorrow."

He grinned again.

"What do we do about Becky? I don't think we should leave her alone," said Kate.

"Agreed. Is there anyone she can stay with?"

"Maybe with Hugh and Gladys. Let me check."

That evening the phone calls were made, the time off was arranged and Roger found someone to teach his Sunday School class. On the phone Gladys said, "Sure, we'd love to have Becky out at the farm. She and Jody will have a ball."

The flight to Las Vegas was calm and uneventful. The DC 10 was full and as he looked over at Kate leaning her head against the seat back, he realized that it had been years since the two of them had gone away together. Too bad this wasn't a real vacation. Roger sipped his Diet Coke and doodled on the Air Canada napkin. Mentally he began going over what might happen in Azuyo. Sergeant Laird and Roger had spent the previous day working out a plan of action. The plan was for him and Kate to get to know the Riverboat proprietor, Goldy Bassino. He and Kate would pose as ordinary tourists from Medicine Hat, Alberta. The less Chester was mentioned, the better, they both agreed.

Neither Kate nor Roger was prepared for the oven-like blast which assaulted them when they stepped out of the airport in Las Vegas. *And I thought Calgary was hot,* thought Roger. They rented a two-year-old silver Chevy Cavalier and headed out for Azuyo. Kate sat in the passenger seat, a tour guide to Nevada opened up on her lap. While Roger fumbled with highway signs trying to find his way through the city to a Route 93 or 95 or an Interstate 515—he couldn't tell which by the map—Kate read aloud: *"The neon memorial to tinseled affluence, Las Vegas, booms 24 hours a day with a heady atmosphere of get-rich-quick. The lure of easy money, the whirling wheels and gaming tables, and numerous plush hotels provide ready entertainment . . ."*

The highways were tangled and crowded. Roger strained forward in the driver's seat. A couple of cars passed him on the right.

"You should go faster in this lane," Kate said.

"I would if I knew where I was going. I want 95, I think. Kate, can you see where that is?"

"No problem." She closed the tour guide and opened the street map of Las Vegas. Three quarters of an hour later they had successfully navigated their way through the city and were on a two-lane highway heading south.

The road to Azuyo wound easily through the desert. A transplanted eastern Canadian, Kate had never been to the southwest, nor seen cactus plants growing wild along the highway. She was enthralled. She constantly urged Roger to stop so she could take pictures. He would have preferred to stay inside the air-conditioned rental, but complied with Kate's requests. They were, after all, tourists on vacation.

It was twilight when they arrived in Azuyo. A large billboard featuring a ten-gallon-hatted cartoon character brandishing a lariat welcomed tourists to *Azuyo—The Friendliest Littlest Gambling Town In The West.* The city was situated beside the wide Colorado River which flowed north into two prime recreational lakes, Lake Mojave and Lake Mead. Hotels dressed in their flashiest neon colors advertised good food, cheap rates, the best entertainment, all night casinos, and millions in winnings.

Roger easily found the Riverboat, a large hotel-casino shaped like an old paddle wheeler. It was entirely outlined in twinkling electric lights which reminded Roger of Hank's patio. They parked the rental and entered the lobby. A few casually dressed people lounged on chairs and talked loudly among themselves. At the counter, Roger caught a glimpse of himself in the floor to ceiling mirror. He was wearing a loose fitting, short-sleeved floral shirt that Kate had picked out and walking shorts. Trying to lose the Canadian RCMP look in favor of what he called the "Miami Vice" look, he hadn't shaved in two days. Kate was always saying you could tell an RCMP officer by his short hair and well-trimmed mustache.

"I don't see how you guys can go undercover," Kate always said, "You can spot a member a mile away."

"Mr. and Mrs. Sheppard? Yes, we have your room registration right here. You're up from Canada?"

"Well, actually down from Canada," said Roger.

The young man behind the counter looked about twenty or twenty-one, was slightly chubby and wore thick glasses; not the sort of person one would expect to see working behind the counter in mega-tourist land. A name tag on his blue suit proclaimed him to be Charles.

"I've always wanted to go to Canada," he said filling out

the forms, and running Roger's VISA card through the machine.

"Must be cold up there," he said.

"Not this time of the year," said Kate.

"You got some beautiful stamps up there," he said.

"Pardon me?"

"Stamps. I collect stamps. That's my hobby. I'm a philatelist, not to be confused with a philanthropist or a philanderer." He smiled at his own joke. "Canada's got some of the nicest stamps. I've managed to get the entire monster series, the history series and the art series. You asked for non-smoking, right? Here's your keys. You're in room 223 in the C-wing. Have a nice day. The casinos go all night and, as a guest at this hotel, you each get one complimentary drink per day. Comes with the room."

"Thanks, Charles," said Kate. "My husband's addicted to Diet Cokes. If you keep him supplied with Diet Cokes, he'll be your friend for life."

A few minutes later they were unpacking in room 223. The room was small with one double bed and an air conditioner which loudly proclaimed its presence. Glancing around, Roger told Kate that the place wasn't noted for its rooms but for its casinos and entertainment.

* * *

As a member of the RCMP, Roger considered himself a fairly worldly-wise individual, knowledgeable and conversant regarding the meaner aspects of society; yet, it was with some embarrassment that he realized that he had never before been inside a casino. A casino was not the sort of place Roger chose to go on vacation. To him, vacations weren't meant to be spent inside crowded, noisy, neon-lit rooms in the company of a lot of strangers. To him, vacations were meant to be spent on boats in the middle of cool lakes with lazy fishing lines dragging behind.

After they unpacked, Kate and Roger found themselves walking through the casino in search of a place to eat. The rooms of the casino were filling up rapidly; individuals marked their territories next to slot machines and Blackjack tables with squat glasses partially filled with amber liquids. Roger and Kate passed one wide-berthed woman in purple stretch pants who sat on a stool between two slot machines, a large plastic bucket of quarters in front of her. Mindlessly, she plunked them in one machine after the other. When Roger made a friendly comment to her, she ignored him.

In the center of the room, half-moon tables overlaid in green felt beckoned individuals to come and lose more money.

Behind them stood an array of somnolent-looking card shufflers who seemed to make no attempt at being merry. Among the milling crowd walked the "change" people. Pushing their little carts they looked like ice cream vendors dispensing dollar gambling tokens for real money, or handfuls of quarters and nickels for bills. The main casino was already becoming cloudy with smoke. Kate waved it away with her hand.

Roger walked over to a change girl, a dark-haired young woman in a short pink leather skirt. He asked for a dollar token.

"You only want one?" she asked.

"That's right," said Roger. "We're tourists from Canada. We've never gambled before. Thought we'd kind of edge into it."

Shaking her head she dispensed one token for him.

"Tell me," he said, "You been here a long time? Working here I mean?"

She looked over at Kate and then at Roger as if they came from the moon, and then she shuffled away.

Giving Roger a playful punch Kate said, "So what are you going to do now, Sherlock?"

He flipped the token into the air and then looked at it. It was identical to the one found on Tom's body.

On their way out they noticed a young, bouncy blonde in a change-apron laughing with one of the customers. She seemed to have a little more life than the rest of the zombie-like crew.

"Hi," Roger said, walking over.

"Hi, yourself," she answered. "You-all need some change or what?" She had one of those deep southern drawls.

"Yeah, give me two tokens. Here's a couple bucks."

"Last of the big spenders." She grinned and reached into the pocket of her apron.

"We just arrived here from Canada. This is all sort of new to us. It'll take us a while," said Kate.

"There's no time like the present to start, I always say. Whereabouts in Canada you-all from?"

"Medicine Hat, Alberta," answered Roger.

"Medicine Hat? What kind of a name is Medicine Hat?"

"A strange one."

She laughed. "That's for sure."

"Actually it comes from an old Indian legend. A Cree medicine man was said to have lost his headdress there while fleeing the ruthless Blackfoot."

"Did they ever find it?"

"Find what?"

"The hat."

"I have no idea. That part's never mentioned in the story."

"Well, that would be my first question." She giggled and said, "Azuyo's the same. It's an old Indian name too, but I forget what it means. You ever been to Toronto?"

"I grew up near Toronto," said Kate brightly.

"No kidding! You ever run into a Ron Porchensko? He's

from Toronto and goes to my college."

"That city's pretty big. Can't say that I have."

"You're a college student?" asked Roger.

"Yeah. In Texas. This is just a summer job for me."

"You like working here?"

"It's okay, I guess. Some of the people are weird. But you get used to them. It's a job. Pays well. And that's what counts."

"Pays well. You must have a good boss, then."

"Yeah, I never see him."

"That'd be Goldy Bassino, wouldn't it?" said Roger.

"That's him. You know him?"

"Heard a lot about him."

"Well, he's all right. Not here much, though. I hear he's mostly out on his plane or on his boat. Who knows where he goes?"

"I take it you don't?"

"Me? I've only ever met him once. He wouldn't know me if he saw me on the street. There's over 300 people working here at the Riverboat. But one thing I will tell you, he's sure fixed up the place. I've been working here three summers, but we used to come here as a family when I was little. And the place was nothing like it is today."

"In what way?"

"Oh, it's much bigger now. He added that other hotel unit over there," she pointed through the lobby. "Fixed up the boardwalk down to the river and expanded the casino. It's a really nice place now. You-all wouldn't know it from what it used to be."

"How long has Mr. Bassino owned the Riverboat, do you know?"

"Around six years I think. But I'm only guessing."

Later on Kate asked Roger, "How do you know so much about Medicine Hat?"

"It was part my research—and also, I'm a whiz at Trivial Pursuit."

* * *

There were a few times during the years after Madeline left the Smiths when she and Tom weren't together as a couple. The night she left the Smiths she moved into a downtown apartment in Calgary with some of Tom's friends. Then for a while she lived with Greg, someone Tom knew through a shared drug connection. With Greg she moved into a crack house in Calgary known to Calgary residents and police as *The Tower*. She remembered the place as having reinforced doors, bars on the windows and lots of people lying around on the floor—there was little furniture. She remembered strangers coming and going at all hours of the day and night, neighbors complaining about hypodermic needles on the lawn, and being afraid. Mostly, being afraid. Greg and Madeline stayed in a dumpy third-floor room and she kept to herself a lot. Between Greg and Tom she was kept well supplied with what she was now calling her *nightmare pills*.

Her nightmares got steadily worse. She'd go for a couple of weeks without one and then, suddenly one night, she would wake up screaming, frantically trying to scrape the blood off her clothes, her arms, and out of her hair. The pills kept these terrors at bay.

Occasionally, downtown she'd see girls her own age with their bags of books and frayed jeans huddling together, and she would feel a momentary pang of sadness. Every so often she would think about Jillian. What was she doing now? Would she remember who Madeline Westmier even was?

She reached over and grabbed a few more chips from the passenger seat beside her. The remains of four days of chips and pop cans and fast food containers were scattered all over the seat and the floor. Tom would kill her if he saw it. He was always so particular about his car. A green sign along the side of the road told her that Azuyo was 21 miles away. It was cool in the air-conditioned car, but ahead of her the road shimmered with yellow heat.

She thought about Greg then, and how she had finally escaped him. It was Greg who had gotten her into drugs in a big way; strong stuff, much stronger than the pills Tom gave her at the Smiths. Even now she could remember the all-night parties, waking up in strange unfamiliar beds covered with unwashed sheets. Occasionally, she would see Tom; he was living with some girl named Tina, but mostly it was Greg.

A few months after they moved to The Tower she began to be afraid of Greg. He would threaten her a lot and even hit her once or twice. He told her he would kill her if she walked out. She thought about her mother and father and believed him.

One chilly afternoon she found herself alone in downtown Calgary, although she had no recollection of where she was going or why she was there. She looked up at the side of the tall buildings and saw a billboard. It was tattered, and the edges of it flapped in the breeze. Funny she should remember that part of it. On it a barefoot girl sat hunched against a brick building hugging her knees, her head down. Across the top it read, *Someone out there cares,* and then the words *Shepherd Centre* and a telephone number.

When she had arrived back at their room, Greg stood in the doorway, his massive shoulders heaving.

"Where you been?" he bellowed.

"None of your business."

"It is my business, when I'm keeping you in smokes and clothes."

"Yeah, Greg. This is great. This place is great. Everything

I dreamed of." For some reason she was feeling strong. Maybe it was because she had memorized the phone number on the billboard.

He had grabbed her shoulders and shoved her against the wall and slapped her face. Over and over he hit her. She screamed and struggled but he held her firmly. He told her to shut up and he hit her again and again. Downstairs she heard other voices, but of course they would ignore her. The figure which loomed over her suddenly became the figure of her father.

"Daddy, don't hit her, please don't hit her!" she screamed over and over until she slumped down against the kitchen wall.

Before she slipped into unconsciousness, she heard Greg say, "You are nuts, woman."

A few hours later she drifted back into consciousness; her head hurt and her flannel shirt was stained with blood. Greg was gone. Probably downstairs. She grabbed her blanket and her mother's tea cup, and walked down the back stairs and out the door, not even bothering to close it behind her. She ignored the stares of the people on the C-Train, who moved away from her when she boarded. She kept her head down and wrapped the blanket tightly around her, the cup in her lap.

Madeline got off at Tom's stop and blindly made her way through the street to his apartment, her blanket dragging behind her like a bag lady's shawl. She banged wildly on his door, pressed the buzzer and called loudly. No answer. Finally, shivering with cold, she lay against his door.

When she awoke she was lying on the couch in his living room. He was smoking in a frayed armchair across from her. Short-skirted, leggy Tina was sitting on his lap and giggling.

She sat up.

He regarded her calmly, "Greg beat you up?"

She put a hand to her face. It felt swollen and it hurt.

"Why'd he beat you up? What'd you do to him?" he asked.

Her head ached and she held it with both hands.

"I gotta go," she said rising.

"Yeah, and where you goin' to go?" he asked. "Back to Greg's so he can shove you around some more?"

She shook her head and looked down.

"Face it. You're a loser. You got no place to go, so you might as well stay here."

Tina giggled again.

She stayed. Two weeks later she discovered she was pregnant. Tina helped to arrange an abortion for her, but two days before her appointment she miscarried. She was sick in bed for a month.

All of that seemed so long ago now even though only a few years had passed. Three years ago Tom and Tina broke up and Tom and Madeline moved back to Chester together.

Madeline munched on a handful of popcorn. She needed something decent to eat, she thought, like a hamburger or a pizza. Azuyo couldn't be much farther now. She began to see more and more signs of life, side-of-the-road motels and little red and white houses with white stones for lawns, odd-looking cactus plants where evergreens should be. She passed gas stations and gift shops advertising genuine Indian crafts.

A pang of loneliness struck her just then. No one who had ever meant anything to her had stuck around—not Jillian, not Bethany, not her mother, not Tom.

She fumbled for a cigarette from the case of Camels on the seat beside her, lit it and opened her window a crack. Sweltering waves of heat filtered into the car. The brochure said the Riverboat had a pool. That would be nice.

CHAPTER 12

The girl who stood by herself at the front desk didn't look more than eighteen or nineteen, although she was probably older. Her eyes darted here and there, and her hands shook as she held onto a tattered gray duffel bag and an old beige quilt folded loosely into a square. Yet, her clothes looked brand new; a pale blue tank-top style tee shirt and matching shorts, and sunglasses perched atop her head.

"Can I help you?" asked Charles.

"I'd like a room."

"Any particular kind of room? Single? Double?"

"I don't care, just a regular room."

"Are you here alone?"

"Yes, I am." She turned to look around her toward the front door. "Does that pool out there belong to this hotel?"

"Yes, it does."

"Well, do you think I could have a room which looks out over it?"

"I don't see why not. Our most popular rooms overlook the river, however, and we've got a few of those left."

"No, thanks. I'd like the pool side. I like swimming a lot."

"Will you be paying with credit card?"

"Is cash okay?" she asked tentatively.

"Of course," he laughed. "Cash is always acceptable!"

She paid him cash for a week in advance and signed her name, Bethany Hadecker from 21 Spring Road, Los Angeles,

California. He was from Los Angeles, too. He wondered where Spring Road was. He gave her a room in the A wing, the old wing, room 454.

She took the key, leaned toward him across the desk and said quietly, "I have one more question. Is that parking lot okay to use?" And she pointed across the street to an abandoned gas station with a *For Sale or Rent* sign in the window. "Can I park behind that old building?"

"I don't know. I guess so. But we've plenty of parking here at the hotel, valet service even, for a slight charge."

"I know but, well, it's my uncle's car I drove and it's brand new. He told me not to park it anywheres it could get bumped. I have a very eccentric uncle."

"Sure, I guess so . . ."

"Thanks."

"By the way, I'm Charles. If you need anything, just let me know, Bethany."

"Thanks, Charles."

"Oh, I almost forgot, here's your drink chits. You get one complimentary drink per day."

"Oh, thanks." She took the chits, stared at them for a few seconds and then stuffed them into her bag.

Then she left, tentatively turning, looking all around her and walking slowly, carefully toward the elevator, a corner of her blanket dragging behind her. He began to wonder about her, so small and so fearful, so alone and so sad. And so pretty. What is she running from, he wondered. He decided that she needed someone to keep an eye on her.

* * *

Pale green cactus plants lined the red tiled walkway which led to the front of Mario's Italian Bistro in Bullfrog, Arizona. Leaving Kate and the current novel she was reading by the Riverboat pool, Roger had hopped into the rental and driven across the bridge into Bullfrog. He was meeting Azuyo County Sheriff Andrew Lund for lunch. Lund had chosen this restaurant for its privacy and because it was definitely out of the way of the general gambling and tourist population of Azuyo. Gambling was illegal in Arizona. The less they were seen together the better, Lund had told him over the phone.

"Mr. Sheppard, Mr. Lund is waiting for you in the back," said the hostess who carried with her two leather-covered menus.

"Would you care for a drink before lunch?" she asked.

"Maybe a Diet Coke."

He followed her through a coffee shop with Formica-topped booths, past a sign which read *Dining Room Closed* and back into a more formal area with cloth-covered tables.

He was unprepared for the young man who waved at him from a booth along the back wall, out of sight of the front door.

Earlier that day Kate had laughed, "He's a U.S. sheriff so he'll probably be fat . . ."

"Smoke cigars," added Roger.

"Have a southern drawl," she said laughing.

"And carry around two 357's."

"And he'll probably want to know where your red serge and horse are."

The preppie-looking slim young man in jeans, casual shirt and loose tie, therefore, didn't fit any stereotypes.

"Hi," said the young man extending his hand. "I'm Sheriff Lund. Andy."

"Roger Sheppard," said Roger shaking his hand.

"I've heard a lot about you. I spoke to Sergeant Laird earlier."

Roger smiled.

"He filled me in on the whole Anderchuk thing. Iced tea for me," he said to the approaching waitress.

"That sounds good," added Roger with a wave of his hand. "Can you change my Diet Coke to an iced tea?"

"Like magic," she said and retreated into the kitchen.

"Nothing lowers the old body temp like a cold glass of brewed iced tea," said Andrew sitting down and producing a thick file from the empty seat beside him. "Canada's a beautiful place. But you can't get a decent glass of iced tea up there, just that sugary mix stuff. Last summer we drove around British Columbia—Vancouver, Victoria, and the entire time we were there we couldn't get a decent glass of iced tea to save our lives. Beautiful country through."

Roger smiled. "Did you make it into Alberta?"

"Banff, and then up to Jasper. Fantastic country. The Columbia Ice Fields—breathtaking."

"But no iced tea."

"No iced tea," he said laughing.

The waitress approached with two tall glasses.

"Ready to order?" she asked.

"A couple more minutes, Theresa," said Andrew.

"Is this place safe?" Roger asked quietly when she left.

"Yes, very. I know the people here. Personally. We can talk here."

"That's good to know. What do you recommend?" asked Roger opening his menu.

"Everything's good. The pizza's great. Closest thing to Chicago that I know."

"Chicago?"

"That's where I'm from. Grew up on the north shore— that's just north of Chicago proper—went to the University of Illinois, and then did my graduate work in criminology at the University of Chicago."

"Graduate work?"

124

"My Master's thesis was on gaming-related crime. Don't ask me why I was interested in that being from Chicago. We moved out here so I could finish my research, and we sort of never left. We like it here."

Graduate work? This guy was no Boss Hogg. "Who's the we?"

"My wife, Candy and I."

"One lunch-sized Pepperoni pizza," he said to the returning waitress.

"Extra cheese, Mr. Lund?"

"You got it."

"I'll have the same," said Roger closing his menu and handing it to her. "I trust his judgment."

When she left Roger said, "They know you here."

"As I said before, this place is safe. I guess I've earned a special place in their hearts. My wife and I had just come out from Chicago around four years ago. About a month later Mario's nineteen-year-old son was killed in Azuyo, caught in the crossfire of some cocaine traffickers. I got to know the family quite well then. I can assure you that they're on our side."

Roger nodded and glanced at the file.

Lund continued, "How about you? You have children?"

"Two daughters, both teenagers."

"Teenagers. That must be fun. I have two daughters too, ages three and five."

"Then you have a lot to look forward to."

Soon after the food arrived, the small talk ended and Lund said solemnly, "Maybe we should get down to business." He picked up his fork. "We've known for a long time that Gabriel or *Goldy* Bassino, as he is called, is involved in criminal activities—extortion, drug trafficking, prostitution. He owns a string of hotels and casinos along the river and businesses in California, but so far we haven't been able to pin anything on him and get it to stick."

"And that's where I come in."

"Right. You're a stranger. We've long figured that Bassino has been bringing in drugs from Mexico and South America. This Canadian connection is new and has us worried."

"You're not the only one."

Over lunch they discussed the plan whereby Roger would pose as a businessman from Medicine Hat feeling out Bassino about setting up a drug connection in Alberta.

"I'm not sure about phone calls between us," said Lund when they were finished. "The fewer the better I think. But we are having you protected, especially your wife."

"Thank you," said Roger rising.

"Check," said Andrew motioning to the waitress.

She called out, "Mario says it's on the house this time."

"Tell Mario thanks and that one of these days I am going to come in here and pay him for all the meals I've eaten!"

"No problem, sheriff."

As Roger closed the restaurant door behind them, his gaze was drawn to a little fish symbol above the pictures of the various charge cards that Mario's accepted. It was an ichthus, the Christian fish with a few Greek letters inside.

"An Ichthus," Roger said quietly.

"A what?"

Roger pointed at the fish and said, "The ichthus is the Christian symbol. It was used by the early church, much like the symbol of the cross is used today. Is Mario what you would call a Christian?"

"A Christian?"

They were walking slowly down the path toward their cars under the white-hot sun.

"Well, he's religious. You got to respect the guy for that. He's about the only person I know who makes his religion part of his everyday life. And he's just about the nicest fellow you'd ever want to meet, too." He paused and added, "He's invited us a couple of times to go to church with him." They had reached their respective vehicles.

"Maybe you should take him up on it," said Roger unlocking his car door.

"I just might someday."

Roger arrived back at the Riverboat to find Kate still lounging in the shade by the pool, her book in her lap.

"Get your suit on," she called to him.

"Mr. Sheppard, hey, Mr. Sheppard!"

He turned. Charles was waving and running toward him.

"Do you have a minute? I got a few new stamps today, from Canada. Thought if you had a minute I'd show them to you."

"I'm going to cool off in the pool now, Charles. But let's make a date, have a Coke sometime and I'll have a look at all your stamps then."

"Sure. Great. I just happen to be on my break now is all."

"Great, Charles. We'll get together some time."

"That'd be great. I got some postmarked from Toronto today, from the Northwest Territories, Vancouver, even from Alberta. You're from Alberta. Ever hear of a town called Chester?"

Roger was instantly aware. Chester?

"Hey, Charles, maybe I *could* spend a couple of minutes looking at your stamps."

The young man smiled from ear to ear. "Wait here. I'm on break now. I'll be right back."

Roger pulled up a white plastic chair next to Kate, adjusted the umbrella on the table so that most of himself, Kate and the table was in the shade.

"Postmarks from Chester?" she said raising her eyebrows.

"Might be interesting," he agreed.

A few moments later Charles ambled toward them, a green

three-ring binder under his arm.

"Here are the new ones I got today," he said opening the binder and displaying various plastic pages. "I haven't had time to put them in my regular album yet. Haven't even taken them off the envelopes. This binder is only temporary. I just put them in here to protect them."

Roger found himself looking down at an envelope addressed to Mr. Goldy Bassino, the Riverboat. The postmark was Chester, Alberta. Roger picked it up. There was no return address.

"Where did you say you got these?"

"My boss. Well, in his garbage. Look, here's an Australian one that one of the guests let me have."

But Roger was still fingering the envelope. "Uh, can I borrow this stamp for a day or two Charles?"

"Why sure, Mr. Sheppard. You really like that stamp, huh?"

"I really like this stamp, Charles."

Back in his room he examined it. No return address. He'd have to somehow get it over to Lund's office. Get it up to Calgary. See if the handwriting matched Tom's. Or Flip Schmidt's. Or Wes Romaine's.

* * *

That morning Madeline bought a gun. She sat on the floor in her room and carefully cradled the gun in both hands, the way the man who sold it to her did. It was cold and heavy; she didn't realize that guns were so heavy.

Earlier that morning she had no clear idea of where she was going to go. Where do people buy guns? She had walked up and down the strip wearing the new sunglasses and wide-brimmed denim hat that she'd purchased the day before. She walked past restaurants ranging from fast food to fine dining, bright video arcades, casinos, clothing stores advertising the best in beach wear, jewelry and Indian craft stores. But no gun stores. She ventured down a few side streets. Here she passed less expensive clothing stores specializing in not-quite-the-best in beach wear, sandwich shops, video arcades and casinos which were not quite so bright and cheery. But still no gun stores. Then she ventured down some side streets off those side streets and passed a few seedy-looking bars, a place to get one's fortune told, a couple of greasy-looking coffee shops and a pawn shop. She stopped in front of the pawn shop. It's grimy window was crammed with tarnished trumpets, bright blue bass guitars with sparkles embedded in their flesh, drums, stereos and radios piled one on top of the other and an assortment of grimy metal kitchen chairs and scuffy dressers. But no guns.

Nevertheless, she entered. The place was dim and deserted. She heard classic oldies coming from a tinny radio. She saw an oily-looking yellow-haired man in a navy tee shirt who sat behind the counter writing numbers in a book. She was the only customer. Good. He didn't look up when she approached. She stood there for several seconds alternately looking at him, at his book and at the array of guns under the glass counter in front of her. She'd come to the right place.

Finally, the man shut the book and looked up. "Something you want?" he asked.

He was missing two front teeth, and those that remained were yellowed and craggy. She tried not to look at them.

"How much are the guns?" she asked.

"You want a gun?"

"Yeah."

"One of these guns?"

"Yeah."

"What do you want it for?"

"None of your business."

He smirked and she looked away. There was something loathsome about that smirk. He said, "I can't sell guns to pretty little women without no reason."

"Okay then, it's for protection."

The man grinned again. "Aw, what's a pretty thing like you need protection from?"

She ignored his question. "Can you please tell me how much one of these guns is?"

"I don't think you want these guns. These guns are collectors' guns. I don't sell protection guns. I'm not in that business."

Madeline didn't understand. Guns were guns as far as she was concerned. She was sure that the guns in front of her would do just fine. She pulled out her wallet and began flipping through a packet of hundreds. She watched his eyes widen.

"Well, now, maybe I *can* be of some assistance."

He led her into a back room where he pulled out a locked chest from underneath a table. In it were guns, lots of guns. He brought out a little black handgun, carefully cradling it in both hands. "This here's a good one."

"How much is it?"

"Kind of expensive."

"How expensive?"

"I can sell it to you for $750, and that's a steal."

It seemed like a lot of money to Madeline. But then again, she had no idea how expensive guns really were. He saw her pause and then went on. "I hate to do this, but for you, 'cause I know a pretty thing like you needs protection, I'll sell it for $700 and I'll throw in a round of shells."

"How about $650 cash, throw in a round of shells and you show me how to use it?"

"Done."

And now she was back in her room. She wrapped up the

gun in a hotel hand towel, wrapped the shells in a face cloth and placed both of them in her nightstand underneath the little Gideon Bible.

Then she leaned back against the pillows, picked up the remote, flicked on the TV, and dug out her cigarettes, balancing the large ceramic ash tray on her lap. She'd do it tomorrow. Tomorrow she would confront Goldy Bassino with her gun. Tomorrow he would talk. Tomorrow he would have to tell her who killed Tom. Maybe *he* killed Tom. A place far inside of her began to be afraid. Her hands trembled on her cigarette and she inhaled deeply. She reached into her duffel bag for a small plastic bottle of sleeping pills. Only a few remained. This worried her somewhat. She took two with water.

Still only afternoon but she decided she was hungry. She dialed room service and ordered the most expensive item on the menu, steak and lobster and a bottle of wine. Make that two bottles. When it arrived she wrapped herself up in her mother's quilt and sat cross-legged on the bed watching TV and picking at her food. She poured the wine into her mother's tea cup and, as the evening progressed, she drank both bottles that way.

Madeline woke to the sound of someone tapping on her door. Tom! Janice! She flung off the quilt spilling the scraps of unfinished supper all over the bed. She blinked her eyes. The sun was streaming through her windows and some guy on TV was inviting everybody to his neighborhood.

Madeline glanced at the digital clock beside her bed. 9:03 A.M. As she shed layers of sleep, she remembered where she was and fumbled to the door. "Yes," she said hoarsely. Her head ached. Oh, did it ache!

"Housekeeping."

"Go away," she yelled at the closed door. The knocking ceased.

An hour later, showered and changed and feeling somewhat better, although certainly not one hundred percent, Madeline approached the front desk.

"I wonder if I could see Mr. Bassino," she said in the most authoritative voice that she could muster.

Charles looked up from where he was sorting through a binder of what looked like old letters. He hastily shut it.

"Oh, hello, Miss Hadecker. You want to see Mr. Bassino?"

"Yes, if he's in."

"Well, you're out of luck. I'm sorry to say he's not here." Not here? "When will he be here then?"

"Maybe later this morning. Maybe tomorrow, maybe not for a couple of days. I don't always know."

"Well, where is he?" She tried to keep her voice steady. She had counted on his being there today. Right now. She was ready for him now. If she even had to wait an hour she might lose her nerve. She held the new little purse made of colorful fabric scraps close to her. It was just big enough for the gun. She had bought it yesterday with the gun in mind.

"Probably at one of his other businesses."

She was aware that Charles was regarding her closely. Too closely? Was he a part of the conspiracy against Tom, too? How could she be sure of anybody down here?

"If it's really important you could write down a message and I'll see that he gets it when he calls in for his messages."

"Well tell him . . ." Madeline had to think fast. "Tell him it's about my . . . my brother, Tom Anderchuk." She enunciated each syllable of Tom's name, pronouncing it slowly and clearly. "And that I know everything." She looked at him carefully, but saw no flicker of any kind of recognition in his eyes.

"Okay, I'll tell him it's about Tom Anderchuk," he was writing down the name on a pad of paper, "and that you know everything."

"Right. Thanks." She turned to go.

"Miss Hadecker! Bethany, wait!" he called.

She turned and he continued, "Bethany, I was wondering if, maybe, if . . ."

"What?"

"Well, I was just thinking . . ."

"Yeah?"

"Never mind."

Charles spent the next hour chastising himself for losing his nerve with Bethany. All I wanted to do was a simple thing like invite her for an ice cream or a movie and I can't even do that! I'm sure she thinks I'm a jerk, a class-A jerk straight from nerdville, he mumbled to himself as he sorted through the guest records.

His work finished early, Charles decided to take advantage of the quiet morning to sort through his stamps in Mr. Bassino's office. His boss was out of town, so what the heck? Plenty of times Mr. Bassino has *me* working late on *my* own time; it's time I did some of *my* work on *his* time, he thought. He picked up a stack of envelopes and began flipping through them, placing the Canadian ones in one pile and the U.S. and foreign in another and wondering what it was about Bethany that attracted him. It wasn't just her prettiness. Azuyo was crawling with pretty girls and he seldom felt the same pull. No, it was something else. Her whole demeanor spoke a certain vulnerability. It was like she was crying out for someone to protect her. Yeah, and that's another thing, he thought, I've probably got her figured out all wrong. I read too many fantasy novels where the poor, vulnerable princess ends up being rescued from all manner of evil by the charming prince. Get real, man. This is reality, not some fantasy world!

He had just about finished arranging the letters. The U.S. envelopes—unless he thought Josh would need them—along with the common Canadian and foreign ones were headed for the shredder. The other Canadian envelopes he placed in a file folder and put it inside his binder to take up to his room. This evening he would make himself a cup of hot chocolate, sit in front of the TV, fill a bowl full of warm water and remove the stamps to be set in his album. Boy, do I know how to spend an evening, he muttered to himself. I'm a real barrel of laughs—regular party animal!

At 11:30 A.M. he grabbed his latest Terry Brooks novel from underneath the counter, said goodbye to Lucia and headed for the coffee shop.

The place was still fairly empty. The lunch crowd wasn't expected for another forty-five minutes, so he found himself a quiet table near a window, ordered a 7-Up and a cheese-burger plate and opened his book. He looked up when his drink arrived and there sitting at the table next to him, with her back to him was Bethany! I'm being given a second chance, he thought. The gods are looking down upon me with favor! Don't blow it this time. He grabbed his drink and his book and headed over.

"Hi, Bethany!"

She looked up, a half-smile crossing her face.

"Are you alone? Can I join you?"

"Suit yourself."

He sat down. She was drinking coffee, he noticed. And there was a full pot of it on her table. She must like coffee.

"So, how's it going? You enjoying your stay?"

"Yeah, it's okay."

"So, nice weather we're having, don't you think?"

"Yeah, nice."

"So, you from L.A.?"

"Yeah."

"So, I'm from L.A., too. Whereabouts in L.A. you from?"

"Spring Road area."

"Yeah? I've lived in L.A. all my life. Where is that area?"

"It's around Spring Road."

Time to change the subject. "So, you going swimming today?"

"Don't know. Maybe if I get to feeling better."

It was then that he noticed that she was looking a little green around the edges.

"You not feeling well?" Dumb question.

"No, not too hot. I think I had too much to drink last night."

"So, partied last night, huh?"

"Not really."

"So, uh, I hope you're feeling better."

"Yeah, me too."

"Well, uh, Bethany, I was wondering if maybe you'd like to go a movie with me sometime? Maybe miniature golfing or something?" Dumb, dumb, Charles, he thought, why'd you have to go and mention miniature golf, only nerds play miniature golf!

"Miniature golf sounds like fun."

"Really? Great!" His cheeseburger plate arrived.

Bethany looked at it, turned green and left abruptly.

"I'll call you about mini-golf then," he called to her quickly-retreating figure.

CHAPTER 13

"That girl, Madeline Westmier, we still can't locate her."

"Still?" Roger said into the pay phone. "She's been gone over a week."

Lavoir said, "Her neighbor, Janice Wallinger, has no idea where she is either, and she says Madeline never goes anywhere without telling her. Madeline hasn't called her. Her car's gone, too."

"Have you checked her apartment, her bank account?" asked Roger. It was sweltering in front of the pay phone outside of the hotel. He wiped his forehead, then shaded his eyes with his left hand.

"We didn't get a warrant. Laird said it might not be relevant to the case."

Roger was in no mood. "Get a warrant, man! She's part of a murder investigation," he yelled into the phone. "I don't care what Laird says. I don't relish the thought of finding her body on top of a garbage heap somewhere, too. Get an APB out on her car. Find out where she went. Find out all you can about her. She may have gone to some relative."

"Will do."

He returned to their room to find Kate sitting at the desk writing a letter on the hotel stationery.

"Let's get some coffee," he said.

"What's the matter with you? You get up on the wrong side of the bed or something?" She folded the letter. He noticed it was addressed to Sara.

He shrugged. "I don't know. I guess I'm a little keyed up. I meet with Goldy today."

"You'll do fine. You always do. Just give me a couple minutes and then let's get some breakfast. I could use some breakfast."

He sat on the edge of the bed and watched her brush her hair. It was thick and dark.

"I really should do something with this mop," she said sweeping it off her shoulders and into a barrette. This was something she said at least once a week. And at least once a week Roger would answer, "Why? I love it that way."

"Why? I love it that way," he said.

She frowned, and Roger noticed something deeper, worry lines around her eyes, a certain unsteadiness to her hand. She said things like "You'll do fine," and "It's in God's hands," but they were words that only masked a deeper uncertainty. I shouldn't have brought her here, he thought. Even though they prayed, and Lund promised that his department would keep an eye on her, he still worried for her.

She turned and faced him with a smile. "You're deep in thought."

"Just thinking about you. You'll be all right. It'll be all right."

She went into the circle of his arms. "I know."

* * *

"Thanks for meeting with me," said Roger.

Goldy Bassino in the flesh was not at all what Roger expected. With a name like Goldy, Roger expected someone fair-haired and tall. Instead, Goldy was dark, small-boned and fine-featured. He was impeccably groomed and his black-gray hair was slicked back into a pony tail which curled neatly over his shirt collar.

Goldy sat with his elbows on the desk, his fingertips together, regarding Roger calmly. "I'm always delighted to meet satisfied customers," Goldy said.

"Well, I'm more than just a satisfied customer. I came to say personally what a change you have made to the place. The last time the wife and I were here was probably six, seven years ago. When we walked in a couple of days ago I said, 'Honey, I'm going to personally meet the man who is responsible for this new and improved Riverboat.' I especially like what you've done with the boardwalk. Six years ago it was just a dirt path."

"Well, I'm delighted."

Roger watched him intently. He was smiling, but was there a certain wariness to his expression? A certain darting of the eyes? Or was it Roger's imagination?

"Actually," said Roger, taking a seat, "This is more than just a social call. Up in Medicine Hat, that's in Alberta—I don't know if you are familiar with our Canadian provinces— there's a group of us interested in bringing this kind of resort there. Alberta is wide open for this sort of thing. And I'm thinking that my partners and I could use your kind of input."

"And what kind of input would that be, Mr. Sheppard?"

"Advice, consulting. We are prepared to pay, and please call me Roger."

"I'm a very busy man."

"I appreciate that. And I wouldn't be here if I didn't think this arrangement could benefit both of us."

"How so, Mr. Sheppard?"

"We are looking for a U.S. partner for our venture."

"What is it exactly that you do, Mr. Sheppard?"

"Investments, real-estate, you name it."

"And you want to open a casino resort in Medicine Hat,

Alberta?"

"That's our plan, yes."

"What about your gambling laws?"

"We're applying for a special permit. There's a big push for tourism, especially along the U.S.-Canada border. I'm confident the rules can be bent for the kind of resort we envision."

Goldy was quiet for a minute, and Roger wondered how far he could continue the charade. After a moment's pause Roger said, "I don't think you would regret making an investment in Canada."

Goldy did not answer, but rose and walked over to the window where he stood, hands behind his back looking out toward the river. Roger took the opportunity to quickly scan the office—spacious, modern furniture, large glass desk, computer, filing cabinet, wall safe. A small stack of letters was on his desk. He could almost make out the return address of one—*Orchard Fr* is all he could see. He resisted the urge to reach out and gently nudge the top envelope away, knowing that if the window was reflective at all, Goldy would have a clear view of him. Instead he sat smiling, hands folded in his lap.

Finally Goldy turned and walked back to his desk, "Well, Mr. Sheppard, you have intrigued me. Have you brought a proposal, a prospectus with you?"

Roger rose. "I can get that to you in a day." He casually bumped the desk dislodging the letter. Quickly he scanned the return address—*Silver Springs Orchard Fruits, Bakersfield, California*. Fortunately, Goldy didn't seem to notice but steered him toward the door signifying that the meeting was over. He would have to call Laird later on and get that phony business proposal faxed to him.

Later that afternoon the three of them, Roger, Kate and Goldy were sitting out on Goldy's private balcony drinking iced coffees.

"Business is booming up in Canada. Good things in Alberta," said Roger. "It's the right time I think for a joint U.S.-Canadian partnership. Condos, luxury hotels, casinos, right along the border."

Far out on the river Roger could see a couple of those snowmobiles on water. Sea Doos, they called them, or was it Jet Skis?

"I've never been to Canada," said Goldy softly, placing his coffee cup on the table and taking a cookie.

Liar, thought Roger.

Kate said, "You would love it there, Mr. Bassino. It's a large, beautiful place. So many natural resources, unspoiled lakes."

"And it's the land of opportunity now," said Roger leaning toward him.

"But you have tight, very tight government restrictions."

"Minor hindrances," said Roger with a grin. "There are always ways around government restrictions. And we are a lot more open to casino type operations than we used to be. Our government itself is in the lottery business now. Strange turn of events, interesting conflict of interest, I would say."

"I would have to see a full prospectus," said Goldy.

"You got it."

"And my own board of directors would have to approve."

"You got it."

"I would want the names of all your partners."

"You got it."

"And I would do personal checks on all of them."

"You got it," said Roger with a grin.

* * *

"I hate it when you have to lie."

He and Kate had changed into shorts and running shoes and were standing on a cactus-strewn hillock overlooking the city. Roger was beginning to think this trek was a mistake. The heat in this dry place was unbearable; a dry sauna-like heat which evaporated body sweat before it had a chance to materialize.

"It's not lying," said Roger turning a small stone over in his hands and looking at her.

"Pretending to be some sort of a real estate agent from Medicine Hat. What would have happened if he'd asked you some technical real estate questions that you wouldn't have been able to answer?"

He smiled, "You would have bailed me out!"

"Maybe, but," she hesitated, "it sure feels like lying to me. I know you're going to say it's part of your job . . ."

"You're right. It's part of my job."

"But to lie to get the truth out, there's got to be a better way. The old ends justifying the means . . ."

"Goldy's involved in something. I'm sure of it. Certain expressions on his face, certain looks. I've been a cop long enough to see that. These are the bad guys, Kate. We're the good guys."

"But what you said wasn't truthful," she protested.

"You want the truth? I'll tell you the truth. The truth is a murder in a small town. The truth is dozens of kids in Chester hooked on drugs. The truth is runaway kids in Calgary caught in prostitution and drugs. The truth is places like The Tower that openly deal drugs and snub their noses at ordinary citizens. The truth is thirteen-year-old prostitutes and their fourteen-year-old pimps. All of them destroying what life they may have because of drugs. That's the truth, Kate."

"But Roger, how can you pretend to be something that you're not to Goldy? Doesn't that conflict with the Christian principle of honesty at all costs? Hey, stand next to that cactus, the big one. That would make a neat picture." She placed the camera next to her eye.

"Smile now," she said.

"You're aiming into the sun. It won't come out that way."

"Down here you aim into the sun no matter which way you turn."

"How about if I look down?"

"Smart aleck!"

The brown, sandy soil didn't look like it could support any sort of life, yet tiny yellow cactus flowers grew in abundance. He bent down to examine one.

"Rahab did it," he said rising and twirling a yellow flower between his fingers.

"Rahab did what?"

"Rahab lied to protect the spies and God honored her. She's even mentioned in the Hebrews chapter eleven hall of fame. *By faith the harlot Rahab did not perish with those who did not believe, when she had received the spies with peace.*"

"You have it memorized."

"I've always drawn strength from that verse. Whenever I question my own involvement in law enforcement, and I *do* question it, Kate, I always go to Rahab. And then there was that girl who hid David's friends in the well."

"Maybe you're right. I just worry sometimes, you know. These are dangerous people. Sometimes I'm afraid. I pray about it, but I still end up being afraid."

"I know," he said.

* * *

It was quiet in her kitchen the day Marjorie Romaine cracked the files on her husband's computer. When she had found the Visa receipts a few days earlier she carried them into the kitchen and checked the calendar which hung above the phone. The last week in April, the dates on the Visa receipts, Wes was attending a two-day meeting in Edmonton. Supposedly.

She dialed the Town Office.

"Paula. Hi. It's Marj Romaine. Yeah, these dates at the end of April—April 23-25—wasn't that the Rural Economic Development meeting in Edmonton? Yes, I thought so. And where was the meeting? The Edmonton Inn? Thanks ever so much Paula, you've been a big help."

Marjorie could imagine Paula sighing on the other end— Wes' wife checking up on him again. Well, if she did nothing else, she would liven up their coffee-break conversation that morning. Well, that's just too bad, thought Marjorie. I've got to find out and I've got nothing to lose, she said putting a hand to the scab on her face where the bruise was just beginning to heal.

Her next call was to the Edmonton Inn. She was a little smarter now after her fiasco call to the Riverboat.

"Hello," she said. "This is Paula Davis with the Town of Chester. We're filling out Wes Romaine's claim receipt for the Rural Economic Development Meeting held there April 23-25 of this year—Oh, he never checked in? Well, maybe he stayed with friends. Thank you very much. We'll check on that."

So Wes had lied. He *was* seeing someone else! And he and the little twirp, whoever she was, had spent the weekend down in Nevada at some gambling joint she'd never even heard of!

She tore the guest room apart then, underwear and socks and neckties she threw all over the floor. She checked the pockets of his suits and these, too were strewn on the floor. She looked for a name, a match book cover (although Wes didn't smoke), lipstick on a shirt collar. But she found nothing. She had no information—except the receipts.

And the computer, of course. She stared at it. She was convinced that all his lies were stored in its inner mind on magical things called mini bytes.

She took it down and placed it on her lap, but had no idea of how to even turn it on! This is hopeless, she thought. Why didn't I pay more attention when Wes would sit in front of it for hours? But no, she sat in front of the TV crocheting baby sweaters for her grandchildren. Why didn't I sign up for that computer course at the library? *The library*. That gave her an idea. Nancy, down at the library, had a little computer like Wes's. She knew it because they sometimes talked about computer stuff.

Half an hour later, makeup applied deftly to hide her bruise, Marjorie was chatting with Nancy in the library office. All her volunteer work with the library plus the fact that she had been on the board for two terms, president for one, couldn't but help.

"I was wondering, Nancy, if you might have time to show me how to run your little computer. Wes is giving me his to use, and of course he's so busy and away so much, what with his council work plus his business—it looks as if learning to run the thing will be up to me."

"Of course Marj. Why don't you bring it in and I'd be happy to help you over lunch or something."

"I was thinking more of yours. I don't have Wes's yet. I thought maybe it would be better if I learned how to operate it before I got his."

"How about lunch today then?"

That was yesterday. Now all she had to do was follow the page of directions she and Nancy had written out. She flicked on the computer and stared at the dark screen. She pressed the button, and with a little *ding* the computer screen brightened. So far so good, she thought. Then she hit a roadblock. A little box in the center of the screen demanded a password.

Nancy hadn't mentioned passwords. She flexed her fingers. Password. Password. What would Wes use for a password? She typed his name, his mother's name, his nickname when he was a kid, his sister's name, his business name, but nothing worked. All she got was *invalid password.*

She got up, stretched and walked around a bit. Think Marjorie, think, she told herself. She wandered out into the kitchen and poured herself a glass of orange juice from the fridge. Then she made herself a piece of raisin toast. Then she called her friend Sheila. They chatted for twenty minutes about nothing in particular. Then she turned on the TV news and watched CNN for a while—some storm at sea. *Suddenly she knew.* His boat, his one love in life, the thing he treasured most. He had a sailboat moored in a Vancouver harbor. Every summer he took it out for a week by himself. When the kids were younger, they used to go out as a family. But that was a long time ago.

She hurried back to the kitchen table and typed Sea Queen. Like magic, the file opened. Ah, Wes, I know you too well, she thought. You can't keep anything from me.

What appeared on the screen was a set of files marked *Letters, Ledgers* and *Dates and Shipments.* Carefully, methodically, she read through them all. At first the picture was very cloudy, but as the entire picture came into focus, Marj was horrified. It wasn't another woman Wes was courting. His mistress was power and money and drugs. She was absolutely positive that what she was reading on a warm, quiet afternoon in her kitchen in Chester was vitally important, extremely frightening, and would change forever her relationship with her husband and his relationship with his children. Nothing in their lives would ever be the same again.

She could turn the computer off, hang the clothes up again and pretend she had never read it, or she could call Corporal Roger Sheppard now. A few months ago there was a story about him in their little Chester newspaper. He was heading up the anti-drug operation in Chester.

In measured steps, Marjorie walked toward the kitchen wall phone and dialed the number for the RCMP detachment in Chester. She asked for corporal Roger Sheppard.

* * *

"Now here's a kid who's had no breaks." Clayton's gravelly voice boomed over the long distance wires. Standing in the afternoon sun, Roger held the receiver of the pay phone up to his ear. This checking in with Chester on various pay phones throughout Azuyo was becoming a nuisance. Although the phone in their room was probably safe, Roger preferred not to trust it.

Clayton continued, "She was put in a foster home when she was thirteen. Ran away three years later. Her foster mother said she was incorrigible."

"You talked to them?" Roger pulled his ball cap down over his eyes. Waiting behind him for the phone was a large lady in a flowered tent dress who was frowning under her straw hat. Roger turned his back to her.

"By phone. They're in Vancouver now. A Mrs. Bernice Smith said Madeline was so difficult that she and her husband haven't taken another foster child since. I don't think Madeline would have gone there. Apparently Herbert Smith, the husband, had some sort of nervous breakdown shortly after Madeline left."

"What about before she was thirteen?"

"That's the sad part. She lived with her parents in Manitoba. An only child. Her father, Madden Westmier, is currently out at Kingston serving a life sentence for the murder of his wife, Celeste Westmier. That would be Madeline's mother. Sounds like there was a lot of abuse."

"Manitoba? How did she end up in Alberta then?"

"Things are kind of hazy on that point. Personally, I think it was a Social Services royal foul-up. The records have it that she was moved to Alberta for her own safety. They didn't find Madden until three months later. Oh, yeah, and it was Madeline who found the body. He had slit her throat with a kitchen meat carving knife. Not a pretty sight, apparently."

Roger shut his eyes against the sun.

"She was thirteen then," Roger mused. "She get any kind of counseling? Any help?"

"That's another part of the foul-up. From what I can gather, Manitoba thought Alberta was taking care of it, and Alberta thought Manitoba had already taken care of it."

"What about this Madden? Could she have gone there?"

"Not likely. We've contacted the prison. Madeline has never written or visited."

"I don't wonder why."

"They told me he's always asking about her, though. Always talking about her. She's named after him—Madeline—Madden. His mother's name was Madeline. He was named after his mother, and his daughter's named after him."

"The legacy continues."

Roger waved a fly away from his face and thought about the fair-haired girl with the red eyes who insisted, *My name's not Madeline. I don't answer to that name. Not now. Not ever.*

"Oh, yeah, and we got into her apartment," he continued. "Most of her stuff is still there it looks like. It's hard to tell. Janice was with us. She's worried too. Said her duffel bag, blanket and some tea cup were gone. Janice also said she took the flower."

"Flower?"

"Yeah, she looked at the table and then said to me, 'Oh,

she must've took the flower.' Also, she hasn't touched her bank account. Has fifty-six dollars and thirty two cents in a savings account."

Roger thought about the thousand dollars she'd turned over to the police. Had there been more?

"Anything on that envelope we faxed yesterday?"

"Nothing yet. It doesn't match Tom's writing though. Calgary told us that much."

"How about Flip Schmidt? Anyone found him yet?"

"He was supposed to be back to work on Monday but he didn't show. One of his employees is madder than stink. I guess Flip was supposed to come back and relieve him so he could go fishing in the north."

"Keep looking for him."

"Will do—also, we're getting besieged by calls from Marjorie Romaine. Says she has to talk to you. No one else will do. Of course we can't tell her where you are so as far as she's concerned, you're away from your desk every time she calls."

"Let me have her number. I'll call her from here. Keep on this, Clayton. Find that girl. And Clayton . . ."

"Yeah?"

"Sorry about my mood yesterday."

"No problem."

He hung up and the flowered lady huffed and puffed and glared at him as she walked to the phone.

CHAPTER 14

Madeline squinted into the bright sun as she wandered down the sidewalk. She was moving aimlessly with no clear direction. Maybe she should just go home. Pack everything into the Camaro and head north, back up to Chester. What was the matter with her anyway? A few hours after she had run out of the restaurant, Charles had called her on the phone to tell her that Goldy was back, he had delivered the message and would she like him to make an appointment so she could see Mr. Bassino? She had said yes, but then when she hung up she grew so terribly afraid. She called Charles and canceled. Oh Tom, Tom, she thought. Why did you get mixed up with these people?

She reached into her pocket for the oversized sunglasses she had purchased that morning at the hotel gift store. She was buying lots of sunglasses, the lenses in each pair just a little darker than the pair before. The only time she felt safe was when she was safely hidden behind sunglasses and big floppy hats. She had checked the Camaro that morning. It was still safely parked behind the old gas station.

She still had lots of money, she thought to herself as she walked. Maybe she should drive over to California, see Disneyland. A profound loneliness began to grip her then. Tom had always wanted to go to Disneyland.

She wandered up to a sidewalk boutique displaying racks of sequined shirts. A quilted jacket with bright squares of fabric caught her attention. She pulled it out of the rack and examined it. It reminded her of her little gun purse. It was expensive, but unique. She took it inside the shop.

"It's nice isn't it?" said a heavy-set girl in a loose-fitting cotton dress which came nearly to her ankles.

"I kind of like it." Madeline tried it on, moving this way and that in front of the mirror.

"An Indian lady around here makes them," The girl was chattering on and on. "She's quite well known. You should see some of the other stuff she makes. It looks terrific on you, by the way."

But Madeline wasn't listening. At the top corner of the mirror she glimpsed the face of a tall blond man gazing at her intently from behind a rack of flowered trousers. His face looked vaguely familiar. But when she spun around to face him, he was gone.

"I think that jacket really suits you. It's so unusual, and you have such an unusual bone structure. I wish I was that thin. It's a bit expensive but it's worth it. You'll go home with a unique creation . . ."

"I'll take it," said Madeline reaching into her pocket. Her mind wasn't on the jacket, but on the face in the mirror.

"I'm sure you'll be happy with that jacket. As I said before, it's a one-of-a-kind creation. You won't find another like it probably in the whole world."

"Thanks," said Madeline as she raced out into the sunshine. He had a square face with a strong jaw. Maybe he was a movie star. Maybe she'd seen him on a movie or something. But, no, she was sure she had seen him in person. Maybe he just *reminded* her of someone.

Half a block down she walked past a store that displayed a rack of Bibles. She stopped for a moment. All different colors, but they all said *Bible* on the cover. And not one of them looked like the Smith's little leathery one. She stood there for a long time remembering a vow she had made the night she left the Smiths, that she would never again have anything to do with religion and with the Bible. She backed away. The sign in the window said, *The Azuyo Christian Book Room*. She had never been inside a store which sold Bibles. As she stood there staring at the Bibles, three teenaged boys wearing backwards baseball caps clomped loudly out of the door holding three newly purchased CDs.

"This is so cool, man," said one of the boys loudly.

"It's so great they had his new CD in there!" said another.

"Yeah," said the other, "Awesome."

They sold CDs in there? Madeline was astounded. What kind of a store sold both Bibles and CDs? The next thing she knew she had walked through the door and was standing in front of a rack of Bibles. She picked up a small blue one and leafed through it. What if Tom was right? What if the Smiths really *were* out to lunch? She hugged the volume to her chest. "Oh Tom," she thought, "If you would only come back I would try to read through this book with you. I would listen to you if only you would come back."

A few weeks ago Tom had come to the apartment one afternoon to find her lying on the couch watching "The Young and the Restless."

"Do you go to work today?" he had asked.

She hadn't looked up, "At six."

"That's too bad," he said grabbing a Pepsi from the fridge.

When she didn't say anything he continued. "Tonight is a special get-together at the Centre."

"A get-together? What kind of a thing is a get-together?"

"A party, you know." He sat down backwards on the chair, and wrapped his legs around the chair legs. He had changed so much since he got involved with those people at the Centre, she thought. He was always going to things he called Bible studies and he never did dope anymore.

"You mean they have parties, this group of yours? Bet they're a blast and a half." She tucked her hair behind her ears and settled back on the couch.

"I was thinking," he said, "that maybe you could come with me this time."

"You're thinking wrong," she said.

Tom shrugged and walked back into the kitchen.

He had died two weeks later.

Now as she hugged the little book to her she thought, "I'm sorry I didn't go to the party, Tom."

"Can I help you? Are you okay?" A concerned-looking young woman with long dark hair stood next to Madeline.

Madeline blinked tears out of her eyes. "I'm okay. How much is this book?"

"Oh, that's a popular one with young people. It's an easy translation to read and has all these helpful notes and things. Let's have a look. Here's the price on the back," She pointed.

"I'll take it. Do you sell CDs too?"

"They're right over there against the wall. Would you like a name put on the Bible?"

"A name?"

"Is it a gift, or for you?"

"For me, I guess."

"Well, we imprint names free of charge. You can have your name across the bottom in gold if you'd like."

Madeline looked down. Her name. "No thanks," she said quietly, "I don't like my name much." She put the Bible on the counter. "Maybe I'll get a CD, too."

The girl's eyes followed her as she walked over to the CDs. Madeline stood there for a few minutes. An entire wall filled with CDs and not a group she recognized. She ran a shaky hand through her hair. What was she doing in here anyway? Her sunglasses, which had been perched on the top of her head, clattered to the floor, knocking two CDs off the bottom shelf. The noise made her jump. She dropped the bag with her new jacket. I'm totally crazy, she thought. This whole thing has got me nuts. She retrieved her glasses, grabbed her bag and scrambled past the surprised girl at the counter who held up her Bible and called, "Miss? Miss? What about your Bible?" She rushed out the door and right into the arms of the blond man she had seen earlier.

* * *

"Goldy around?" Roger leaned into the front desk.

"No, Mr. Bassino left about an hour ago, some kind of emergency," said Charles.

"Know where he is?"

"I think he might've gone over to California. Or maybe even down to Mexico. He's got businesses all over the place."

Roger whistled through his teeth. "California! Mexico! What's that guy do in all these places? More hotels? More casinos?"

Charles smiled, "Unfortunately the only business I'm acquainted with is the hotel here."

"He'll be gone for a while then?"

"He's supposed to be back day after tomorrow. That's what he told me. He took his plane I think."

Grinning, Roger said, "Some guys have it all, Charles, and then there's you and me."

"You want me to leave a message for him if he calls?"

Roger said, "Yeah, tell him I've got that prospectus he wanted to see."

Roger leaned into the counter and spoke quietly, conspiratorially. "You know anything about his orchard in California?"

"No, sir, I really don't."

"We're thinking of driving over there. Maybe we'll stop in

to see his orchard."

"Well, have a good time."

Roger nodded, paused and then said, "You got any more stamps?"

Charles's face lit up. "You want to see some of my newest? I got a couple more of the Elvis ones, not like I'm a great Elvis fan or anything, but his stamps are collectors' items, already. But as you know, I'm mainly interested in Canadian stamps."

"Got any more of them?"

"You interested in Canadian stamps, Mr. Sheppard?"

"Very much so."

"Let me go get my stamp albums."

"What about that binder? There were some interesting stamps in there, I thought."

He bent down and retrieved the binder from underneath the desk.

"I bet Mr. Bassino's impressed with your collection," said Roger.

"He doesn't know a thing about it. He's said on more than one occasion to make sure I shred all his envelopes."

"Really? He tells you to shred everything?"

He nodded and placed the binder on the counter. "Here, you can look through them. If you're interested in trading, maybe we could work out a deal." He pushed the book toward Roger. Roger began picking up envelope after envelope looking for what, he wasn't sure, pretending to examine each stamp with a practiced eye.

He came across an envelope postmarked Bakersfield, California. He picked it up and turned it over. No return address. Near the bottom of the box he struck gold. An envelope addressed to Silver Springs Orchard Fruits, Bakersfield, CA and postmarked from Chester, AB. No return address, but now he had a definite connection.

"Can I borrow this for a while, Charles?"

Charles looked surprised. "You want *that* one? That's just an ordinary everyday Canadian stamp. That one was going into the shredder for sure. What I do is gather up all of Mr. Bassino's letters and put them in this binder. Then when I have time, I go through them and shred the ones that are worthless."

Roger was carefully examining the envelope, turning it this way and that. Charles leaned toward him and said, "Do you know something I don't know? Is this one worth something?"

"It's worth a great deal, Charles. A great deal."

Charles's open-mouthed gaze followed Roger as he turned and walked away.

* * *

"Hey! Whoa! Where are you going?" He held tightly to her arms as she struggled to get free.

"You! Let me go! I don't know who you are or why you keep following me, but let me go!"

Inside, the surprised sales girl, still holding the Bible, was striding toward them through the store.

"You bumped into *me*, lady!" he said looking down at her, his hands still holding tightly to her shoulders. "You come running out looking like you've seen ghost. Why don't you watch where you're going?"

"*Me*? Why are you following me?"

"I'm not following you, but hey, we better get outta here before we have the Bible-thumpers on our backs."

"Let them! Let them call the police!" But Madeline allowed herself to be led away down the street.

"And you *are* following me," she said.

"I'm not following you."

"Yeah, well, how come you're always showing up where I am?"

"Maybe *you're* showing up where *I* am."

"I doubt it," she snorted.

He finally let go of her arm. "You're staying by yourself at the Riverboat, right?"

"You *are* following me! I don't like people following me."

He stopped on the sidewalk and put his hands up in a playful gesture of surrender. "Okay, you caught me. I *have* been following you. I'm at the Riverboat too. I guess when I saw you, and realized you were all by your lonesome, I decided to try to meet you, your being so pretty and all."

She groaned. Oh great, she thought, just what I need. She stood on the pavement and looked critically at him. He wore faded green cotton shorts and a beige tank-top which revealed a lot of upper body muscle. He was deeply tanned and had dark blond hair which kept falling into his eyes. They began walking together down the street.

He said, "Hey, you want to get a drink or something?"

"I don't know. Maybe."

He chatted about how he was an apprentice cabinet-maker from San Diego and had come here by himself to get his head together. He was just coming off a bad relationship, he said. Madeline nodded a lot but said little. He led her into a sidewalk cafe where he ordered two beers. After a while he looked across at her, "You look sad," he said.

"If I am, it's none of your business."

"Sorry." He held his hands up once more.

After a while she said, "Well, if you must know, a whole lot of things been happening to me lately. I came down here to forget things."

For a long while she said nothing. Then, "My husband died a little while ago. I'm a widow."

"Oh. You married?" He gave her a quizzical look.

"Was married."

"You don't wear a wedding ring."

"Who are you, Matlock? No, I don't wear a wedding ring. I'm not married now. I told you. He died. From brain cancer."

"Most widows wear their wedding rings for a little while."

She looked across at him and sipped her beer. "I buried my ring with him," she said. "It seemed the right thing to do at the time."

"I'm sorry to hear about your loss," he said looking at her intently. He really did look like a movie star, she decided.

"Yeah. Well."

"Look," he said. "Here we are having a drink and I don't even know your name, but maybe we could be friends."

"Bethany."

"What?"

"Bethany. My name's Bethany."

"That's a pretty name."

"I think so."

"I'm Mitchell," he said.

She looked up at him. His blue eyes were almost chilling. Then he smiled.

CHAPTER 15

"Something's on your mind." Kate leaned across the car and put her hand on Roger's arm. In the back seat were their bathing suits, towels, and a six-pack of Diet Cokes in a cooler. It was Saturday morning and, like real tourists, they were heading up to a public beach on the lake. Lund was scheduled to meet them there.

"It was just that last conversation with Clayton," he said, his hands guiding the Chevy up the highway next to the river. "I don't quite know what to make of it."

"Tell me."

"Madeline Westmier, that girl I've told you about . . ."

"Tom Anderchuk's girlfriend."

"Well, she's been missing for a week now."

"You told me that."

"Last night her apartment was ransacked. Janice, her next-door neighbor, called the detachment when she heard sounds. Apparently, she'd heard noises from that place all evening and just assumed Madeline had come back. She says she intended to go over as soon as she got her baby to sleep. When she heard loud male voices, she called us. She told Duane that she looked out of her window in time to see a blue car pull away. She didn't get the license and doesn't know the make."

"People are so wonderfully observant," remarked Kate.

"When Lavoir and the guys got there, the place was totally

torn apart—a professional job; cupboards pulled out, furniture methodically taken apart, television in bits and pieces all over the floor, and of course, no finger prints of any kind. These people were so good they even managed to erase most of Madeline's and Tom's . . . Say, can you reach back and grab me one of those Cokes?"

Kate leaned over the back of the seat unloosing a Diet Coke from its plastic holder. "And Madeline's not around?"

"Gone, despite the fact that Roberta told her not to leave."

"Maybe she's gone, not of her own free will," said Kate fiddling with the flick-off tab on the Coke.

Taking the Coke from her he said, "That's what worried me at first. But why would her kidnapper neatly pack up her bags, and even pack the flower I sent?" He paused. "And why break into her apartment now? She's been gone for a week." Roger took a long drink from the can and shook his head. "That poor girl's really had a life."

"You told me. You know, I don't even know this girl, wouldn't know her if I saw her on the street, and yet I've been praying for her."

That was so like Kate, thought Roger. "Lavoir also said that Marjorie Romaine's in the hospital in Calgary. Roberta has been in to see her. Two black eyes. Broken wrist. Bruises all over. She was burglarized in the middle of the night she said. Three men who came into the house wearing ski masks."

Kate shook her head, "That poor woman. Did she have a lot stolen?"

"Nothing was taken, she said."

"Curious. There's a lot in that house that would appeal to thieves, I should think."

"Roberta said that Marjorie was very, very shaken."

"Well, I don't doubt it for a minute!"

"The thing that bothers me is that she wanted to talk to me. I tried calling her but couldn't get through. And now this."

"Does Wes have anything to do with this other mess? Is that the sign for the beach up there?"

"I think so—to both questions. Think of this. Wes buys Flip's Deli. Tom writes Flip's name on a U.S. bill. Flip is on vacation now, some little gambling town in Nevada. But we can't find him. When I leave the deli, I see Wes pulling out very quickly from the back. And then there's Goldy Bassino. Somehow, somewhere, all of these things connect." He pulled into a parking space. "Lund's supposed to meet us in about an hour. I'm going to run some of this stuff by him."

"Well, let's forget about everything for just a few minutes and have lunch."

He grabbed the cooler and blanket with one hand and they walked down to the sand, hand in hand.

* * *

After they had eaten a leisurely lunch of deli-made subs, little bags of chips, fruit and bottled iced tea, Andrew Lund pulled up to shore in his 50 HP Bayliner. Roger and Kate gathered their belongings and climbed in. The interior of the boat was a study in blues; dark blue upholstery, pale blue carpeted floors, and navy blue controls. As they sped out toward the center of Lake Mojave, the water disappeared underneath them like molten glass.

Lund wore a pair of faded brown swimming trunks, the kind of black rubber sandals they sell in athletic shoe stores, and a faded and very old 49-ers tee shirt. On his head was an Oakland A's baseball cap. In the distance the shoreline, with its lifeless ocher hills reminded Roger of pictures he'd seen of the planet Mars.

"This would be a good place to make Mars movies," yelled Roger above the roar of the engine.

"What?" yelled back Andrew.

"Mars movies. Movies about Mars."

Andrew grinned. "I think they do," he called.

"What?"

"I said I think they already do."

"This whole shoreline reminds me of pictures I've seen of the surface of Mars, like the ones NASA sent back."

"They are," said Andrew grinning. "NASA never went to Mars. They just came out here to Lake Mojave. Figured it would be cheaper."

"Go figure."

In the back seat Kate laughed.

Later on, when the boat had slowed, Roger said, "I think someone should check out that orchard in Bakersfield, the Silver Springs Orchard Fruits. The one I told you about."

"I've got two deputies working on that, plus I've notified the Bakersfield police department," answered Andrew.

"Would it help if I went?"

"You?"

"I've done plenty of undercover work. Bassino doesn't know who I really am. I'm a stranger to everyone down here."

The tops of Roger's thighs were red and felt hot. He reached back into Kate's bag for their ever present never-go-any-where-without sunscreen and lathered them up again.

They were making their way into a populated area of the lake Water-skiers sped past them along with jet skiers and racing boats They passed a couple of houseboat yachts with people in various stages of relaxation on their decks—sunning, drinking and chatting.

"What about Kate?" Lund asked.

"What about me?" she called from the back.

"Do you want to go to Bakersfield?" asked Roger.

"Would love to. I'm a tourist, you know."

While the lake sped away underneath them, Lund and Roger talked about Bakersfield, Goldy Bassino, Tom Anderchuk and the increasing drug problem on both sides of the border.

"We could probably pull out of here tomorrow," Roger said to Lund as they sped back to the beach.

"Give me another day on this," said Lund. "Plan to go on Monday. Tomorrow's Sunday. Take tomorrow off."

Close to the shore, Roger jumped out, helped Kate out, then waved as Andrew Lund sped off down the lake again.

* * *

She held tightly to his waist. It was fast. It was fun and for the first time since Tom died, Madeline actually found herself laughing. She looked down at her feet, fascinated by the funnel shaped pattern that the water made against her ankles as they sped down the river. She had never been on a Sea Doo before. It wasn't like a boat as much as a motorcycle on water. The wind whipped her hair across her eyes and in a few moments whipped it back again. She kept a firm hand around Mitchell's waist.

"You okay back there?" he yelled.

"Fine! Fine!" she called back.

It was Saturday morning. Last evening after their somewhat unorthodox meeting, Madeline and Mitchell had eaten supper in the sidewalk cafe. Then they had wandered from casino to casino all along the strip until well after midnight. Mitchell was attentive and kind and Madeline found herself relaxing in his presence despite herself. Sometimes his eyes disturbed her but she ignored that, so hungry was she for a friend.

This morning he had even let her try the Sea Doo by herself. She spilled it half a dozen times but under Mitchell's patient tutelage, she had finally gotten the hang of it. Now they were on an extended tour of the river and Madeline realized that she had not had so much fun in a long time.

They beached the Sea Doo on a sandbar out on a wide part of the river. The sand was delightfully white and Madeline ran up on the beach. "Ow, ow, ow," she shrieked and backed into the water.

"Should've warned you," he said. "The sand is hot enough to burn the bottom of your feet."

"Now you tell me."

They sat down at the water's edge, and she listened to him describe his childhood in California. When he asked about her childhood she just sat and looked across at the stubbly hills. Some things were painful, and she was getting so tired of making up stories.

"You're awfully quiet," he said to her.

"Just thinking," she said scooping up a handful of sand and letting it run through her fingers.

"About what?"

She looked down and said nothing.

* * *

Charles knew of that guy, that Mitchell Standish guy, who was suddenly taking this enormous interest in Bethany. Mitchell Standish was well-known in Azuyo for having a different girl on his arm every week, always an out-of-town girl. The Azuyo locals were on to him. He wondered what story Mitchell had concocted for Bethany. Was it his, "My girlfriend dumped me and cleared out my bank account" story, or "I'm just coming off a bad relationship" story? He knew all about Mitchell from the receptionists. Lucia and Donna and Jennifer had all had run-ins with the scuz bucket and he had listened when they compared stories. And now he was with Bethany! A part of Charles cursed himself for not getting there first.

This morning he'd seen them leave with bathing suits and towels. Had he stayed overnight in Bethany's room? Charles tried not to think about that. The day was going unbelievably slow for him. He looked at the clock: 10:10. After he was sure a half hour had passed, he looked at the clock again: 10:17.

A clear, sunny day, a Saturday when normal people are lying out on beaches or out on boats and here he was, stuck inside, trying to keep Mr. Bassino happy. His boss had walked in this morning in an incredibly grumpy mood. And Charles couldn't believe his reaction when he'd been called into the office around lunch time. Mr. Bassino had reamed him out, cursing and swearing, while Charles sat in a chair, hands folded in his lap, looking down at his feet.

"What do you mean, you don't shred everything that comes through here? That's part of your job. I don't care one whit that you collect stamps. I don't pay you to collect stamps. I pay you to be my office assistant. Maybe I should fire you and you could collect stamps full time!"

And then he had bent down and placed his face right next to Charles'—so close that Charles could smell the cigarettes on his breath and the oily fragrance of his aftershave. *"Shred ev-ery-thing!"* he said enunciating each syllable.

Charles had nodded, apologized profusely, practically got down on his knees promising that nothing like this would ever happen again, and that no one had seen his stamp collection; he hadn't shown it to anyone. What he meant was anyone important. For the rest of the day Mr. Bassino icily ignored him. And now six minutes before he was due to get off at 4:30, Charles had a splitting headache.

From underneath the receptionist desk, Lucia reached for a paperback. "You got two days off—here's the new John Grisham—get lost in someone else's problems for a while.

Maybe his highness will be in a better mood when you get back on Tuesday."

He fingered the book. "Yeah, maybe I should read something like this for a change."

She smiled at him. "Oh, yeah, I forgot. You only read books about gnomes and trolls and fairy princesses."

Charles gathered his belongings and glanced up at the clock. "I'm outta here. I'm history. See you Tuesday morning."

"Take care, and have some fun this weekend, will you?"

Charles took the elevator to his room, shed his uniform, took two Tylenols and a shower. Sitting on his couch, a cold ginger ale in his hand, he made a decision. He picked up the phone and dialed Bethany's room.

"Hello."

"Hello, Bethany, this is Charles."

"Oh, hi, Charles."

"I don't know if you're busy or not, but would you like to meet me for coffee or something?"

"Right now?"

"Sure, that is unless that's inconvenient or something."

"Well, I don't have anything for a while yet." She paused. "Sure, I can meet you now."

They decided to meet in ten minutes at the Rose Cafe, one of the hotel's ground-floor watering holes.

An hour later they were sharing a plate of nachos and talking. Actually talking, much to Charles's delight. Perhaps the day wouldn't be a total write-off. She told him she was from L.A.— he never did figure out where the Spring Road area was—and he said he had lived in L.A. all his life. He asked if she often went on vacations by herself and she said not usually. He told her he was headed for his last year in computer science and he hoped one day to develop software. She said she'd never tried a computer, and he told her he'd let her try his one day. She mentioned that she was going to school in the fall, too. But she didn't say where.

There was a pause in their conversation; Bethany picked up a nacho in her right hand and seemed to regard its generous topping of salsa and sour cream. Then she said, "I'm just curious. Did you ever meet anyone named Tom Anderchuk?"

"No, I don't think so. Your brother, right? Is he from L.A., too?"

"No, he was here at the Riverboat at the end of March or early April."

"I didn't start work this summer until the end of April."

"Oh, you would have missed him, then."

"Yeah, I guess so."

Madeline looked down into her half-empty cup of coffee. Charles couldn't help himself. He said, "I see you got a new boyfriend."

"So, what of it?" She was still looking down, not at him.

"Bethany, I hate to say it, but he's not the most honest guy in the world. I'd watch it with him."

"You know him?"

"Everybody does. His reputation precedes him."

"I'm not sure I believe you. He seems nice." Her sunny smile of a few minutes ago had been replaced by an uneasiness. She seemed restless suddenly, looking past him at the clock on the far wall and then back again at her small purse.

"What I'm saying is the truth. I know that guy, and listen, Bethany . . ." He leaned across the table and took her small hand in his, a gesture he would never have made had he given himself two seconds to think about it. Her hand felt cool and smooth.   ". . . If you ever need someone to talk to, I live here in the hotel, room 635 in the C-wing."

"I gotta go. I gotta meet someone."

She withdrew her hand and walked away.

CHAPTER 16

The video arcade was crowded and noisy with the rat-a-tat of computerized guns, the grunts and groans of fallen video heroes, and the clamor of children as they eagerly fed quarters into the machines to become war hero, jungle adventurer, space traveler, or kick boxer. Every hotel sported these arcades, often several rooms of the latest in video babysitters for the parents who had entered their own dream world of big winnings in the casinos next door.

Mitchell was good at the shooting games. An expert shot, Madeline noticed. Her own hand-eye coordination was somewhat lacking by comparison. After a rather poor score on X-Men she said, "Boy, I'm sure wasting my money."

"Do you like boating?" he asked her suddenly.

"Boating? You mean like on your Sea Doo? Sure. Fine."

"No, I don't mean Sea Dooing. I'm talking serious boating, as in yachting, as in a well-stocked bar, able to sleep eight, air-conditioning, all the latest appliances, kitchen, TV-VCR. I'm talking major houseboat, babe."

They were standing next to a pin-ball machine and over the whirring and clanging she had to strain to hear.

"It's out on Lake Mojave," he said. "Belongs to a friend of mine. Sometimes he lets me use it. I could try to get it next weekend if you'd come with me."

"I don't know how long I'm staying."

It was all happening too fast. She had met him only yesterday and already he was talking about a weekend on a house-boat.

She said, "I just don't know, Mitchell."

"What's not to know? You're here for a holiday. I'm here for a holiday. I've got a boat. So what's not to know?"

"Let me *not know,* okay? I don't have to have a reason for everything."

She was becoming confused. Should she believe Charles that Mitchell was a low-life? Or should she trust her own instincts? The truth was, her own instincts had never been that hot. And the part that was confusing was that she was beginning to like Charles. Maybe not like so much as trust. But Charles didn't know her. To him she was Bethany Hadecker, a fictional character from L.A., a nice girl who was going to school in the fall. Well, maybe that part was true. She had planned to go to school in the fall in Calgary. With Tom.

She blinked her eyes a couple of times to get rid of the tears that were forming at the edges. Charles didn't know that she was not a nice girl—that she was Madeline Westmier, high school dropout, druggie, father in prison, mother dead, pregnant once. She didn't deserve someone like smart Charles who collected stamps and wrote computer programs and probably got straight A's. Even if Mitchell was everything that Charles said he was, he was the kind of guy she deserved.

A little girl around six or seven bumped into her just then. She was following an older boy winding his way through the arcade and whining, "You never let me try. Daddy said you should let me try."

Madeline looked down at the girl, at her cherubic face and white-blond hair held off her face with a couple of little flowered barrettes. She reminded Madeline of Bethany. Fictional Bethany. Bethany who sat on a wall praying while she listened patiently to Madeline's tears and longings and hopes and dreams.

There was a time when Madeline talked to Bethany every single night. After supper, if the Smiths weren't going to a church meeting, Mr. Smith would retreat with a cup of Earl Grey tea and the paper to what he called his den. Actually, it was a spare bedroom off the dining room.

Then she and Mrs. Smith would clear the table and wash the dishes. Mrs. Smith dried the dishes with brisk, efficient motions, making it a chore for Madeline to keep ahead with the washing. During those times Mrs. Smith always said the same thing. "And did you have a fine day, Madeline?"

And Madeline would always nod and answer, "Yes, Ma'am." Mrs. Smith had instructed Madeline to call her *Ma'am*.

Madeline always said, "Yes, Ma'am" even if it wasn't a fine day, even if the nightmares had kept her up all night until she got up and vomited into the toilet. She always said, "Yes, Ma'am" even if the kids at school picked on her because she didn't have real parents. She always said "Yes, Ma'am" even if teachers humiliated her in class because her homework wasn't done. She always said "Yes, Ma'am" even when she had to read aloud in class and the kids snickered at her faltering reading skills.

The teachers were probably right. That's what Mrs. Smith said. The few times Madeline had asked Mrs. Smith to help her with her homework, Mrs. Smith had stood over her and clucked her tongue and said, "You must learn to do this by yourself, Madeline. That's how independent thinkers are made."

So Madeline learned to always say, "Yes, Ma'am, everything is fine." Even when it wasn't.

After the dishes were put away and the kitchen returned to its spotless condition, Mrs. Smith would take her needlepoint into the front room. Madeline would trudge to her back room where she spent the evening talking to Bethany.

After she met Tom he would sometimes come to her window and she would sneak out with him and go to the Seven-

Eleven. If the Smiths ever knew about these adventures, they never said anything.

"You're awfully quiet," said Mitchell leaning down and looking into her eyes. "You act so rough on the outside, but I know that's not the real you."

Madeline backed away. There was something about his face, about his eyes which momentarily frightened her, that sense that she had seen him somewhere before. He put his arm gently around her shoulders and they walked out of the arcade, out of the building and down the wooden steps toward the river.

"Come on," he said, "Let's think about something else."

They sat close together in the dark on a wooden bench overlooking the wide river. The casino sounds were distant, a part of another world. Mitchell touched her hair and said softly, "You need someone to take care of you. You shouldn't be alone."

She looked out across the water. The night seemed to go on forever. Maybe she should just trust him. He had been so friendly and understanding these past few days. She felt a little dizzy as she leaned against his shoulder. Perhaps it was all the wine she and Mitchell had drunk earlier, or maybe it was the stress of the past few weeks, the sense of finality—Tom was gone, and now she was truly on her own. But she needed someone, someone who wouldn't cringe at the real Madeline Westmier.

She said to him quietly, "I want you to come to my room. I have to show you something."

In her hotel room she said very quietly, "My name's not Bethany."

Mitchell's eyes widened. "It's not?"

"No." She spoke slowly without looking at him. "My name's Madeline, and I need . . . I need a friend."

He moved closer to her, "Your name's Madeline?"

She looked down, "Yeah. That's my name." Then she said, "I really need a friend, Mitchell."

"You got one, babe."

"I need a friend to help me do something." She was quiet for a moment before continuing. "I wasn't married, Mitchell. I've never been married. My husband didn't die of brain cancer. I . . . I had a boyfriend named Tom. I'm from Canada, not California. He was killed in Canada. I think the person who shot him is down here somewhere. I think it's the guy who runs this hotel, or if he didn't do it, he knows who did."

"Slow down. What are you saying? Start over."

She walked over to the nightstand and got out the gun.

Mitchell backed away, his hands up, "Hey, whoa, wait a minute, hold it—What's going on?—Where'd you get that?"

"I need you to kill him for me, Mitchell. I need you to kill the person who murdered Tom."

"Wait a minute, Bethany, or Madeline, or whoever you are. You got the wrong guy. I'm not into killing dead boyfriend's murderers."

She sighed and looked toward the floor.

"Mitchell." Her voice cracked. A low sob emanated from deep within her. "I thought you'd be my friend. I don't know what to do. The police aren't doing anything. They're glad he died. They think he was just a bad kid."

Mitchell walked toward her shaking form, pried the gun gently from her fingers and placed it on the bed. Then he put his arms around her. "It's okay, babe. It's okay."

It was several minutes before her sobbing ceased. "Come on," he said gently, guiding her toward the couch. "Tell me all about it."

And so she did.

* * *

"I'd like to ask prayer for someone I met on Friday." A tall, dark-haired girl was on her feet in the sanctuary. She talked animatedly with her hands. "Well, actually, I didn't meet her, I don't even know her name, but she came into the store and took this Bible from the shelf and was hugging it to herself and kind of crying . . ."

Roger and Kate were sitting halfway up in the center section of the church. Yesterday, after their picnic on the lake, they spent a few hours wandering the streets of Azuyo. At the Azuyo Christian Bookroom they saw an advertisement for this church and decided to attend the following morning. Roger recognized the girl from the store.

She continued, "I went over and asked if anything was wrong. She said she wanted to buy the Bible. Well, to make a long story short, she never bought it. She bolted out of the store. I don't know—I can't seem to get her out of my mind. I feel like the Lord is asking me to pray for her. So, I wonder if we could pray for her this morning."

"Why don't we pray right now?" said the pastor from the front. "Is there anyone who would take this request?"

Roger judged the pastor of this congregation to be about his own age, a kind face, brown hair streaked with gray, and a mustache bordering on handlebar. A woman sitting near the front raised her hand. When he nodded, she rose and prayed.

The congregation wasn't large—maybe 200, a nice, average-sized church, large for Chester standards, small for Calgary, but there was an informality about the service that impressed Roger. They met in a brand new building on a hill overlooking Azuyo. Announcements followed the prayer time and he and Kate followed along in their bulletins.

"I want to remind you," the pastor was saying, "that the 24-hour prayer vigil for the city of Azuyo begins Tuesday. For those of you who are unfamiliar with what we do here, we join with other churches in the Azuyo area twice a year for 24 hours of non-stop prayer for Azuyo. Individuals or groups sign up to pray for half-hour intervals around the clock. From eight in the morning until ten at night the churches are open for prayer. If you sign up for the night hours, you are expected to pray at home. There is a sign-up sheet in the back. I believe there are some half-hour slots still open."

Twenty four hours of prayer for a city, Roger mused. Chester could sure use that. He made a mental note to talk to Pastor Phillips about it when he got home.

In keeping with the theme, the Pastor's message was on prayer. Roger listened with rapt attention when he gave examples of disciples standing firm against the enemy in the book of Acts. He turned to Ephesians 6 and urged the congregation to clothe themselves in the armor of God. He spoke forcefully, eloquently, and Kate took copious notes in a small notebook she always kept with her Bible. As the pastor continued speaking about standing firm, Roger thought about Chester, a little town which seemed to have more than its share of problems. In his daily game of cops and robbers, it was easy for Roger to forget the meaning of verse 12: *For we do not wrestle against flesh and blood, but against principalities, against powers, against the rulers of the darkness of this age, against spiritual hosts of wickedness in the heavenly places.* He reminded himself that people like Goldy Bassino are not the deceivers. They are the deceived, deceived by Satan who promises life and riches, but who delivers death and poverty.

On the way back to the Riverboat Kate said, "Boy, after a message like that, I can't imagine that whole church not signing up to pray."

After a leisurely lunch in the hotel dining room, Roger left to meet Lund to go over a few last-minute items regarding the Bakersfield trip. Kate said she was just happy to take her

Bible and notebook down to the pool. She wanted some sun and a chance to review the morning's sermon.

* * *

"What do you think you're doing?" she demanded.

"I'm sorry. I just get jealous. You weren't calling an old boyfriend were you?"

"I was calling my friend, not that it's any of your business!"

"A girlfriend?"

"Yeah, a girlfriend."

"From Chester?"

"Yeah, from Chester!"

Madeline never thought it would happen, but Mitchell was starting to bother her. He hadn't left her alone even for a second since she told him about Tom last night. He was always asking her questions about her past, about Tom, about Chester. Even questions about hers and Tom's apartment, and stuff like—did Tom have a safety deposit box at the bank, and where did Tom keep his valuables, and how much money did he have in the bank.

She was sorry now that she had ever told him. He had insisted on taking the gun. "It's too dangerous for you," he said. "When the time comes I'll get rid of the guy that murdered Tom."

Putting the telephone down Mitchell said, "I'm sorry, Babe. I just get so jealous sometimes. You're the best thing that's ever happened to me. Here, let me punch in the number for you." The phone was cradled in his lap and she snorted and sat back on the couch and sighed.

"Okay. I don't care. Dial it."

He punched in the numbers one by one as she recited them.

"Here, all set." He handed her the phone.

"Gee, thanks," she said sarcastically. She pressed the receiver to her ear and scowled at him.

"That's funny," she said.

"What's funny?"

"It says the number's been disconnected."

"She probably didn't pay her bill."

"That's possible, knowing Janice."

He got up, walked to the dresser and fingered the tall vase which held a dry, droopy rose.

"Who gave you this?" he asked.

"I got it when Tom died and none of your business."

"Like at his funeral?"

"Something like that."

Mitchell sat on the couch and fiddled with the remote control changing from program to program.

Madeline said, "Would you *please* find one program and stick with it?" She was becoming testy. Actually she wished he would leave so she could have some time by herself.

"There's nothing good on Sunday mornings anyway, just those religious jerks asking for money in southern accents."

He flicked off the TV and turned to her. "I'm sorry if I'm so possessive. That's what gets me in trouble in all my relationships."

"Remember, Mitch, we said no strings?"

"I remember. I remember." His blond hair fell onto his forehead. "So what do you want to do? You want to do something today or what?" he asked.

"I don't want to do anything. I feel like sitting here for a change."

"Madeline," he said brightening. "I've got this great idea. How about I go up and see if I can get that houseboat I was telling you about? I could probably get it earlier than next weekend."

Madeline sighed and shifted her position on the couch.

"Go ahead," she said. "Go see your friend."

When he left, Madeline tried Janice's number. It was answered on the second ring.

"Hello." Madeline recognized Janice's shrill voice.

"Hi, Janice. It's me, Madonna."

"Madonna! Holy cow! The cops are looking for you and everything! I been worried sick. Where are you? You okay?"

"I thought your phone was disconnected."

"What! What are you talking about—disconnected? Nothing's been disconnected except your brains for leaving without telling no one where you're going! You know your apartment was broken into!"

"My apartment!" Madeline nearly dropped the phone.

"Yeah. I was over there with the cops. Everything's all apart. Them burglars were awful quiet. At first I thought you were back when I heard noises. I was goin' over after I got Sam to bed when I heard men's voices yelling. It was me that called the cops."

Her apartment broken into! Why?

"What did they take? My TV and stuff?"

"No, heck, they tore the TV apart. I never seen nothing like it. The cops think the guys who broke in were looking for something."

"Looking for what? Did the cops say what? Did they catch the guys?"

"Not as far as I know."

Madeline could hear Samantha whimpering in the background. "Hey, Madonna, hold on a minute will you? Don't go away, okay?"

Madeline heard Janice making cooing sounds to the child until Samantha's whimpers turned to giggles. Whatever Janice was, she was a good mother.

"Samantha's giving me fits here. I think she's teething.

Where are you, Madonna? Where'd you go? I heard one of the cops tell one of the other cops that he thought you were kidnapped. You okay?"

Kidnapped! "I'm fine. I drove down to Nevada in Tom's car." Why would the cops think she had been kidnapped?

"What are you doing down in Nevada?"

"Well, I thought I figured out who killed Tom, but now I'm not so sure."

"Hey, you're losing me, Madonna. You think Tom's murderer is in Nevada? Samantha, shh, shh. This kid's going to drive me crazy. Do the cops know about this?"

"No way. But I'm thinking about coming home. I think I hit a dead end. Give Samantha a hug for me, okay? Tell her I'll be home soon."

"You just better get here right away. Even your boss called me, as if I knew anything anyway. Oh, yeah, the police said I'm supposed to tell them where you are if you ever call me."

"*DON'T*, Janice. Please don't."

"Okay, okay. We never had this conversation, okay?"

"Thanks."

When she hung up the phone she stomped around her hotel room throwing things into her duffel bags. Her television broken apart! That TV cost her the equivalent of two paychecks. And Mitchell! Whatever number he dialed, it certainly wasn't Janice's. What a jerk. Why am I always letting people take advantage of me? He seemed so nice last night. I should never have gotten hooked up with him. I should have listened to Charles. "I'm going home!" she said aloud, "Going today and no one's going to stop me."

Outside the window the pool sparkled invitingly in the sunshine. The place was almost deserted, too, except for a woman in a white one-piece bathing suit and a big floppy hat who sat reading under an umbrella.

She paused for a moment. She had paid for a week in

advance at this place. She had three days left. They probably wouldn't give her money back if she left early.

Her TV set! So what? She still had money left. Lots of it. She'd buy a new TV. She could get five TV sets if she wanted. She'd break up with Mitchell. In three days she'd leave and drive to California. By herself. What was in Chester for her except for a torn-up apartment and a boring job? Maybe she'd call Charles. "Maybe I'll just go on being Bethany Hadecker forever," she said to her reflection in the window glass.

She changed into her bathing suit, grabbed her towel and headed toward the pool.

CHAPTER 17

She was so angry that she dropped her towel on a white lounge chair, did a swift surface dive into the pool and swam five lengths of front crawl almost without thinking. I can still do this, she thought to herself. I can still out-swim everyone I know, including, I bet, that stupid Mitchell, plus those stupid idiots who broke into my apartment. I'll never go back to Chester. I'm going to take Tom's money and go to California. Get a job and buy a little house with an Olympic-size pool in the back. I'll swim every day! I'll show them. I'll show everyone.

But she'd do one thing for sure today. After her swim she'd walk right down to the desk and ask Charles to get her a different room. And she wouldn't tell scum-bag Mitchell where it was.

The water was warm and felt good gliding over her body as she switched from the front crawl to the breast stroke. The lady in the white bathing suit across the pool looked familiar. Madeline was sure she'd seen her before, and not just at the Riverboat. She shook her head and said to herself, "I got to get out of this place. I'm going crazy here. First, Mitchell looks familiar, and now this lady." She took a breather by the side of the pool and the woman smiled down at her.

"Do you swim professionally?" The white-suited lady was talking to her. Madeline looked up at the woman shading her eyes against the blinding sunshine.

"No," she said.

"Are you a life-guard or an instructor, perhaps? You really are good."

"No, not really." Who was this lady anyway? Why did she look so familiar?

"Have you ever thought of teaching swimming? You seem to be a natural."

Madeline was breathing hard. She hoisted herself up on the side of the pool and said, "I'm out of shape now, though. That's what smoking does."

"You're a real natural."

"Thanks."

"Are you from around here?"

"From California," she lied.

"I'm Kate," said the lady. "Kate Sheppard."

"I'm Bethany."

After a few minutes of small talk in which they discussed the weather, the pool, the heat, Madeline noticed a small pink book lying on the ground beside the woman.

Madeline had to ask, "You read the Bible?"

"Why, yes, I guess I do," she answered.

"Why?"

The woman paused, picked up the book and placed it on her lap.

"All of the answers to life are found in this book."

"I used to have a boyfriend who read the Bible."

"Have you ever read it, Bethany?"

Madeline frowned. "I tried reading it once but it didn't make any sense to me."

"What part didn't make sense?"

"Well the whole thing, actually. I'm not such a great reader. I couldn't understand it very well."

Kate smiled. "Sometimes it's not the easiest book to understand. There are a lot of modern translations which make it easier, though."

Madeline remembered the girl in that Bible store who said, "This one is quite popular with young people," then she thought of Tom leaning over his little Bible at the kitchen table, reading it slowly and painstakingly, his fingers moving along carefully under the words.

"Did your boyfriend ever talk about the Bible to you?"

"He tried but I never listened."

"Where's your boyfriend?"

Madeline looked away, "He died."

"Oh, I'm so sorry to hear that." Kate put her hand on Madeline's arm. "You must miss him very much."

Madeline's eyes misted. "I do. He was a good person. I know that now."

"Do you have a Bible, Bethany?"

"Only my boyfriend's, but I don't know where it is. Probably his sister took it."

Kate held the Bible out to Madeline. "Would you like this one?" she asked.

"But it's yours."

"It would make me happy if you took it. Really."

Madeline took the book. "Thank you," she said very quietly.

"Are you okay?" Kate asked gently. Madeline shifted on the cement of the pool deck and frowned.

Kate said, "Why don't you pull up one of those chairs? It's a lot more comfortable than the cement and less hot."

Madeline dragged a white plastic chair over and sat across from Kate. She felt strangely drawn to this friendly and sincere-looking woman. And she was intrigued by a person who read the Bible like Tom. Answers to life? Mrs. Smith never told her that. All Mrs. Smith said was that it was *required*.

"What did you mean when you said the answers to life?" she found herself asking.

Kate said, "This book talks about a person, Jesus Christ, about how much He loves us, how much He wants us to love Him. But our sin separates us from Him. He paid the penalty for our sins when He died on the cross. All we have to do is trust Him. Am I going too fast for you?"

"A little. My boyfriend said those same things." She paused, then said, "I've done some really stupid things since he died."

"We all do stupid things sometimes."

Madeline went on. "Yeah, but I do *really* stupid things. I got involved right away with this real loser."

"And you want to get out of this relationship?"

"Yeah. He's always around. Always bugging me. Always following me. Do you think the desk would give me another room?"

"Another room? I don't see why not. They don't seem to be too full. Why do you want another room?"

"Because Mitchell, that's the guy I'm talking about, is always in my room. He has a key to my room, and I need some space. It's not like I asked him to move in or anything! I just need some time to think."

Kate smiled. "Sounds like you do need a new room."

"Yeah, I just hope they can give me one. I've got three more days here."

"Where's this boyfriend now? Waiting for you in your room?"

"No, thank goodness. I feel real bad, I just met him on Friday, and he was real nice then, but now I think I made a mistake. But I don't want to hurt his feelings. He's sort of nice, but kind of jealous."

"Well, you can be gentle with him. Do you want me to pray for you?"

"Pray for me? Well, um, okay."

Madeline rose, suddenly afraid that this woman would start praying right here and now. Except for the Smiths perfunc-

tory mealtime prayers, Madeline had never heard anyone pray—
at least, not for something like a boyfriend problem. "I better
go," she said nervously.

"Bethany," Kate called after her. "If you want to talk
anymore, I'm in room 223. I'll be here for a few more days,
anyway."

"Thanks."

As Madeline made her way back into the Riverboat, a
bellhop accosted her. "Is that Mrs. Sheppard by the pool?"

"Yeah, she's down there."

The bellhop hurried toward Kate, a worried expression on
his face.

* * *

Madeline hurried into the hotel, head down, towel around
her shoulders, her new book pressed against her chest and
bumped square into Charles who was on his way out. He
was dressed neatly in Khaki shorts and a cotton shirt. Slung
across his shoulders was a backpack.

"Hey," he said steadying her shoulders with his hands.
"You're in a hurry."

"Yeah, I'm in a hurry," she muttered, "I'm in a hurry to
get out of this place."

"What's the matter? What happened?"

"You were right, Charles. You were right about that stupid Mitchell!"

His hands were on her shoulders and she was trying to
keep the tears from squeezing out of her eyes. She dabbed
them with her towel.

"You want to talk?"

"You look busy."

"Not too busy. It's my day off. I'm heading over to the
philately display at the museum."

"Philately?"

"Fancy word for stamp collecting. Why don't we sit over here and talk a bit?" He steered her over to a quiet corner of the lobby where the couches formed a cozy circle. She sank into a large, overstuffed chair and drew her knees up under her. Her new pink Bible was on her lap. She saw Charles eyeing it.

"What do you have there?" he asked.

"A book a lady gave me at the pool—you were right about Mitchell!"

"I would never say I told you so. It's just that I've heard so much about him from the receptionists and even a few of the guests in years past."

"Mitchell lives around here? He told me he's from San Diego."

"A cabinet-maker, right?"

She smiled slightly, "Yeah. That's not true?"

"That guy wouldn't recognize a cabinet-making tool if he tripped over it. He's a chronic liar. You have to understand, Bethany, that some people can't function unless they are lying, forever making up stories about themselves."

Madeline looked down and fingered the book on her lap. She was no better than Mitchell. Her whole life was a lie. She began to cry again. Openly this time.

"Hey, it's okay," said Charles gently. "He really hurt you, didn't he? What a jerk!"

She kept her eyes averted from him when she said, "He wants me to go on some houseboat with him. As if I'd even consider it now. I'm going to ask for another room. Do you think they'd give me one?"

"I will personally see to it. Come with me." He rose and extended his hand. She took it and within a few minutes she had a new room, a new key and Charles even arranged for a bellhop to move her belongings to the new room.

That settled, he asked her, "How would you like to come to that stamp display with me?"

She paused. I am a liar, she thought. A chronic liar, just like Mitchell. I don't deserve to be seen with a nice person like Charles. "I don't think so, but thanks," she said. "I'm kind of tired. I think I just want to be alone for a bit."

"I understand. Maybe I'll call you later. Okay?"

"That would be nice."

"Maybe supper or something."

"Miniature golf would be nice."

"Miniature golf it is then."

* * *

Before Roger reached the elevator, the girl behind the counter called out, "Oh, Mr. Sheppard, I almost forgot. You got a message here."

She handed Roger a little pink message note. Roger frowned. Why was Clayton calling him here? Following Lund's strict instructions, he had told the Chester RCMP *not* to contact him here at the Riverboat.

Still fuming, Roger entered their room to find Kate still in her white bathing suit and sitting on the edge of the bed, her head in her hands.

She looked up and he saw that her eyes were wet. "Gladys called. I think we should go home."

"What happened? What's wrong?"

He sat down beside her and took her hands. "What happened? Is Becky okay? Is it Sara?" His mind was racing.

"It's Becky, and she's okay, but she and Jody plus Jerry, who drove them, went to some party down by the ravine. There was drinking and some drugs." Kate reached for a tissue. Then she said, "Duane and Clayton arrived and hauled all the kids in."

"Becky and Jody?"

"Clayton, bless his heart, drove them out to Gladys and Hugh's. Hugh, I guess, was fit to be tied."

"I can imagine."

"I don't know what happened to Jerry."

"Have you talked to Becky?"

"Not yet. They're grounded on the farm. Hugh and Gladys didn't even take them to church this morning. They tried calling us, but couldn't get through. I guess the police found quite a lot of drugs out there."

Roger clenched his fists, rose and began pacing in the small room. How dare his daughter get involved in something like this! He'd ground her until she was thirty!

"Gladys says it's already all over the church, too. Sometimes I wish that Hank Pfeiffer would mind his own business. According to Gladys, he organized some sort of, quote, 'prayer meeting for our wayward kids.' Pastor Phillips is still on vacation, you know. So now the rumor mills will be running overtime—mountie's kid selling drugs!"

"How were the girls involved?"

"They weren't. According to Gladys they just happened to be at the wrong place at the wrong time."

"I'll say."

"I want to go home, Roger."

"We'll both go."

"No. You stay. If bringing these drugs into Chester has anything to do with what's going on down here, I want you to stay and find it. Stay and do your Rahab thing."

While Kate packed, Roger, ignoring Lund's orders, called Clayton from their room who told him that the girls were probably just innocent bystanders who had stumbled onto something they didn't know anything about. He said that he and Duane had confiscated some cocaine, some hashish and plenty of alcohol. Not a major drug bust, hardly enough for the newspapers, just your average, everyday cache for an evening in Chester.

"Kate will be coming home. I'm going to stay," Roger said.

"Madeline Westmier is still missing. So is Flip Schmidt."

"Keep looking for them."

"Will do," Clayton said.

"And Clayton, thanks."

An hour later Kate and Roger were driving north to Las Vegas. When he had dropped Kate off at the airport, he headed west to Silver Springs Orchard Fruits in Bakersfield. Knowing how close his daughter had come to the drug problem, Roger was more determined than ever to stop it.

CHAPTER 18

Her new room was at the back of the hotel and her window overlooked the river rather than the pool. From it she could see across the water to Arizona. She walked around her new room, flicked on the TV, then flicked it off again, wishing she had gone with Charles to that stamp collecting thing. Glancing at the new Bible on her dresser, she called down to the front desk and asked to be transferred to Kate Sheppard's room.

"I'm sorry, she and her husband checked out about an hour ago."

Checked out! She had told Madeline she was staying for a while. Where did she go? She picked up the pink Bible and then put it down again. She had to admit to herself that she was afraid to read it, afraid that if she did, the words would be as nonsensical as they were a dozen years ago. A restlessness stole over her as she looked out into the evening; she realized just how lonely she was. She saw clusters of people laughing, talking and walking down the boardwalk next to the river. Everyone had someone to be with and somewhere to go.

Throughout the afternoon she called Charles' room periodically, but he was always out.

She lay down and flicked the TV on again, just for the sound of people and voices. She changed into a pair of loose fitting shorts and Tom's oversized Calgary Flames shirt. She grabbed the Bible from the nightstand and opened it. Kate had underlined certain parts of it in red. She flipped back to the first page and read, *To Kate, all my love, Roger.* Kate Sheppard. Roger Sheppard. Roger Sheppard. What was familiar about that name? She shook her head and put the Bible down on her nightstand. She was really going crazy, totally berserk.

Even though it was early, she was tired. She hadn't been sleeping well. She got up and fished through her duffel bag for her pills. When she pulled out two empty pill containers, she panicked. Then she remembered. She had taken the last one last night. They were all gone now.

A year ago Tom had gotten an enormous supply for her, at least she thought it was enormous then. She had carefully counted them out on the kitchen table, before dropping them into clear plastic bottles. She figured that if she took one a night they would last two years. But most of the time one was not enough. Many nights she would wake up screaming and sweating with her fists in her mouth, shaking uncontrollably. She would get up and grope around in the dark until she found her bottle. She'd swallow a couple, often without the benefit of a glass of water. Then she would wrap herself in her mother's quilt and sit in front of the TV until they took effect.

A few months ago Madeline had approached Tom for more. He was sitting at the table, his head bent over a thin book with large print.

"Tom," she had said softly, "Can you get me some more pills?"

He looked up at her. The booklet flipped closed and she could see that it was *An Easy-Reading Study Book of Mark.*

"Madeline. You know I don't deal drugs any more. I told you that."

"But Tom, I need them. I can't sleep without them." She

paused, "Could you get them just one more time for me? Just one more time, I promise."

"I can't, Madeline. I've broken contact with those drug people forever."

Madeline became angry. She had fumed around the kitchen. "It's not like these are *drugs,* Tom. I could go to any doctor and get a prescription. Any doctor would give me a prescription!"

"So, go to any doctor."

She had stormed into the living room cursing and screaming at him.

Later that evening he had said, "Madonna, I'm sorry I was so uncaring. It's just that I'm concerned about you. You really got to get off those things. They're gonna kill you. They're killing you already." And then he had gone on about some girl named Jenny at the Centre who had been hooked on drugs, and how this Jenny was someone that Madeline should go and talk to. "They can help you down there. They really can. They helped me. I don't even smoke cigarettes anymore!"

"Well, bully for you."

She cuddled up on her bed in her mother's quilt and sobbed as the police sirens on the TV movie she was watching rose to full crescendo. When the story broke for commercial, Madeline heard someone fiddling with the lock outside her door. A second later Mitchell stood in the doorway, a bouquet of daises in his hands and smiling from ear to ear.

* * *

"How'd you get in?" she demanded.

"It's just my charming nature. Actually, the maid let me in, after I begged and pleaded that my ladylove had accidentally locked me out."

He extended the daisies toward her. She turned away.

"What kind of a reception is this? It took me a long time to get your new room number. I almost wore out my charm, and why'd you switch rooms anyway?"

"I like the view better."

He walked over to the dresser, removed the dead rose from the tall vase, threw it in the wastebasket and replaced it with the daisies. "There," he said arranging them, "Much better."

Madeline was on her feet in a minute. "How dare you touch my things, Mitchell!"

She rushed toward him but he grabbed her arm. She was no match for him.

"That was *my* flower, Mitchell!"

"It was dead."

"I don't care. I was keeping it."

"You always keep dead flowers?"

"I always keep special things."

"What's so special about this flower?"

"That's my point, Mitchell. You're so possessive. I hardly know you and you're jealous. That's why I got another room. I want you to leave me alone."

He smirked. She didn't know how to interpret that look and moved away from him.

"I need some space is all. Maybe tomorrow. Call me back tomorrow, okay?" she said quietly.

"But I came to get you now."

"Get me for what?"

"For the houseboat. If we're there in half an hour we can have it."

"No, I'm staying right here."

There was silence for a few minutes, then he reached for her shoulder and turned her around. "I don't think so, Madeline Westmier."

She was startled, "How do you know my last name?"

His gaze was steady.

"You looked at my driver's license," she said accusingly. "You're always in my face, Mitchell. I told you, I don't *want* to go out on that houseboat."

"You have no choice, Madeline."

She was becoming frightened. What was going on here? What did she really know about Mitchell? Was he some crazy lunatic?

"Get out of here or I'll call the front desk."

"I don't think so, Madeline. Your friend, Charles, won't even be able to help you."

She attempted to loose herself from his grip. He held tightly to her arm.

She gasped. In his right hand he was holding a gun. *Her* gun. And he was pointing it at her.

Stunned she said, "Mitchell, I . . . what do you want?"

"You know what I want." His face contorted into a cruel grimace.

She was suddenly very, very frightened. "I don't know what you want," she said. Her shoulders shook under his grasp. He pushed her roughly into a chair.

"Mitchell, please let me go."

"Shut up!"

Keeping the gun trained on her with his right hand, he dumped her bags onto the bed, and began rummaging through them with his left. She winced when he touched her mother's tea cup. Then he pulled out the dresser drawers. They were empty, but he pulled them all the way out and examined the spaces behind them. He pulled out the end-table drawer and threw the Gideon Bible on the floor, its pages fluttering. Picking up the little pink Bible he said, "What's this?"

She said nothing.

"I said, what is this?" His voice was louder.

"A book."

"Yeah, this book didn't help what's-his-face," he muttered throwing it to the floor. Then he scattered the contents of her makeup case all over the bed. He grabbed her and shoved her into the bathroom where he told her to climb into the tub while he methodically examined the toilet tank, the space behind the tissue holder and underneath the sink.

"Where is it?" he growled.

She cowered at the far end of the tub, shivering.

"I said where is it?"

"I don't know what you're talking about, Mitchell. Where is what?"

"Don't play dumb with me! Let's go."

"Go?" she whimpered.

"To the houseboat, and we're going to walk very calmly through the lobby, right past the front desk, and you're not going to say nothing, right?"

They walked out the front lobby past little knots of happy tourists. Mitchell pushed her roughly into the back seat of a large silver car with black windows. He slammed the door and then climbed into the passenger side. She pressed herself against the far corner. The driver was skinny, hawk-nosed and wore an oversized fishing hat and clip-on sunglasses. He didn't turn or acknowledge her presence.

She drew her legs up under her and huddled against the door. Loud, classical opera from the radio filled the car's interior.

Just out of Azuyo Mitchell turned to the driver. "Is everything all set?" he asked.

"No one's too happy. They want the book, not the girl."

Mitchell said, "It's not there, Ray. I've looked everywhere, and I mean everywhere."

"No one believes you."

Mitchell scowled and said nothing.

"He's paying you to find it."

The air conditioner blew cold air against Madeline's knees. She shivered and her teeth chattered. Outside her window, dry, pale, scrub brush blew across the parched earth. She felt as if she couldn't breathe.

The two in the front stopped talking. Ray frowned and concentrated on the road ahead while Mitchell fiddled with the radio until he found an oldies station.

Ray said, "Leave it alone!" He quickly flipped back to the opera.

About an hour later they turned left down a narrow road. Tires crunched on the gravel. Madeline looked out the window but saw nothing. The only car in a deserted lot, Ray parked under a leafy palm tree. Mitchell opened her door and the blast of hot air was almost welcome, almost comforting. She looked up and saw a short man with a stubby beard sitting some distance away at a picnic table. She fairly fainted with relief.

"Help me," she cried turning toward him. But he ignored her, got up, nodded at Ray, got in the silver car and drove it back down the gravel driveway.

With his hand firmly on her shoulder, Mitchell led her toward a set of steep, rickety steps. Various docks, some submerged, some dangerously askew jutted out into the water at odd angles. A *Closed* sign hung crookedly on the door of a grimy, weathered building. *Lake Mojave Marina* was barely visible across the glass. A couple of the windows were broken. They descended the stairs. There were very few decent-looking boats tied up to the docks. The few that were there were mostly rusting hulks covered with molding, rotted canvas. One of the clean-looking boats was the massive houseboat at the end of the dock. Several boards in the dock were missing, and Madeline stumbled a few times. Beneath her the water looked cool and inviting. If she could just jump, she knew she could swim. But then again, Mitchell still had her gun aimed at her beneath the jacket draped over his arm.

And then she saw a man, a few berths over, high up on the mast of a sailboat with ropes hung around him, a man wearing a beige hat practically hidden behind the sail he was adjusting. Should she scream? They could shoot him, too, just as easily as they could shoot her. Should she wave? No, for the same reason. It was obvious that Mitchell and Ray hadn't seen him. They were only scowling and looking at their feet as they marched her toward the houseboat.

In the end, all Madeline did was to half-heartedly squirm out of Mitchell's grasp. If the man in the sailboat was looking, all he would see was that she really didn't want to be here. So what?

The houseboat was immense. The name along the side was *The Maria.*

"Mitchell," she protested in one final effort, "Why are you doing this? What do you want?"

He grunted and said, "I want you to get on board."

He shoved her onto the deck and through a cabin door. Inside, the boat was everything Mitchell told her it would be—plush carpets, furniture, kitchen, bar, TV, VCR, air conditioner.

Mitchell pointed the gun at her. "Sit down and don't move."

She sat. He kept the gun trained on her as he grabbed a beer from the fridge, flicked it open and drank deeply.

With Ray at the helm they moved out of the bay and slowly up the lake. Hours passed, it seemed to her. Still, she sat on the couch, Mitchell across from her with the gun. In the front of the cabin, around a kitchen table, sat two other men. Spread out on the table in front of them were papers. Madeline could see little stacks of money. The money! Could that be what they were looking for, the money she had found in Tom's car? Did Tom steal money from these men and they wanted it back? Somehow, that didn't fit with Tom. But what was this talk in the car about a book?

Several hours later as night was beginning to fall, they pulled into a secluded bay.

* * *

By late afternoon Charles was back from the Philately display. He decided to call Bethany. All afternoon he'd been planning it. Here were the plans: He'd call Bethany and they'd drive out of neon-ville and across the river to a nice restaurant in Bullfrog. He wasn't quite presumptuous enough to make reservations, but he knew a couple of restaurants that didn't require them.

After dinner they'd walk beside the river. From the Arizona side Azuyo would be a pretty sight, with its bright, fluttering lights reflecting on the water. They would sit and talk and he'd find out all about her. She lived in L.A. He was from L.A. Maybe they could see each other in the fall—just as friends. She said she was going to school in the fall, although she didn't say where. Wouldn't it be neat if it was the same school he was going to? Maybe they could meet occasionally for lunch in the SUB, or go to a movie. He had halfway decided to pursue this Campus Fellowship thing in the fall. Maybe Bethany would be interested in that. Just maybe. After all, she had a Bible with her. He would ask her about that Bible. She was too upset earlier to talk much about it. Get a grip, Charles. One day at a time.

Back in his room he dialed her new room. No answer. Okay, so maybe she went down for something to eat. He decided to search the hotel restaurants so he could find her before she ordered. Or if she had already eaten, the plans could be changed to *dessert* across the river.

He took the elevator and, starting with the second floor, scanned all of the Riverboat's restaurants, lounges and coffee shops. Nothing. So maybe she's in the casino. He checked. She wasn't there. She could be walking on the boardwalk. By herself? Somehow he doubted it, but he jogged down to the boardwalk, nearly colliding with a hand-holding couple on their way up.

"Why don't you watch where you're going, buddy?"

"Sorry," he said.

She wasn't there either. She liked to swim. Nearly out of breath, he jogged back up to the pool. But the pool area was empty, too. Twilight now, and neon was beginning to grip the strip. Soon, it would be alive, an organic, pulsating city. Down at the boardwalk again, he looked up at her room. Something about it troubled him. The drapes were open and fluttering out of the open window onto her balcony. The lights were on, and he could also glimpse the flickering of her television. So? Lots of people leave their lights and TV on when they go out.

Could her phone be out of order? Back inside he took the elevator to her floor and knocked on her door. No answer. Where could she be? Returning to the front desk, he saw Maria, one of the chambermaids on Bethany's floor.

"Hey, Maria," he called.

"Hola, Charles," she said with a wide smile. Her thick black hair fanned around her face. She wore purple lipstick which matched a large set of dangly earrings.

"Maria, do you remember the girl, the blonde girl, Bethany, in room 476?"

"Si, I remember her."

"Have you seen her?"

"She leave."

"Leave?"

"Little while ago. I give her boyfriend key."

"You *what*?"

"Her boyfriend. He had flowers. So nice."

Panicked now, Charles turned and grabbed his master key from the board and headed up to room 476. Ignoring the elevator, he took the stairs two at a time. "Bethany!" he mumbled as he unlocked her door. She was gone, of course, but stepping inside, he really became alarmed. All of Bethany's belongings were scattered: on the floor, on the bed, on the dressers, even on top of the television. "Bethany," he muttered, "What's going on?" The dresser drawers had been pulled out and lay on the floor, a bouquet of daisies in a glass vase was tipped over, the glass shattered.

The bathroom was worse. The toilet tank cover had been removed and was lying on the sink. The tissue dispenser was on the floor, all of the tissues ripped out and scattered on the counter, the shower curtain was ripped from its moorings.

One name came to his mind—Mitchell. She was with Mitchell. And it was obvious by the looks of the place that she hadn't wanted to go. He'd taken her against her will. Abducted her, and kidnapping is a crime.

Slowly he walked through the debris and back into the main part of her room. He made his way through the jumble of clothes and picked up her phone.

"Get me the Azuyo county sheriff's department," he said to Lucia on the desk.

CHAPTER 19

Even though he had arrived very late in Bakersfield the previous night, falling into an exhausted sleep in the first hotel that looked decent, by nine in the morning Roger had showered, breakfasted and was ready to pay a visit to Silver Springs Orchard Fruits.

If Goldy Bassino was not on the premises, he would be Pete West, of Greenside Pesticides, Your Environmentally Friendly Pesticide Company. If Goldy Bassino *was* there, he would be "just stopping by to see the operation."

Along Route 99 he saw a large white sign edged in silver. It read *Silver Springs Orchard Fruits*. The long driveway was flanked on both sides by small evenly-spaced bushes covered with tiny, orange flowers. A good quarter of a mile later the drive opened up onto a large estate. The white buildings were impressive and reminded Roger of pictures he'd seen of southern plantations. He pulled into a space marked *Visitor Parking* and got out. On each side were precise rows of green trees, most of them laden with fruit.

The breeze was refreshing, the sky was clear and the view from the orchard was magnificent. Set on a hill, Silver Springs Orchard Fruits overlooked a rolling green valley. In the distance, between two rows of trees, he caught a glimpse of a figure in white adjusting a sprinkler. Except for the figure between the trees, the place seemed deserted.

He walked toward the building marked *OFFICE*. A sign

on the door read *Closed—Back in 20 minutes*. He stared at the sign wondering why proprietors put up signs like this. How was the customer supposed to know when the twenty minutes had started? He knocked on the door. No answer. He opened the screen door and tried the door. Locked. Through a small space between two venetian blinds he could see that the office, like the grounds was tidy and organized. A large metal desk held a computer, fax machine and telephone. Then his gaze was drawn back to the building itself, to the facing boards. A paint chip. He picked at it with a fingernail and then stood back. Here and there all along the front of the office, the paint was chipping, revealing a dirty gray under-coat.

Roger turned and followed a sidewalk which led around to the back of the office and ran parallel to a wide driveway. He found himself in a large parking area facing a series of ware-houses. Butted against one of the doors was the back end of a semi-trailer. It looked as if Silver Springs was not only an orchard, but a fruit-packing plant as well. He walked over and peered through one of the windows. He saw crates and baskets. But no people. He tried the door. Locked, too. Roger backed up and looked at the building. Like the office, this one also seemed in disrepair. Sagging shutters, peeling paint— the majestic Silver Springs Orchard Fruits was falling down around itself, he thought.

Walking back toward his car he was startled by a voice behind him, "Can I help you?"

He turned. Standing in front of him, a husky young woman in plaid shorts, a stained yellow blouse and white sun-visor was carrying a file folder and munching on an orange.

"Oh, hi, yeah. Goldy around?"

Her eyes narrowed, "Goldy? You mean Mr. Bassino?"

"Yeah."

"No."

"You know where he is?"

"I never know where he is. The more he stays away, the better. He's supposed to be here later. That's all I know."

"Later, when later?"

"Don't know and don't care." She spit an orange seed on the ground.

"You work here?"

"Have for nine years." She pointed, "In the office."

"I take it Goldy is not your most favorite person."

"You take it right. Now, what would you like?"

He extended his hand and smiled. "I'm Pete West, Greenside Pesticides. I heard Goldy was the owner here and thought I'd pay him a visit."

"Well, you're wasting your time. The amount he knows about raising fruit you could put on the head of a pin."

Roger looked around. "This looks like a pretty successful operation to me."

"Only because of the Rolands. Mr. Bassino," she spat out the name, "bought them out around a year ago but if you ask me, they were forced out."

Roger raised his eyebrows. "What makes you say that?"

"Alls I know is I come to work one morning and there's Mrs. Roland sitting on the porch crying her eyes out. Now, the Rolands, they knew fruit. They built this whole place, they made it what it was. I know things were a bit tough the last couple of years, what with the drought and then the flooding, but as I kept telling Mr. Roland—a couple of good years and you'll be on your feet again. Don't give up."

"But you stayed? You work for Goldy now?"

"Yeah," she said dryly. "Mr. Bassino kept me on. Don't ask me why. I told Mr. Roland I was going to quit, and he persuaded me to stay on. He says, 'Felicia, this is your job, this is your life. You stay so's that this orchard don't completely fall apart.' Even the pickers are upset. The Rolands always treated them well."

"Bassino doesn't?"

She grunted, "He don't know the meaning of the word."

They talked as they walked. Behind the shed was a large white house with a wide veranda. In front of it was a blue four-door sedan.

"Is that where the Rolands used to live?" asked Roger.

"Yeah, it used to be a nice place."

"Does Goldy live there now?"

"Heck, no. No one lives there. That car belongs, I think, to one of his shareholders—board members, he calls them. All's they use the main house for now is meetings."

"Meetings?"

"Yeah, I don't know what all. But listen, you want to talk pesticides, and here I'm going on and on. You new with Greenside?"

"Brand new."

On closer look, the house needed a major paint job, and a new roof. Clearly, times had been tough for the Rolands.

A few minutes later, from a side door emerged two men. One of them was Goldy Bassino. The other was Wes Romaine. They were frowning and arguing loudly. Although Roger was fairly sure Goldy wouldn't recognize him with his hat, sunglasses and the beginnings of a beard, he shrank back against the building and put his hand up to his forehead as if to shade his eyes against the sun.

The two got into the car and pulled away. As they backed up to turn, Roger got a clear look at the back end of the car. It was a rental car. He memorized the number.

"Felicia," said Roger after the car had left, "Do you have a list of Goldy's shareholders? Maybe I could talk to them individually about my product."

"No can do. I don't do anything like that anymore for Mr. B. I don't know—maybe he don't trust me or what. And would you believe it? He even changed the phone number over there at the main house. It's unlisted. And don't ask me what it is."

* * *

"What do mean I'm not authorized?" demanded Roger.

"With all due respect sir, this badge and ID from Canada mean nothing to us here. You must have authorization from a police department here in the United States to get that kind of information."

At the counter of the car rental agency Roger stood with his fists on the counter. He said, "First of all I have to wait in line for half an hour and then you tell me I'm not *authorized?*"

The thin man in the loose-fitting brown suit behind the counter regarded him coldly. "I'm sorry sir. Those are the rules that I operate under."

"I'm with the Royal Canadian Mounted Police!"

"That may be fine and dandy in your country, sir," said Mr. Brown-suit, "but I have to abide by the rules in my own country. We just can't let any police department from any country in the world come walking in here and get confidential information like the kind you're requesting."

"Canada!" said Roger, his temper beginning to flare. "We're talking about Canada. We, sir, are not at war. We are friends. Canada and the United States are friends."

Mr. Brown-suit stared at him. People in line behind Roger began whispering to each other.

"Do you have a phone?"

Without looking up he pointed with his pen, "There's a pay phone over there, sir."

Fortunately Blazovick was in and in a matter of minutes Roger had the authorization he needed. Mr. Brown-suit reluctantly told him that the blue Chevy Impala had been rented to a Mr. Flip Schmidt, from Chester, Alberta, Canada.

Bingo.

* * *

Charles was beyond panic. The police were taking his request entirely too lightly. Last night when he had asked to speak with Sheriff Lund, he was told that Sheriff Lund was out on an important matter and would he like to talk with someone else. Sure, he said, and proceeded to tell his story to a bored-sounding deputy.

"Maybe the girl just wanted to go back with her old boyfriend," said the monotone.

"No! It's not like that. Her room was torn apart!"

"Maybe she's just a messy housekeeper."

Charles hung up. He paced around her room. He sat on the edge of her bed and ran a hand through his hair. He got up and paced some more, and then stopped and looked out of her window to the river below. He sat back down on the bed and wondered if this was the time when people prayed. His friend, Josh, prayed. But how do you go about praying? And who do you pray to? And how can you be sure someone is listening? At twenty minutes before midnight he had dialed Josh's number.

"Hey, dude, how's it going?" asked a sleepy-sounding Josh.

"Sorry, did I wake you?"

"No, I had to get up to answer the phone anyway. What's up?"

"I guess I just need to talk to somebody."

"Talk away."

"Maybe to pray for me, for this girl I know."

"Girlfriend?"

"No, just a friend, but a friend in trouble. Her old boyfriend, a real sleaze bucket, has kidnapped her. I know that sounds bizarre and melodramatic, but that's what I believe happened. She didn't want him hanging around her anymore, so I go up to her room and she's gone and her room's been totally torn apart. I called the police but they're not taking it very seriously. I'm going to call them again tomorrow."

"Go on."

"And I guess I just want someone out there to know. Maybe you could pray for her or something. I don't know."

"I will pray. What's her name?"

"Bethany."

"Okay. I'll pray for Bethany."

"Thanks Josh, thanks for being a friend."

"No problem."

"Go back to sleep."

"After I pray."

When Charles hung up the phone he became more convinced than ever that Bethany had been kidnapped. There underneath a pile of her cosmetics was her wallet. People don't go anywhere without their wallets.

He picked it up. It was a bright pink plastic wallet with a picture of a kitten on the front. It looked like the kind of wallet that little girls would use. Maybe he should check it out, maybe there would be something about Mitchell's houseboat in there. He unclasped and opened it. The billfold part was thick with bills. All hundreds! He pulled them out and counted them. Seven! What was Bethany doing with seven hundred dollars in cash? It filled him with fear, but it could be as simple as not believing in bank machines or traveler's checks.

He put the money back and then unsnapped the little photo-holder section. He flipped through. Most of them were of a freckle-faced guy with an impish smile. An old boyfriend? Her brother? Near the back was a black and white one that had been taken at one of those shopping mall photo

booths. Their faces were close together and they were making faces. Both of them were sticking out their tongues with
their fingers in the sides of their mouths.

In the last plastic slip was her driver's license. He pulled it
out. It wasn't hers. It belonged to someone named Madeline
Westmier who lived in Chester, Alberta, Canada. The picture
was Bethany but the name was Madeline. He dropped the
wallet and the license onto the bed. What was going on? He
felt hurt suddenly, hurt and angry that this Bethany or Madeline
or whoever she was had lied to him. Of course she wasn't
Bethany from L.A. For a long time he couldn't place her
accent. She was from Canada! She spoke with the same
nuances of speech as the Sheppards, also from Canada. But
why would she register as Bethany Hadecker? He remembered that when she checked in, she faltered on her own
name. But he also remembered the lost-looking girl who dragged
a quilt into the hotel—a quilt! When hotels always supply
blankets and during a time of year when no one needs blankets anyway! H e took her wallet and made his way absently
down the several halls and elevators to his own room.

Tomorrow he would take her wallet down to the police
station. But now, the full light of Monday morning sun had a
cleansing effect on his brain. He picked up Madeline's wallet
and looked at it again. He couldn't go to the police. He
hadn't even known her real name. He could imagine bored-
voice: "You're sure a girl's been kidnapped, a girl you've
only known a few days—a girl who didn't even give you her
real name!"

No, he'd have to find her himself.

CHAPTER 20

Noon hour traffic was heavy as he headed across town to the Bakersfield police station. Would spotting Bassino and Romaine be enough to get a wire tap on the unlisted phone in the main house? Probably not. Sure would help, though, to find out what goes on inside that place.

Traffic was slowing and Roger wondered if some accident up ahead was causing the slow-down, or was this the way it was supposed to be? Fiddling with the radio dial he found a Christian music station, one that didn't pound his head with rock and rap. He found himself humming along to a classical guitar rendition of *Faith of our Fathers*. It was soothing. He stared ahead of him into the traffic and thought about his phone conversation earlier that morning with Kate and Becky. Before leaving for the orchard he had called home. Becky had answered on the second ring.

"Hi, Becky. This is Dad." He was still angry. How could his daughter, the daughter of a police officer get involved in a drug party? Did she do these things just to spite him or what? Sara never gave them any trouble like this. Why did Becky continually try his patience?

"You okay, Becky?" he had asked.

"I guess."

"I talked to Constable Lavoir . . ."

"Mom told me."

"He said he took you and Jody to Jody's house."

Becky was silent.

"You still there, Becky?"

She said, "Why do we have to go over it a million times? First with Jody's mom, then her dad. Then Mom, now you. Everyone in church knows and they all blame me and not Jody. It was an accident, Dad. We were driving around with Jerry. We saw smoke from the campfire down at the ravine. We just wanted to see who was down there. We hardly even knew anyone there anyway. We were just standing around, and all of a sudden, a million cop cars are roaring down the road. Even Mr. Lavoir doesn't blame us."

Roger sighed. He suddenly felt very old, very weary. "You had no idea there were drugs there? That drug *dealing* was going on there?"

"I told everybody already. I never saw any drugs. I wouldn't know what drugs look like if I saw them. We weren't even in the main part of the party. I didn't know most of those people anyway."

"Becky," he said quietly, "I believe you. But just associating with people and driving down to parties which you know are questionable wasn't very bright . . ."

Roger was aware of a whimpering sound. Could she be crying?

"Becky?"

She sniffed, "Here's Mom."

"Kate?"

"Roger! I'm glad you called. Things are okay. They really are. Becky's okay. When I got in last night we talked, really talked until past midnight. I think she's going to be all right. She's scared mostly."

"Honey, do you want me to come home?"

"No, Becky and I are okay. We even prayed together last night, for the first time in—how many months? No, you stay and do what you have to do."

"Are you okay, Kate? I miss you."

"I'm fine. It's only been a day!"

Then Kate had read Sara's latest letter to him. Sara was thoroughly enjoying Spain, she wrote, but was getting tired of the heat, and looking forward to her first year at the University of Calgary. Her day began around 7:30 A.M., then it was hammering nails and hauling cement for the new church building. Almost every evening she and the other young people took their guitars and visited some of the rural villages. Usually a missionary spoke. Sometimes they would give their testimonies through an interpreter.

"It gets really hot here around lunch," she wrote. "Just when you feel like you can't lift another finger, it's lunch time. Lunch is really long. Most of the Spanish church workers take a nap after lunch. It's so hot then. We don't get back to work till about two or two-thirty or even three. Sometimes we sleep. But most of the time we sit in a shady spot and talk. That's when I get most of my letters written. Like this one. I'm learning a bit of Spanish, and I'm going to see if I can take it at university in the fall."

The letter went on to describe Donaldo, a little village boy who often came to help the student workers. "He's the cutest little fellow you ever saw. He's always wanting to help carry stuff."

She continued, "The church is going up nicely, It's almost done. The guys are finishing the building and I got elected to do the landscaping. I am really enjoying that."

"Well," Roger had said to Kate. "At least one of our daughters is on the right track."

"Roger," she said sharply. "Don't say that. They're both fine girls."

During the last quarter of an hour Roger could have sworn his car hadn't moved two feet, and then he saw why—a gigantic neon right-arrow sign. Moving four lanes of traffic into one had to be some sadistic highway construction engineer's idea of fun. The guitar had finished and an orchestra was playing *Eternal Father Strong to Save*, complete with trumpets and fanfare, while he sat still in the precise spot on the highway that he had been during *Faith Of Our Fathers*. Next to him a man in a gray Mercedes was drinking coffee out of a travel mug and talking on a cellular phone. Listening to the music Roger began to think about his impatience and his temper, a constant struggle for him. The man at the car rental counter was only doing his job. And Becky was just being a teenager. He prayed for her then, thanking God that she was not a part of the drug-taking group but only a bystander. He thanked God for his wife, Kate, and even her sharp rebuke, "They're both fine girls." Good thing God didn't judge him the same way he judged people. He prayed for Sara, that God would give her strength through the hot weather as she worked with the Spanish people.

He also prayed for Madeline. He felt a deep sense of urgency that she was in danger. He prayed that it wasn't too late. Then he prayed for Goldy and Wes and Flip, disillusioned by power and money, yet needing a Savior.

Hours later—it seemed—Roger pulled into *Visitor Parking* at the Bakersfield Police station. When he was barely inside the front door, a large man who hastily introduced himself as Sergeant Phil Blazovick hustled him quickly down the hall.

"We may have enough for a wire tap," he said. To Roger's raised eyebrows he said, "Your sergeant, Roy Laird, called about half an hour ago. I guess your wife was in a panic. The morning paper in Calgary ran a picture of Madeline Westmier and your wife recognized her. Also, a neighbor of Madeline's called. Madeline called her the other day . . ."

"Recognized her? From where?" he asked incredulously.

"From the Riverboat, down here. You want coffee?"

Roger nodded and Phil raised a hand, "Blair, get us a couple'a javas please, pronto."

Turning back to Roger he went on, "Your wife said she talked to her yesterday in Azuyo. Said she was going by the name of Bethany. I guess your wife gave her a Bible or something. They had quite a chat. Madeline was complaining to her about an over-protective boyfriend, name of Mitchell, and your wife was giving advice."

Kate met her? Down here?

Roger stopped in his tracks and looked at him.

Blazovick went on.

"Also, last night one of the Riverboat employees, a Charles Howarth, reported that Bethany—the name she was going by—was supposed to meet him but never showed up."

"Have you talked to Charles today?"

"We can't find him. It's his day off. He could be anywhere."

The coffee arrived and Roger drank his hot and black, hardly bothering to taste it.

Phil continued, "Now the only Mitchell I know is Mitchell Standish, one of Bassino's hired thugs."

"Have you been to the Riverboat? Checked her room?"

"As we speak. And we're getting a wire on that orchard pronto. Lund's getting one for the Riverboat."

* * *

Deputy Frank Hickle was a thin, wiry black man who had confided to Roger in the van on the way out to the orchard that he'd been involved in numerous wire tappings before. He was also up for promotion, he said, and if this operation was successful, it should be a sure thing. He and Roger sat next to each other in the back of the van and his non-stop bragging, foul language, lewd comments and bad jokes were beginning to grate on Roger's already-frayed nerves.

Driving the van was Blazovick. Next to him was another black officer, Deputy Harold Rochester, a large and thoughtful man who reminded Roger a little of Clayton Lavoir. It was late afternoon and they were heading out to the orchard where Roger and Frank would place the wireless tap on the phone lines just outside the main house. The receivers would be set up in an abandoned garage less than a mile away.

When they passed a couple of well-endowed working girls of the night, Frank let go with a string of profanities that made Roger turn to him, his mouth open.

"Zip it, Frank," said Harold looking back over his shoulder.

To Roger he said, "He's a good cop but he thinks he's Eddie Murphy."

But he was a good cop. That's what Rochester had said. And this became evident when the two of them, Roger and Frank, made their way across Goldy Bassino's orchard in the twilight. All attempts at dark humor were gone. Deputy Frank Hickle was in control.

Night fell as they crept through the underbrush as noiselessly as possible. It was clear and moonless. There was also a bit of a chill to the air, and Roger was thankful that he was wearing his black turtle-neck. In the main house lights blazed behind drawn drapes.

A gust of wind blew the shrubbery and lifted and whipped Roger's now-longer hair against his cheeks. He brushed the hair strands back with his hand. In a few moments, Frank had climbed the telephone pole, found the phone wire and inserted the tap.

* * *

It had been a whole day since they arrived in that bay and

she still didn't know what they wanted. For an entire day they had kept her tied to a chair while they talked and argued and watched television. The screen was just out of her view.

She was learning a bit about her four captors. First, there was Mitchell who mostly aimed the gun at her and glared. Then there was Ray, the driver of the car that brought them here. He sat at the kitchen table drumming his fingers against it while he pored over what looked like long ledger books. Then there was Roly, the pudgy one who talked loudly, walked loudly and was constantly red in the face. "Why'd you bring her here anyway?" he'd rant at Mitchell. "It's gonna bring us nothing but trouble!" He continually paced, lighting cigarettes, dousing them half-smoked into ashtrays or throwing them overboard, circling the deck, scowling, picking up a Reader's Digest from the well-stocked bookshelf, flipping through it, then putting it down again, all the while muttering, "It's not going to work," until Mitchell would yell, "Will you shut up already?"

Curly-haired, friendly-looking Flip was the one she felt the least frightened of. It was Flip who gently untied her hands and brought bowls of soup, or glasses of water. It was Flip who untied her feet and hands and walked her to the bathroom a few times a day. Flip would talk to her, too. Out of earshot of the others he would say, "You know, you really should give them what they want. I know these people, they always get what they want eventually."

The television was on now and Madeline heard the theme song of Sesame Street. Roly sat down in front of the set, a banana in his hand. Without a word, Ray rose from the table, flicked off the TV and motioned for the three of them to follow him into the front room. They sat in a circle with Madeline in the center. She looked from one face to another. Mitchell and Roly glared at her. Ray looked noncommittal and bored, and Flip looked worried and kept rubbing his nose and frowning.

The five of them sat for several minutes, silently looking at Ray, waiting for Ray to begin. He seemed in no hurry. Finally he spoke, "Miss Westmier," he said, "You have something that belongs to us. And we would very much like to have it back."

She shook her head, unable to speak.

"Where is it, Miss Westmier?"

Her throat felt closed up. Her mouth was dry.

Roly rose and leaned toward her, his face just inches from her own, "Did you hear him? Are you deaf? Where is it?"

"Let her be," said Ray quietly motioning him away. He turned to her again, "Just tell me where it is and we'll be done with all this."

"It's in my hotel room. My hotel room and the car," she whispered.

"Which is it, your hotel room or the car?"

"It is not!" interrupted Mitchell, "I would have found it."

He ignored Mitchell and continued, "Let me repeat my question, where is it, your hotel room or your car?"

"Both places."

"Tell me something, how can it be in two places at the same time?"

"I divided it up."

"You took it apart?"

She nodded. The men looked from one to another. Mitchell started laughing.

"Why did you tear it apart?" asked Ray.

"I didn't want to lose it. But I already spent part of it."

Roly rose once more and leaned toward her. "Are you some kind of idiot? Where is the book? The book your punk boyfriend stole?"

"Sit down," Ray commanded.

She looked from one face to another around the table.

"What book?" she said.

Roly spoke again. "The book, stupid. The book that got Tom killed, the one that's gonna get you killed." He grabbed her arm.

"I don't know what you're talking about!" She began to sputter. "I don't know anything about any book."

Mitchell got up and grabbed a beer from the fridge. "The book, Madeline. I've looked all over your entire room, all through your car. Where did you put it?"

"I don't know what book you're talking about," she said quietly this time.

Mitchell downed about half of the beer, then wiped his mouth with the back of his gun hand.

Ray spoke again. "We're equipped to stay out here for days—days and days—until you decide to tell us where the book is."

Flip spoke for the first time. "Madeline, Goldy Bassino will be coming out maybe tomorrow. You'll want to remember where the book is before he comes."

Ray glared at him.

"I don't know what you're talking about."

"I don't know what you're talking about. I don't know what you're talking about," mimicked Roly.

Ignoring Roly, Ray regarded her evenly. "I admire your stubbornness," Ray said quietly. "Too bad it won't help you in the end." He clucked his tongue. "I do so hate killing people . . ."

She turned to Mitchell. "Mitchell," she pleaded, "I thought you were my friend."

He leaned back his head and laughed, his face contorting as he spoke. "Tom was easy to kill. The jerk kept praying the whole time I had the gun aimed at his head—praying, praying, praying. His God didn't help him. Don't expect Him to help you either."

Tears flooded her eyes. Mitchell was the one who had killed Tom! Mitchell! Someone she trusted. A sob caught in her throat as she remembered the video arcade and wandering down the streets of Azuyo and laughing on the Sea Doo as it sped down the river in the sunshine.

Ray leaned toward her, "Miss Westmier, we need that book. Now we can stay here as long as it takes. But you are not leaving until we have the ledger."

CHAPTER 21

The inside of the garage where the monitoring receiver was housed was stuffy and overly warm. The sole window was a grimy square of glass up high on the wall, and the only fresh air came from a 12-inch space under the garage door which had been propped open with a brick.

For the past day, Roger was in and out; first to the police station to speak with Sergeant Blazovick, then back to the garage to talk to whoever was on duty there, then on the phone to Chester or to Lund in Azuyo. He'd retreated to his hotel room last night when Blazovick had finally ordered, "Get some sleep!" But he was up early trying to puzzle out the events of the past two weeks. By quarter to eight he had arrived at the Bakersfield police station and was talking to Blazovick. By nine he was at the garage with Rochester pacing back and forth, a styrofoam cup of gritty coffee in his hand. The telephone monitor was quiet, even though they knew that Goldy, and probably Wes, were staying at the orchard's main house. It gave him some comfort that Lund's deputies were combing the area for a large silver car fitting the description of the one seen leaving the Riverboat.

While Roger paced, Deputy Rochester sat at a table and wrote in a small spiral notebook. Sweat pooled on Roger's forehead and he wondered if they were somehow on the wrong track.

Little conversation passed between them as Rochester bent

over his book. Roger walked over and looked down at the large police officer. The pages were filled with lines of words, some crossed out, and pen marks. It didn't look like a police report.

"Are you working on a report or something?" he asked casually.

"No," Rochester said softly. When Roger looked at him quizzically, he put down his pen, closed the book and said, "Just a hobby of mine. It sometimes helps me keep my head together. Keeps me from going crazy."

"What does?"

"Poetry. I write poetry."

"*Poetry?*" Roger realized he'd said it too loudly, expressing too much surprise.

"Yeah, poetry."

"You write poems?"

"Yeah," he said smiling, "Just something I do in my spare time."

"Wow." Roger had never met anyone who actually wrote poetry. "What kind of poems?" he asked.

"Police poetry."

"*Police* poetry?"

"Yeah, you know, close-to-the-edge type stuff—drugs, knives, the smell of blood, what it *really* feels like to be looking down the barrel of a 45."

Roger shook his head. He never read much poetry. Well, actually he had to admit that, except in school, he had never read *any* poetry.

"It's a hobby, but I hope it's going to start paying for itself soon. I'm having a book of poetry published next year."

"Wow, well—wow! Congratulations! What's the name of it?"

Rochester smiled. "It's tentatively being called *Blue Lines* but the title's still up for grabs."

"Wow," said Roger again, shaking his head.

"Yeah," said Rochester smiling.

Roger sat down on a rickety folding chair and took the final sip from his coffee cup. There was more to this cop than meets the eye. He wondered if Clayton Lavoir was also a closet poet. After a few minutes he said, "Do you think you could send me a copy of your book when it comes out?"

"I don't see why not."

Just then Rochester put his hand up. A call was coming in.

A voice Roger didn't recognize said, "We're out on the boat now and we've got the girl. She keeps saying she doesn't have the book."

"The girl is lying."

Roger recognized Goldy's clipped voice.

"Yeah, well, she says she doesn't know what we're talking about."

"The girl is a pathological liar. May I remind you that we will be out there soon, myself and Mr. Romaine. And we'll be wanting to know the whereabouts of the ledger. Is the fruit shipment ready?"

"Ready."

"Well, at least you've gotten one thing right. And the imported sauces?"

"Ready, but Flip wants to talk to you about that."

"I take back what I just said."

There was a click on the phone. Goldy had hung up. A book? Fruit? Wes Romaine? Earlier that day Laird had told him that Wes Romaine had booked into the Hilton in Ottawa. He had picked up his registration package and name tag and, for all intents and purposes, was in attendance at the city officials' annual conference in Ottawa. Marjorie had confirmed it. From her hospital bed in Calgary she had nodded, yes, he was in Ottawa. No, he hadn't called her, but she had no reason to believe he wasn't there.

"I say we find that houseboat," said Roger rising.

"I say you're right."

Roger drove quickly back to the station where he talked with Blazovick, then called Lund.

"Where would you guess that boat to be?" Roger asked.

"It could be anywhere, even off the California coast, but my guess, given Goldy's proximity to Azuyo, plus the fact that I don't think they would drive the girl all the way from Azuyo to California, is that it's either Lake Mojave or Lake Mead."

"Great. Shall I head back in my rental?"

"No, we'll arrange a flight. It'll be quicker. We had another new development about half an hour ago. A kid came in here with Madeline's wallet. Seems she was staying at the Riverboat under the name Bethany Hadecker. He confirmed that Madeline and Mitchell were heading out on a houseboat."

"I'll see you in an hour or so."

* * *

"Boy, did you miss all the excitement!" said Lucia to Charles when he arrived at work that morning.

"Excitement?"

"The cops, yesterday afternoon, crawling all over the place. Just like in the movies!"

"The cops were here?"

Lucia smoothed back her hair and leaned against the counter. "Yeah, and they kept asking for you."

"For me?" Charles stared at her.

"Yeah, but I guess they didn't find you or you'd know what I was talking about."

Charles spent yesterday driving aimlessly up and down the lake looking for Bethany or Madeline or whoever she was, and a houseboat. Good luck, there were hundreds of houseboats out on the lake. Yesterday everybody and his dog decided to go boating. Occasionally he'd stop, get out of his car and peer out onto the lake with his binoculars. A couple of times he considered renting a boat but scrapped that idea when he realized that that would be even more futile than his car search. By late afternoon he reluctantly gave up his search, drove over to the Arizona side, went to a double feature science-fiction movie, and got home just before midnight, using the employees' elevator to avoid the lobby. And now to find out the police had been here!

"What did they want? Did they say?"

"It was about a hotel guest that disappeared. They asked me about her. That girl from California, Bethany Hadecker. I saw you talking to her the other day. Maybe that's why they wanted to see you."

Ahh! So the police were finally taking his phone call seriously. Well, it was about time.

"If you ask me," said Lucia pushing her glasses up on her nose, "I think she just left. So what if she didn't check out? She paid in advance, so what's the big deal?"

"The big deal is that she was kidnapped, Lucia. I know what it's all about now. Bethany was kidnapped, taken against her will by your friend and mine, Mitchell Standish. I called the police Sunday night."

"Mitchell kidnapped her?"

"Yeah, that's what I think. That's what I told the police."

"How do you know he kidnapped her?" Her brown eyes were wide.

"Oh, just some things—things she told me. She was afraid of him. She told me he wanted to take her out on his houseboat. She refused. We were supposed to meet. To make a long story short, I went to her room and it was totally wrecked."

"Wrecked?"

"Yeah, signs of a struggle. Her clothes and stuff were all over the place. So I called the police."

"Well, they sure took you seriously. About five cop cars showed up and millions of cops, and her room's all cordoned off. No one can get in there."

"Wow!" They really *were* taking his request seriously.

He asked, "Is Mr. Bassino in? Does he know about this?"

"No, to both questions. And that's another funny thing," said Lucia reaching down to adjust the hem of her skirt, "Remember how he said he was going to be in yesterday? Well, he didn't show, no message, nothing. You haven't heard from him, I don't suppose?"

"You're kidding, right? We didn't part on the best of terms Saturday."

"Oh, yeah."

* * *

Shortly after noon, Andrew Lund met Roger Sheppard at the airport and drove him to the Azuyo Sheriff's Department. When they arrived, the place was a mass of activity. But it was soon apparent to Roger that there was a definite order within the chaos. Pairs of deputies hurried out with photocopied faxes of Madeline and Mitchell, to search up and down the river and lakes. They knew Goldy would be arriving in Azuyo any minute and plainclothes police were monitoring all the airports, hoping that Goldy would lead them to Madeline.

While Andrew leaned over his desk, phone receiver to his ear, Roger sat at a smaller table leafing through a thick report of Goldy Bassino's activities. As he skimmed it, a picture began to emerge of a shrewd businessman. It looked as if Goldy routinely bought up businesses that were failing such as the Silver Springs Orchard and the Riverboat. Maybe such as Flip Schmidt's Deli? But why?

Andrew hung up the phone and Roger said, "What book are they looking for? Do we have any idea?"

"Whatever it is, we're fairly sure they haven't found it yet," answered Andrew.

"Tom must have hidden it well."

"Sheriff!" A young female deputy rushed into the room. "We've got someone who saw a person fitting Madeline's description board a houseboat with a group of men. Max and Joanne just called it in."

"Where?" Lund grabbed the phone.

"The old marina."

"Let's go," said Lund. He and Roger hurried out and climbed into Lund's police cruiser.

"We're lucky it's Lake Mojave and not Lake Mead," said Lund squealing out of the parking lot, "It's a lot closer."

About twenty minutes later Andrew steered the patrol car down a gravel drive. He explained that this was the old marina. A new, more modern facility had just been built farther up the coast. This one was in the process of being systematically shut down.

* * *

How long had she been here? She wasn't sure, although a couple of nights had passed, with her sitting scrunched up, her ankles and wrists still tied to that chair. They just kept after her, on and on, about some book. Tom never told her about any book. Why wouldn't they just listen to her? Mitchell was getting more and more insane. Late last night she heard a shot fired. She tensed and then listened to the argument that followed. Ray, who had never raised his voice above a monotone yelled, "Do you want to blow this whole thing? Shooting out on the lake for no reason. You stupid jerk!" Then she had heard Mitchell mumbling and then Ray again: "I've half a mind to leave you here with the girl when we blow this ship apart."

Blow this ship apart! Madeline's hands trembled in her lap when she remembered last night's conversation. They intended to kill her, all because of some stupid book. She strained against the ropes, but they were tight. She knew that if she could just get free she could jump overboard and easily swim to the shore. And then what?

Today, all of her captors seemed unusually tense. Even Flip, especially Flip. He still came and got her up a few times a day, but he spoke little to her, and looked away when he brought her small plates of food at regular intervals.

There was a crack in the curtain on the window next to where she sat which gave her a hairline view of the desolate shoreline. There was nothing out there, just beach and scrub brush. Where were they?

Over and over she replayed Tom's last hours in her mind, trying to remember something, anything about a book. Before he came into her apartment that night, she had heard the sound of the car hatch closing. Probably that was when he was stowing the box with the money and maps. Tom had walked into the apartment, eyes bright, wearing an ugly, strange jacket. He had said, "I've got one more thing I gotta do. I've got to try one more time." That was it, *I've got to try one more time.* What did Tom mean by that?

Flip was sitting across from her now, nervously wringing his hands in his lap. She said to him, "I really, really, *really* don't know where your book is. Someone has to believe me."

"I believe you, but Goldy thinks you're just being stubborn."

"What's going on in here?" Roly sauntered into the front room, a can of beer in his hand.

"Give her a break, will ya? She doesn't have the book.

Tom must have given it to someone else."

He rubbed his large-featured face with his pudgy fist. "She has it. She's just being pigheaded. Of course he gave it to her, what else would he do with it? Your mistake was killing him before we got the book from him."

Madeline winced. In the distance she heard the unmistakable sound of an outboard motor. She glanced through the curtain crack but saw nothing. The sound was getting louder. Then there was a flurry of activity on the deck. And then an unfamiliar voice, "Gentlemen, the one remaining piece of evidence to be destroyed tomorrow is that book. I trust you have it now?"

That must be Goldy! She squirmed against her bonds. They had killed Tom, and they planned to kill her, too. She looked down at the knots in the ropes. Her wrists were red and sore. Some of the skin had been worn away. Her shoulders hurt. When she looked up, a small neatly-dressed man was standing over her.

"Ah, Miss Westmier, we finally meet and under such unfortunate circumstances." He was smiling. "I hate giving ultimatums. But if we don't have the book Tom stole by tomorrow, you will be destroyed along with this ship. We will, of course, be miles away in new countries with new identities when that happens."

"I don't know what you're talking about. Tom never gave me a book."

Goldy clucked his tongue. "That's too bad, my dear. It's such a shame when someone so young and pretty has to die."

CHAPTER 22

The man who met them on the dock was deeply tanned, sinewy, wore an Australian bush hat and introduced himself as Len. To Roger he looked like he spent his days running marathons in the hot sun. Next to him, his sailboat was covered in riggings and ropes and other boat-type paraphernalia that Roger couldn't identify. When Len saw the direction Roger was looking he said, "Haven't made the move to the new marina yet. Call me stubborn, but I like the location of this bay." His smile was warm and friendly. The name along the side of his boat was *Predawn*.

He told them that he had been up in his bosun's chair working on the mast when the pair with the girl had walked beneath them. They hadn't looked up.

"So they didn't see you?" asked Lund.

"Don't think so, mates. They were a strange bunch. I kept my eye on them."

"Why?" asked Roger.

"That blonde, a little bit of a thing she was, didn't look happy. She was with two guys, one looked like a California beach bum, a big, hulking brute of a guy with bleached hair. He kept his hand on her, like he was afraid she might bolt or something. They were with this skinny guy, tall. I didn't think too much of it till the other guys began waltzing down the dock toward the boat."

"Other guys?"

"Yeah, two guys carrying briefcases. I'm saying to myself, these mates aren't just out for a little picnic."

"Did you see where they went?"

"Yeah, I watched them. They turned out of the marina and headed north up the lake."

"And this was Sunday? Around what time?"

"I couldn't tell you. I lose track of time. Don't wear a watch. I think it was maybe mid-afternoon, getting on toward evening maybe."

"What's up that way?" asked Roger turning to Lund.

"Only about a hundred miles of bays, beaches and inlets," he answered.

Len said, "Like finding a needle in a haystack, mates."

"Will take us hours by water," said Lund.

"How about the chopper?" offered Roger.

"The police markings are too noticeable from the ground. We could take the fixed wing, but that, too, is a red flag from the lake."

Len interjected, "How 'bout this, mates—I can fly you in my Cessna. I'm up and down the lake all the time. Wouldn't attract any attention."

"Would you be able to recognize the houseboat from the air?" Roger asked him.

"Yeah, no worry. I know that boat. *The Maria*. Odd bunch owns that boat. It sits there for months on end, and then suddenly a whole crew of business-types gets on."

In less than twenty minutes the three of them were high over Lake Mojave in a Cessna 172 Skyhawk. The sound of the engine was hypnotic to Roger as he sat in the back and scoured the lake with binoculars.

He saw people lying on beach chairs reading, playing beach volleyball, water-skiing, wind surfing and eating their picnic fixings under large umbrellas. Three quarters of the way up the shoreline of the lake, Len pointed across the lake.

"There it is, mates," he said.

"You're sure?" said Lund. The houseboat was barely visible and was deep within a secluded bay.

"Yeah, I'm sure. You want me to fly across?"

Lund said, "No. That would attract too much attention. Fly up the lake and then down across that coast. We'll get a better look at it."

"We're wasting time," said Roger from the back.

"I'm thinking of the girl, her safety. They get suspicious and she's history."

"If she isn't history already," muttered Roger.

He was impatient. If he were on a flat surface, he would be pacing. Kate said that he always paced. When he was worried, he paced. When he was trying to puzzle something out, he paced.

Twenty-five minutes later they were flying directly over the houseboat which was anchored some distance from the shore.

"It looks quiet," said Lund. "No movement."

"Maybe they've left," said Roger.

"Let's hope not."

"They picked a good spot, anyhow," said Len. "See how the bay opens up there? You can't see into the bay from the lake. I know that spot. Only fits one boat, too. You never would have found the boat from out on the lake."

"It'll make their escape just that much more difficult," said Lund, his binoculars trained on the bay.

"You want me to call anybody or anything?" said Len picking up his radio receiver.

"No, too much of an open line," said Lund. "We'll have to wait until we're landed."

"Then what?" asked Roger.

"We call the lake patrol, find a boat ourselves and head out there."

"Know what I'd suggest, mates?" offered Len. "See that little inlet over there, about two bays away from *The Maria*?" He pointed up the lake. "It's sheltered and no one goes there, the ground is too rocky. No sandy beach. You go in there and just over the hill is the houseboat. You need a boat, use my speedboat. It's an old boat but it's fast."

Lund nodded. Roger felt like pacing.

Back on shore, Lund ran up to his patrol car, made a couple of calls then grabbed two blue duffel bags from the trunk, and threw them into the dinghy.

"What's in these?" asked Roger.

"Body armor. Radios. Bullhorn. Sunscreen," he said pulling the choke on the outboard and heading them out into the lake.

* * *

The boat's head was small and stuffy. It included a small toilet, a tiny shower and sink in dark mahogany wood. The door behind her was closed and locked. On all previous occasions Flip made her leave it open an inch. But this time when she closed it behind her, he just looked at her with that worried look on his face. She knew he was feeling sorry for her, maybe that would work to her advantage.

She knelt down and carefully, quietly, she opened the cupboard under the sink. In the front were a few rolls of toilet paper and a couple of folded white towels. She felt behind the towels and found a can of powdered cleanser and a small glass vial. She lifted the bottle out and looked at it. The label said wood varnish, but it was empty. She reached into the cupboard again and at the very back her fingers found a large plastic container tipped over on its side. She lifted it out. Liquid chemical toilet fluid. Poisonous. Good.

Quickly she rinsed out the small wood varnish bottle under

the tap and filled it with the poisonous fluid. Then she screwed the cap on very tightly and shoved the bottle deep into the pocket of her shorts, thankful that she was wearing Tom's loose shirt. It was long enough to hide any pocket bulges. The rest of the cupboard was empty.

She could hear her captors in the other room arguing loudly. She pressed her ear against the wall.

Mitchell said, "I say we kill her. They're probably looking for her right now."

"Who's looking for her? No one knows where she is," said Roly.

"Someone's gonna put two and two together."

Madeline hugged her arms to her chest. *Oh, Tom, Tom, what's going on?*

The arguing went on, and she decided to take advantage of the noise to continue her search. She rose and stepped on the toilet seat. On tiptoe she could just see out of the high window. She moved the curtain aside. The shoreline was lifeless and desolate. She felt around the rim of the shower. Maybe there would be some sort of weapon—a screw driver, scissors or something. At the back next to the wall her fingers stumbled onto a little key. She picked it up and looked at it. It was too small to be a house key. It was probably the key to a safe somewhere. She looked at it again. A key. Just a key. But what was niggling at the corners of her thinking?

A loud knock on the door brought her out of her reverie. "Come on out now!" yelled Flip. Quickly she pocketed the key, flushed the toilet, ran the sink for a few minutes, dabbed her eyes with water and then walked out. Without being told to, she sat down sullenly in the chair and allowed Flip to tie her hands.

"Do you have to do that?" She asked plaintively, allowing a few droplets of the water to drip from her eyes. "Look at the marks on my arm."

He stopped tying until Roly said, "Don't be a fool, Flip, make the ties tight."

But Flip didn't. Winking at her, he tied them loosely. She smiled and allowed him to carefully wipe the "tears" from her eyes with his handkerchief.

Mitchell was becoming crazier. Now he was staggering around with a ham sandwich and a beer. Beer was all he ever drank. He walked over to the large window and pushed aside the curtain with his can of beer. Goldy glared at him. He dropped the curtain back in place. Madeline looked away as Mitchell walked past her.

* * *

Almost an hour later Roger and Andrew Lund pulled soundlessly into the adjacent bay. Lund jumped into the water and pulled the boat to shore. On the rocky beach, they donned body armor, clipped radios to their belts and hung the binoculars around their necks. Andrew clipped on his holster. Roger had to be content just to carry a radio. He could not carry a gun outside of Canada.

Behind them at a discreet distance two patrol boats followed. They would unobtrusively stand guard at the entrance to the bay.

"Whatever you do, don't touch the cactus," warned Lund as the two of them crawled up the bank.

At the crest of the hill they lay on the ground and focused their binoculars on the houseboat. A motor boat was tied to the large houseboat. As soon as they saw movement, *if* they saw movement, they would descend upon the bay.

But they saw nothing. Roger's biggest fear was that they were too late, that the boat's occupants had long gone ashore and were already far away.

The only movement Roger saw was a ten-inch cement-colored lizard which crawled lazily in front of them, looked up, regarded them with disdain, and then scuttled off through the cactus and sand.

"Wait a minute," said Lund. And then Roger saw it too— the curtain in one of the cabin's large windows parted and Roger caught a front view of a frightened-looking girl with blonde hair. Then the curtain fell back into place.

"That was her," said Roger. She was still alive but was she all right?

Lund radioed the other two boats. One of the patrol boats which had followed them into the bay contained the sharp-shooters. They climbed over the bank behind Roger and Lund and took their places hidden on the ridge, ready for Lund's command. Lund and Roger descended the hill toward the beach. The houseboat was anchored some twenty yards from the shore.

Lund approached the edge of the shore carrying a bullhorn.

Facing the boat, Lund yelled, "We've got you completely surrounded. Come out with your hands up."

Nothing.

"Come out with your hands up!"

Nothing. Five minutes. Ten minutes.

This could be a long time, thought Roger. Silently, he prayed. He personally knew of standoffs which had lasted hours, even days. Would this be one of those? Dear God, no.

"Come out with your hands up!"

Fifteen minutes. Twenty minutes. Except for the lapping of the lake against the shore, all was quiet. The patrol boats at the entrance of the bay stood like sentinels against the sapphire sky.

Suddenly the door banged open and out staggered a tall man with ragged blond hair. He was holding a girl tightly around the neck and dragging her roughly across the deck. Her hands were tied in front of her. Madeline!

"Get away from here, or the girl gets it!" he yelled.

She screamed and the man clamped one of this large hands over her mouth. Roger saw her eyes widen at the sight of him on the beach.

Andrew walked as close to the edge of the lake as he could. He talked gently to the man, "Put the gun down. You don't really want to hurt her. Just put the gun down. We'll talk after you put the gun down."

"Get out of here!" the blond man said waving the gun. His voice was hoarse.

He's desperate, thought Roger, which was a good news-bad news twist; good news because he might make a mistake allowing them to come in, and bad news because he might do something really crazy.

They stood that way for many minutes, Lund gently trying to persuade him to put down his gun, the man yelling obscenities, and Madeline struggling.

"I'll kill her. I swear I'll kill her!" The man's face dripped with sweat.

"No you won't. You won't kill her. Put the gun down, then we can talk about it."

Madeline struggled and fought against him and Roger could see that she was managing to slowly loose her wrists from the ties. The man seemed not to notice. Be careful, thought Roger, whatever you're trying to do, be careful. And then she was moving her right hand slowly to her pocket. The man waved the gun wildly, cursing at Andrew, cursing at the girl, cursing at the whole world. He didn't notice that she had plunged her right hand deep within the pocket of her shorts. Lund talked gently, the man yelled, Madeline fiddled with something in her pocket, and Roger prayed.

Suddenly, in one quick movement she brought out a small bottle and threw it in the man's face. He screamed in pain. Immediately his fists flew to his face and he let her go. In the next instant Madeline was overboard and swimming swiftly toward the shore.

A shot rang out from the hillside and the staggering man on the ship's deck was instantly felled.

Roger rushed into the water toward Madeline, but she was already on the beach. He grabbed her and led her, sobbing and shaking, away from the water. "He killed Tom," she said, "He told me he killed Tom."

"It's all over," yelled Lund into the bullhorn. "Come out with your hands up, or we're coming in."

A few minutes later, Goldy Bassino, Wes Romaine, Flip Schmidt and two others he didn't recognize exited *The Maria*. The body of Mitchell Standish was removed and the entire houseboat was confiscated as evidence.

CHAPTER 23

Charles was waiting at the police station when Madeline arrived, shivering, damp and swathed in a large blue beach towel. She looked up at him briefly. He smiled at her and she looked away. A policeman had his arm around her and was guiding her toward a back room. He decided he would stay.

He sat down on a plastic chair in the lobby where he could observe the comings and going of the officers. He figured out that this wasn't just some ordinary kidnapping. Mitchell had been shot and killed, he heard. Also, that a major drug operation had been brought down. He still didn't have all the particulars but he knew it involved the boy in the photos in Madeline's wallet. Tom Anderchuk. The name she had asked him about.

A young woman officer approached him. "Can I help you with anything?"

"I'm just waiting to see Madeline, the girl they brought in." He was starting to think of her as Madeline rather than Bethany.

"That may be a while."

"I'll wait."

He stared straight ahead, his hands motionless in his lap. His mind was still too keyed up for much else.

Earlier that morning he had left Lucia at the desk and drove over to the police station. Mr. Bassino wasn't in, so what the heck? Besides, this was a police matter. If Mr.

Bassino had problems with him leaving, too bad.

The same bored-sounding officer had asked him a lot of questions such as, "What is your relationship to Madeline Westmier?"

Wishful thinking mostly, he thought to himself. Instead, he had answered, "Just friends."

He'd told them about Mitchell and the houseboat while the officer jotted down his replies in a small notebook.

"Can you tell me what's going on? Are you looking for her? Will you find her?"

"We're doing everything we can."

Standard police reply, thought Charles.

Charles had driven back to the Riverboat, but every hour on the dot he called the police. "Have you found her yet?"

"No, but we're working on it."

Late that afternoon their reply was different, "We're bringing her in."

Bringing her in! Charles said a quick goodbye to Lucia and headed for the police station, where now he watched the door of the room where Madeline and two police officers were. He strained to listen to snatches of conversation: "Bassino finally arrested. Mitchell dead. Drug ring. Extortion."

Mr. Bassino? His boss? He shook his head. This was major confusing.

Finally the door opened and a sunburned man in shorts and sandals walked toward him. Mr. Sheppard from Medicine Hat?

Charles rose, "Mr. Sheppard?"

"Hello, Charles," said Mr. Sheppard. He re-introduced himself as Roger Sheppard of the Royal Canadian Mounted Police. He said that Charles could talk to Madeline now. The Royal Canadian Mounted Police! What were they doing down here in Nevada?

Charles followed the mountie into the room where Madeline

sat huddled in a towel on a wooden chair. She managed a smile when he approached. The two police officers left and Madeline and Charles were alone.

"They told me you wanted to see me," she said.

"I just wanted to make sure you're okay. Are you okay?"

"Not really," she answered. She ran a hand through her damp hair. "I'm sorry I involved you in all of this."

"You didn't involve me. I involved myself, Madeline."

She looked up at him sharply.

"It's okay," he said, "I know your real name. I know you're from Canada. Are you," he paused, "Are you in some kind of trouble? The Canadian mounties are here and all. You haven't been arrested for anything have you? Is that why I can only see you in this room?"

She smiled, "No, it's nothing like that. They have me protected or something. That's why I have to talk to people here. The police told me they are even going to escort me home to Canada."

Charles rubbed his forehead. "What's going on? Can you tell me? I know Mitchell kidnapped you. I was the one who called the police. But it's more than that isn't it? What's Canada got to do with it? And how come you told everybody you were Bethany Hadecker from California?"

She sighed and looked down. Then she told him her story. She told him about a person named Tom, and drugs, and about how he went straight and started going to church, how he came down here and went back home and was murdered. It was a strange story and Charles didn't say a word, feeling that if he so much as sneezed, she would clam up. Somehow he felt that she needed a friend, that she needed to tell this story. She was leaving the next day for Canada, she said.

It was quiet in the room. The front office sounds were muffled behind the door. He reached across the table for her hands. He gently held them, ever so briefly, looked into her eyes—her sad eyes—and said, "Madeline, you'll be all right."

"I know," she said.

They exchanged addresses and phone numbers and promised to write.

On his way out, the sheriff pulled him aside. "How well did you know Goldy Bassino?" he asked Charles.

* * *

The Goldy—Flip—Wes—Tom jigsaw puzzle, or what there was assembled of it, was dangerously close to being tipped off the card table and scattered onto the carpet. Back at his desk in his detachment in Chester, Alberta, Roger leaned his head in his left hand while he went through the thick file on Tom Anderchuk again. He'd been over the reports a hundred times, and yet he felt as though he was missing something. It wasn't just the book. Goldy, Wes, Ray, Roly and Flip had been arrested in Azuyo for unlawful confinement and uttering death threats. That was all. Even though the houseboat had been gone over inch by inch, all of the incriminating evidence—if there had been any on the boat in the first place—had been destroyed before Goldy and his buddies came on deck smirking with their hands up. Divers had searched the entire lake bottom in the bay and had come up empty. What was needed was the book, the magical missing link. Goldy wanted it. Roger wanted it. Madeline knew nothing about it. Tom was the only one who knew where it was and Tom was dead.

Roger read again from the transcript of the phone conversation, *The girl is a pathological liar. May I remind you that we will be out there soon, myself and Mr. Romaine. And we'll be wanting to know the whereabouts of the book. Is the fruit shipment ready?*

Book. Fruit. Roger pressed his fingers against his forehead. His headache was worsening. What did it all mean?

Behind him Adele said quietly, "Marjorie Romaine is here. She wants to talk to you."

"I thought she was still in the hospital."

"To me it looks like she should be. She looks pretty bad."

Roger got up and followed Adele out into the lobby. Marjorie sat stiffly against the wall in a wooden chair. The left side of her face was various shades of purple and one eye was swollen shut and crisscrossed with blue and yellow. Her lips were badly chapped and raw. Her left arm was in a cast and with her right hand she clutched a cane. Marjorie Romaine, formerly a striking woman, looked frightened and pale and utterly beaten.

She started to rise as Roger approached her.

"Corporal Sheppard?"

"Mrs. Romaine."

"Corporal, I have to talk to you. I took a cab from the hospital. They didn't want to let me out, but I must talk with you."

He took her elbow and guided her slowly down the hall toward his office. He led her to a chair and sat down next to her.

A few minutes later she was sniffling and groping in her handbag for a tissue. Tears streaked down her blotchy cheeks. Roger grabbed a box of tissues from his desk and handed her one.

"It hurts to cry. Do you how it feels to have it hurt to cry? It hurts my face. I can't even blow my nose."

"It's okay, Mrs. Romaine. Take your time."

"All of this is my fault. I just wanted to come here and apologize as if my apology will change anything. It won't make it right, but I have to talk to you."

Roger grabbed his notebook and opened it to a fresh page. "When I think of that young girl, how she almost died, and it being all my fault . . ."

"Madeline is fine. She's back in Chester and she's doing just fine. Kate's taken her under her wing. How is it all your fault?"

"I knew a lot about what was going on. And I kept quiet."

"Mrs. Romaine, what did you know?"

"I could have prevented this. I knew a lot of things . . ."

Roger leaned forward, "Mrs. Romaine, would you mind if I taped this interview, and if another officer sat in?"

"Oh." She looked helplessly around. "Can it be that nice policewoman who took me to the hospital?"

"Constable St. Marie? I'll see if she's here."

A few minutes later the three of them were sitting in Roger's office. Roberta with her arm around Marjorie's shoulders, Roger with his notebook ready, and on the center of the desk the tape recorder whirring.

"Why don't you start at the beginning?" said Roger.

"Now that he's been arrested, I don't suppose he can hurt me." She paused. Roger waited, his pen poised on his notebook.

She sighed and sniffed. "At first I thought . . . I thought it was another woman, that's why I started spying on him initially. I wanted to find out who she was. When he went on his trip to Ottawa, which I now know was a ruse, he left behind his little computer, quite by accident, I know now."

"His computer?" Roger asked.

"Yes, his portable, you know, those little computers that fit into briefcases? Well, I learned how to operate it. I even figured out his password. Well, I discovered that there wasn't another woman. But what I found out scared me half to death. He was buying up small financially-troubled businesses here in Chester and then using them as drug fronts. He and that crew from Nevada. On the outside it looked all very legitimate and up front. Flip Schmidt's Deli was one."

She looked at Roger. "I tried to call you, but you were out. I wanted to show you the computer. My mistake was in telling Wes. He called one evening. Sometimes I can't keep my mouth shut. Never was good at keeping a secret. It gets me in trouble more times than I can count . . ." She was openly crying now. Roberta rubbed her back and handed her a fresh tissue. "I said to him on the phone, I said, 'Wes, I'm going to the police. I've got your computer and I'm going to the police. You're in Ottawa and there's nothing you can do.' That night was when the men came." She dabbed at her eyes with the tissue. "Three men came into my home when I was in bed. They beat me up. The only thing they stole was Wes' computer."

Roberta asked gently, "Why didn't you tell me this in the hospital?"

"I was frightened, my dear. I'm not stupid. If they had wanted to kill me, I wouldn't be here talking to you today. No, their intent was to frighten me. They succeeded. The message was *Keep your trap shut, lady.* Those people are so evil. They turned Wes into something so evil."

Marjorie grabbed another tissue from the box to stem a fresh torrent of tears.

"Mrs. Romaine," said Roger, "Can you remember any of the information on the computer?"

"A little, I think. There was Flip's Deli for sure. A lot of information was about the Deli, about importing cocaine in crates of salsa. There was also something about fruit, but that was more sketchy."

Flip Schmidt's Deli. Of the five arrested, Flip seemed the closest to breaking. A little pressure applied at the right places, and maybe he would talk. Maybe a promise of plea bargaining and he could be persuaded to testify against Goldy and Wes.

The conference room was deathly still.

"What else can you remember?"

"Not that much, really. There were a whole lot of dates and lists of things, but I didn't understand it all. And I didn't commit it to memory, I'm afraid. I'm so terribly sorry the computer was stolen."

Not half as sorry as I am, thought Roger.

After apologizing a few more times and blowing her nose a few more times, she and Roberta walked to the front. It was plain that she knew nothing more. She was going to go home, she told Roberta, and could someone please call her a cab?

"Are you sure you're all right?" asked Adele.

"I want to go home. I should call my sister in Three Hills. Maybe she can come over for a while or maybe I can go up there. My home has so many bad memories."

"I think that's a real good idea. You shouldn't be alone now. Corporal, can we spare Roberta to drive Mrs. Romaine home? I'll call her sister."

"Oh would you please? That would be so sweet of you."

After they left, Roger began his pacing once again. Pacing and praying. Praying and puzzling and pacing. Less than an hour later Duane and Dennis came barging in.

"Voila!" said Duane, proudly holding up a little blue key in his hand. "This," he said dropping it on Roger's desk, "will unlock all the secrets of the Wes Romaine—Flip Schmidt—Goldy Bassino operation."

Roger frowned. "What it is?"

"It's a key."

"I know it's a key. But what's it for?"

"It's a key to a locker," offered Dennis.

"I know it's a key to a locker, what locker?"

"That's the slight problem," said Duane. "We don't know what locker."

Roger looked at them questioningly.

Dennis said, "Maybe we should tell you the story."

"I'm all ears."

Duane began, "We were at Madeline's just now, following up on a few things, trying to figure out if she could remember anything about this so-called book."

"Yeah, we're still missing the book," said Dennis. "We're in there talking when suddenly she gets this funny expression on her face, like a light bulb going on inside her head."

"She runs outside," Duane continued, "and brings back one of those little cassette recorder things. She opens up the battery compartment and dumps this key out on the table."

Dennis said, "She tells us that she found it with all the money she took and then forgot about it. She says, 'Do you think this might be important?' And I'm thinking—it might be the most important break in this case so far!"

Duane continued, "She said that when she found all the money in the shoe box, she was fiddling with this little cassette recorder trying to get the Playback button to work. For some reason, she opened up the battery compartment which was empty and dropped in the key."

Dennis said, "And then she totally forgot about it."

Duane said, "She doesn't know what the key is for."

Roger said, "I'm willing to bet the mysterious book is locked up in whatever that unlocks."

"That's what we think."

Roger said, "So what are you two waiting for? Go try that key in every locker in Chester and Calgary until you find that book. Make phone calls. As many as you have to until you find that locker. Get as much help as you need."

"Right boss!" The two of them saluted and left.

CHAPTER 24

The drought had still not broken. Heat hung in the night air like an invisible vapor that clung and would not let go. It was late. Kate and Becky had gone to bed. In another week Sara would be home. Roger couldn't sleep. He walked around his living room aimlessly—opening and closing windows, picking up the remote and flipping through the TV channels. Maybe if he tuned his mind onto something else, an old movie or something, that piece of the puzzle which still eluded him would come clear. On TV-CKJY the top news story was still the arrest of Goldy Bassino for kidnapping a girl from Chester. He was already out of prison, and waved to the TV cameras as he made his way to his long limousine. Roger pounded his fist into his hand. The book was still missing. He had assigned every single constable to it—he knew they would find that locker eventually—but would Goldy Bassino be long gone by then?

He turned the TV off and stomped outside onto the deck. The night was alive with insects and the heavy mugginess was wearying. Inside, the house was quiet. That morning Kate had driven Madeline into Calgary to help her enroll for the fall semester at the Alberta Vocational College. Afterward they had gone out for lunch. According to Kate, Madeline was quite interested in the Bible. That, at least, was good. He found a bag of stale corn chips in a cupboard in the kitchen and took it into the living room where he sat down and picked up the paper. It was the same story—RCMP stifled in their attempt to stop mob leader Goldy Bassino. He flung the paper aside and turned on the television. A late night sit-com rerun flickered on the screen with its cheery images and canned laughter where all the problems of life are solved within the space of half an hour.

Lord, what am I missing? He clasped his hands behind his head and stared at the set. The sit-com broke for commercial. He recognized Hank Pfeiffer in one of his old homemade commercials. In one hand Hank held up an orange and in the other a grapefruit urging everyone to, "Come on down and enjoy the hometown shopping experience." Roger leaned forward.

Suddenly he knew. At least one of the pieces was now fitting in place. He got up, made a phone call, wrote a quick message to Kate, and hurried out into the night. As he sped toward the downtown section of Chester, a few drops of wetness splattered onto his windshield. It wasn't until he pulled into the back of Pfeiffer's Independent Grocers that he realized that it was drizzling, the first rain in months. Hank's car was there. Somehow that didn't surprise Roger.

The back door was unlocked and Roger walked through the coffee room. Coffee cups were still stacked in the sink. The stained coffee pot was still partly-filled with cold, dark liquid. Still the same *Peoples, National Inquirers, Stars* and *Calgary Heralds* were haphazardly scattered on the smudgy table. The old, dilapidated couch still leaned against the wall.

Through the office window he saw Hank. The big man was leaning forward, his head in his hands, his shoulders heaving. When Roger stood in front of him, he looked up. His eyes were wet, his nose was red, his large red face was blotched with tears. He didn't seem surprised to see Roger there.

His only comment was, "How did you figure it out?"

"I didn't want to believe it. I kept myself from believing it, that was until I saw one of your ads on TV tonight. You should have pulled those ads, Hank, especially the one with you wearing that old plaid jacket of yours."

"That jacket." He bowed his head as if in excruciating pain. "Tom was like a crazy man."

"Wes bought your place here, didn't he? Along with Flip's Deli. The question is, how much of you does he own too, Hank? Did you come with the deal?"

Hank looked up miserably. "You have to understand something before you come in here and judge me," he said. "All I wanted was my business back. That's all I wanted. You don't know what it's like—this recession and all—I just wasn't making it anymore. I was up to my ears in debt. The big chains in the city—Superstore, Food For Less, Safeway— are squeezing us independents right out of business. You know how long I've had this store? My father had it before me. I worked here as a kid, stocked shelves after school, made deliveries. Forty years ago everybody bought their groceries here. Nobody went into Calgary. An honest businessman could make a decent living. Now, everybody runs off to the big chains. I was drowning. I was so far in debt I was willing to do anything."

"And then Wes Romaine comes along with an offer you can't refuse."

Hank nodded.

"And so you began selling more than fruit."

Hank blew his nose loudly into the handkerchief. "He said I wouldn't have to be involved."

"But you were, of course."

Hank leaned his head into his large hands. "At first I didn't know what was going on. I didn't want to know."

Roger continued, "Soon Wes began hiring his buddies to work, to remove and distribute the drugs from the fruit crates when they arrived. Tom Anderchuk was one of those people. But there was something you didn't count on. Tom found the Lord, became a Christian and then his conscience became so pricked, unlike yours, that he couldn't go on. Instead, he began gathering information about you, about the whole operation. He was going to turn you in. That was a lie about him helping himself to the cash register, wasn't it? When he came to you with the facts, you decided to get rid of him."

"No! It wasn't like that. I told him to leave town. I even offered him money, lots of money, ten thousand dollars."

"Where'd you get that kind of money?"

"From Wes."

"Ahh, a payment."

Hank nodded. "My first payment. Somehow . . ." he paused and ran his hands over his anguished brow and continued quietly, "I couldn't spend it. I couldn't put it in the bank, so I hid it in the pocket of that old jacket. I offered it to Tom when he came. I told him he was going to get himself killed. Instead, he takes the bus down to Azuyo and starts digging up more stuff. He shouldn't have gone down there. Those people are powerful. They're dangerous."

"He took the money with him?"

"No, he threw it back at me. I rubber-banded it together and put it back in the jacket pocket. I keep that old jacket on a hook in the very back of my office broom closet. I haven't worn it in years."

"So Tom goes down to Nevada," said Roger, "and finds out that Goldy Bassino and his crew have set up a Canadian connection to bring drugs across the border. Tell me, what kind of a cut did he offer you?"

"Fifteen percent."

"Fifteen percent?" Roger whistled. "That's not much. I would have held out for more. Was it worth it, Hank? Getting the money? Being responsible for someone's death, but keeping your own business, was it worth it?"

"I never killed anybody. I told you. I told Tom to run. As God is my witness, I offered him money and told him to run."

"God is not your witness, Hank. Not any more. I'm talking about the drugs, Hank. Drugs kill, or don't you know that?" Roger paused before continuing. "And then Tom comes back to see you, and you call your buddy, Mitchell Standish, who just happens to be in Chester, probably checking out Flip's Deli, and he conveniently drives over and shoots him."

Hank's whole body was quivering. "No, that's not how it was. I didn't even know this Mitchell. I never met him."

"But you were here the night Tom was killed. You drove over in your blue van."

Hank nodded and said, "Tom came back to see me. He had all the evidence he said, to put them all away for a long time. Hidden, he said. He said because we both were Christians," his voice shook, "that we should go to the police together. He said the book was in a safe place. But I couldn't go with him. I was scared. Scared to death of what they might do to my family. To my children. To my grandchildren. I told him to get out, take the money. I told him it was in the pocket of that jacket and I pointed to the closet. So he goes over to the closet, grabs the jacket, takes the money out of the pocket and says, 'This is going to the police, too. Thanks, Hank.' And then he does this really crazy thing. He puts the jacket on and starts dancing around and laughing. He says, 'I'm filling the jacket of a really, big Christian businessman. I think this is a perfect fit.' I tell you, that got to me more than anything . . ."

"I bet it did," said Roger dryly. "But not enough to go with him."

Hank bowed his head. "Then he left," he said quietly.

"And then you called Wes."

"No, I didn't . . ."

"What happened then, Hank?"

"Well, I wondered, maybe I should go to the police with Tom, get this thing over with. I tell you the whole thing was really playing on my mind."

"I'll just bet it was."

"A little while later, Tom called again. He said he was on his way down to give me one more chance. I told him, 'Okay I'll go with you.' I had really decided to go with him, by now."

"But something changed your mind."

"My Rosie, I couldn't let anything happen to her . . ." He covered his face with his hands. Quietly he said, "I called Wes. I had to." His voice broke. "Everything would have been ruined. I was scared. But I didn't think anyone would get killed. No one told me that anyone would get killed!" He paused. Roger waited. "I never saw Tom again after that."

"Tom came, however, and Mitchell met him in the parking lot and killed him, and then dumped his body in your dumpster."

"I guess so. I never heard anything."

"You killed that boy, Hank, as sure as if you'd pulled that trigger, you killed that boy."

"Stop it! Please!" He slammed his fists onto the desk. "I know what I've done. But you've got to understand. My business . . ."

"Let's go, Hank."

"Go? Where?"

When he heard the sirens in the distance Hank's hands began to shake. "Please, Roger, brother, can I go home? I'll come in tomorrow morning. You have my word. Let me have some time with my Rosie. She knows nothing about this . . ."

"I'm sorry, Hank. You know I can't do that."

"Roger, brother . . ."

"Don't *brother* me, Hank."

"You don't understand; I didn't want to become rich. I was going to quit, maybe even turn them in myself once I had enough money to buy my business back. That's all I wanted. I had no choice! Don't you understand me? I had no choice!"

"You always have a choice."

It was pouring down rain when Roger led Hank, sobbing and broken, to a waiting patrol car.

* * *

"All this time I thought I was stupid, well, stupider than other people," said Madeline. She set her coffee mug down on an end table and smiled at Kate who sat next to her on the couch.

"But you're not stupid," said Kate. "You're just different. Your brain sees words on a page differently than other people. All you have to do is to learn how to read words the way your mind sees them. That's what that instructor said, right?"

Madeline smiled and nodded.

The four of them—Roger, Kate, Madeline and Becky— were sitting in the Sheppard living room following a late supper of barbecued chicken. The day had been a long one for Roger. The previous evening, less than twenty-four hours before, Hank had been arrested. Roger had spent the day dealing with a subdued Hank, a tearful and nervous Rose who came in with a concerned Pastor Phillips, just back from vacation, and then later with a zealous and obnoxious Chad Williamson.

Hank was arrested. Flip was arrested. Goldy was still free, but Roger was fairly sure that even without the book, their testimony would be enough to put Goldy behind bars. From Nevada, Goldy and Wes were still hiding behind their "no comment" lawyers. At six he left the crew of them in Lavoir's and Laird's capable hands and drove home in the rain with a splitting headache. Basically it had not quit raining since last evening. One thunderstorm after another tormented the area. At home, Kate told him that two papers had called—their local paper, *The Chester Leader*, and *The Calgary Herald*, along with Talk Radio 650 and Chad Williamson from CKJY-TV. So before supper they had turned on the answering machine and were basically ignoring the telephone. If it was Laird, Lund, Pastor Phillips or the detachment office, Roger would pick up at once.

Sitting with her knees tucked up under her, Becky was regarding Madeline without speaking.

Kate was talking now. "They said with a little help, Madeline can get her high school diploma."

"Charles thinks I should, too," she said. "He's been so nice to me. What I'd like to do is go into physical education," she said. "Maybe work at a pool or teach swimming. They told me I could take swimming lessons while I'm going to school, so I signed up for them, too."

"That's great, Madeline," said Roger. "You want to be called Madeline now or Madonna?"

"Oh, Madeline. It's my name. I guess I just have to get used to it." She looked out through the front window. The sky was blackening again. Another rainstorm was impending. Madeline looked over at Becky.

"You are so lucky to have two parents that love you," she said quietly. "Don't ever take that for granted. I would give anything, *anything* to have parents like yours."

Becky nodded and looked down at her hands which were folded in her lap. She was still grounded for the ravine episode and had been strangely quiet since her father had returned. Maybe being driven home in a police car, even if your dad *is* a policeman, is a sobering enough event. Becky's long hair covered her down-turned face and Roger couldn't see the expression it hid.

The phone rang in the kitchen, and immediately Roger heard Kate's soft voice on the recording, "We are not able to come to the phone right now, but if you leave your name and number after the beep, we'll get back to you as soon as we can."

"Corporal!" It was Duane. "Corporal, if you're there, this will interest you . . ." Roger had already risen and was hurrying toward the phone.

"Yes, Duane," he said into the receiver, "What's up?"

"Corporal, we found the book. We finally traced the key to a Greyhound bus station locker in Great Falls, Montana. Tom must have ditched it there. Well, the book is a three ring binder which includes financial statements of small businesses in Chester. Those reporting losses are flagged. As you can guess, Flip Schmidt's Deli and Pfeiffer's Independent Grocers take first place in the book. In the back are shipment dates, orders, letters from Silver Springs Orchard Fruits and the Riverboat. This is like Christmas, Corporal. We've got everything here, everything to put these guys away and throw away the key. Oh, yeah, there was another book in the locker too—a Bible."

"I'll be right down."

EPILOGUE

The morning meeting of the Christian Men's Breakfast Club was unusually restrained. Normally boisterous back-slapping businessmen were speaking to each other in hushed tones. Even the waitresses carrying the coffeepots walked quietly and unsmilingly from table to table. The events which had rocked the small town of Chester were still being felt. It seemed to be the only topic of conversation at the post office, at the coffee shop, at the office, at the hardware store, at the drug store.

At the head table, Roger pondered that today, of all days, he was to be the featured career moment. His notes were completed, with key points jotted down on three-by-five cards in the breast pocket of his uniform. Next to him was the guest speaker, Dr. Bruce Anderson, outspoken Christian physician from Edmonton. His talk was about euthanasia and impending right-to-die legislation in Canada. Next to Dr. Anderson was Phil Ferment, local vice-president of the CMBC. The place next to Roger, the president's spot, was empty. Hastily, Phil removed the extra place setting and stacked it on a back table. He also pocketed Hank's place tag, muttering to Roger, "Terrible thing about Hank."

Roger agreed. Indeed, it was a terrible thing about Hank. During breakfast, conversation was muted. The clatter of plates and forks and knives filled the spaces that conversation normally covered. Plates were not filled twice from the loaded breakfast buffet. Collectively it seemed they had no appetite.

Dr. Anderson engaged Roger in a light conversation about the speed limits on Highway #2 between Edmonton and Calgary, but even that seemed unimportant and trivial. Everyone skirted the main issue.

Breakfast finally over, Phil rose to the podium. After the welcome, opening prayer, and announcements, he turned to Roger and said, "Roger, come up and tell us how the Lord works in your life on the job."

Lord, help me, Roger prayed as he took his place behind the microphone. He placed his cards in order on the podium next to his Bible. Several moments later he began:

"My job is to uphold the law. According to Romans 13, I am one of God's ministers. Let me read that passage." He opened his Bible, *"Let every soul be subject to the governing authorities. For there is no authority except from God, and the authorities that exist are appointed by God.*

Therefore whoever resists the authority resists the ordinance of God, and those who resist will bring judgment on themselves. For rulers are not a terror to good works, but to evil. Do you want to be unafraid of authority? Do what is good, and you will have praise from the same. For he is God's minister to you for good. But if you do evil, be afraid; for he does not bear the sword in vain; for he is God's minister, an avenger to execute wrath on him who practices evil."

He flipped to another marker in his Bible and said, "And then in First Timothy it says: *Therefore I exhort first of all that supplications, prayers, intercessions, and giving of thanks be made for all men, for kings and all who are in authority that we may lead a quiet and peaceable life in all godliness and reverence."*

He paused before continuing. "As a member of the Royal

Canadian Mounted Police, I make it possible for you to lead peaceful and quiet lives. If there were no law, and people to see that the law is upheld, there would be no peace in our communities. Those who practice evil would rule the streets. There would be no quietness, no security in our homes and for our families. All of us would live in fear."

Roger's eyes swept over the group. "I should tell you that most of the time my job is humdrum and tedious—parking tickets, speeding. Television would have you believe that we face the barrel of a gun everyday but most of the time that isn't true. And there are also piles and piles of paperwork." He looked up. He was hoping for a few smiles here. He got none. He looked down at his cards once more.

"The fact that I am God's minister has never been so clear to me as in the events of these past few weeks. As some of you know, I was appointed to head up an investigation into drugs in Chester. And that, I have attempted to do to the best of my ability. These past few weeks have been most difficult. I have to admit that there were times in the past month that I was afraid. I was afraid for my own family, for my wife and my two daughters. But as God's minister, I have to leave my family in His hands."

Every eye was upon him. "Sometimes I feel as if I cannot deal with one more abused child, one more battered wife, one more shattered life destroyed by drugs, one more person living in the gutter, one more individual who feels that the only way to survive is to take up arms against the ministers of God."

He continued, "But just when I feel like giving up, God injects hope into the situation. Most of you may not know that Tom Anderchuk, that young man who was found murdered here in Chester last month, was a Christian."

A few collective gasps went up from the group. The men looked at each other and then at him.

"No, I didn't think you knew that. That's not the kind of thing that gets reported in the news. According to those who knew him before he died, he had given his life to Christ. He had gone through the Drug Rehab program at the Shepherd Centre in Calgary and was being guided and counseled to remain drug-free. Unfortunately, you don't leave the drug world that easily. His girlfriend, Madeline, is putting her life together. Kate and I are confident that she, too, will come to know Christ the way Tom did. That's the good news."

The room was deathly still. He looked down at his notes. "Working together with the sheriff's department in Nevada, we have broken one drug ring. You would have had to spend the last few weeks on Mars not to know that. We can applaud our efforts, the joint efforts of the RCMP, the Azuyo Sheriff's department and the Bakersfield police department, but only briefly. The battle continues. In a year's time there will be another drug ring to break, another abused child, more lives ruined, more businessmen selling themselves out for thirty pieces of silver. The battle continues."

He hesitated briefly, "It was especially sad for me to find out that someone I knew as a Christian brother, someone who has stood before you where I stand," and here his voice broke, "was found to be contributing to the drug problem here in Chester. It makes me question, as I'm sure it makes you question, how could he have gotten so far off track? The expression, *There but for the grace of God go I,* has never been more meaningful because—given the right set of circumstances—we could all be where Hank is today."

He paused. "As a Christian I have to pray everyday that what I see will not send me over the edge, that I will know His will, that my job as *your* minister will not be put to shame. All of us can fall. But," he said very quietly, "God is a forgiving God."

Roger's voice gained confidence, "No, the battle is not

256

over. It will not be over until Jesus comes again to set up a rule of peace on the earth. Then I will be able, at long last, to lay down my gun, never to take it up again."

Roger gathered up his cards, and sat down at the table.

Eighty-seven faces stared at him in silence. Someone in the back started to clap. It was taken up along the sides. Finally, the businessmen of the Christian Men's Breakfast Club were all on their feet in one concert of thunderous applause.